By The Same Author

AMBER ROYER

A CHOCOLATE IS ANNOUNCED

**GOLDEN TIP
PRESS**

GOLDEN TIP PRESS

A Golden Tip Press paperback original 2024

Cover by Jon Bravo

Distributed in the United States by Ingram, Tennessee

ISBN 978-1-952854-20-0

Ebook ISBN 978-1-952854-21-7

Printed in the United States of America

To Jake, for taking care of everything else, so this book could actually happen.

Chapter One
Wednesday

I look nervously into the camera, feeling stifled by this ridiculous tweed skirt suit and ruffled blouse. "Are you sure all this is necessary?"

Chloe Winston sighs dramatically as she comes out from behind the tripod to adjust my felt hat, complete with pheasant feather. She'd wanted to put flour in my brown hair – all the better to make me actually *look* like Mrs. Marple – but I'd drawn the line at that. Really. I'm in my 30s. Chloe is 17, and she thinks I can pull off looking elderly. There had been some flailing about to avoid the flour, the whole canister of which had wound up upended onto Ash Diaz – my former nemesis turned podcast host. And now the latest victim of Chloe's enthusiasm.

He's sitting on a director's chair over in the corner, pouting, as he cleans his square glasses with the end of his signature skinny tie. He's gotten most of the flour off of his purple button-up shirt. And the flour in his dark hair just manages to make him look distinguished, more's the pity, though he's in his 20s and shouldn't be able to pull it off. Ash says, "Come on, Koerber. You want people to come to your mystery weekend, right? It's a perfect chance to highlight this space before you sell it."

We're in the lobby of the hotel where I'm living. My aunt flips properties while my uncle works offshore, and this hotel is her latest project. It isn't open to the public, but she is letting me occupy a top-floor suite, since I provided a lot of the cash to initially buy the place. I love this lobby, now that she's restored it. It has a retro-elegant feel, and a fantastic art deco fireplace that she'd just installed, with green fan-shaped panels on either side. Chloe thought the fireplace would be perfect to add a bit of atmosphere to the video. I pull at the collar, which feels like it might strangle me. We're doing a commercial for the new line of chocolate bars at Greetings and Felicitations, the craft chocolate business I co-own with my fiancé. He's finally come up with a chocolate bar he wants to put his name on. I say commercial, because that's what it is – sort of. Chloe keeps telling me that advertising in the AI age is all about interactivity. You have to have contests, ask for feedback with your customers – play subtle games to keep them thinking about your brand. So we're having a contest to choose a few super fans for an expenses paid weekend at the hotel I live in, to enact a murder mystery party in celebration of the Mystery Flavor bars.

"I guess a few people will get to see the hotel," I admit, "But the mystery weekend is supposed to be selling people on our chocolate."

"It will." Chloe is in full-on director mode. She has her bleach-blonde hair up in a bun, and she's wearing pink jeans, pink pumps and a sequined pink blouse. She says, "You told me I could have free reign putting together the new marketing campaign. And you can blame Mrs. Parker for the Mrs. Marple idea. She's the Agatha Christie fan."

By Mrs. Parker, she means Autumn, my best friend – who just got married a couple of months ago. She's been Autumn Ellis my whole life, so it's hard to get used to her being called by

Drake's last name – especially since she's still using Ellis for her books, so as not to confuse her readers.

I tell Chloe, "Autumn isn't here to substantiate that. I feel ridiculous. And beige is so not my color." I have no idea where Chloe came up with these antiquated clothes. "And I really shouldn't be playing a game riffing on murder when everybody calls me a murder magnet – thanks to Ash over there, and his podcast."

"You're welcome," Ash says.

It's in poor taste. I know that. I've been involved in helping solve half a dozen murders that have happened in, near, or somehow adjacent to my chocolate shop. The true crime crowd come to Greetings and Felicitations and dare each other to try my creations – on the off chance it will lead to literal death by chocolate. I've reluctantly embraced this darker side of my image – despite the fact that my design for the shop is dove gray and pink shabby chic – with a logo modeled after my sweet, innocent bunny Knightley. But Logan had really liked the idea, probably because he used to be a cop, and he wants to pay tribute to the puzzle solving we've done together.

I couldn't tell him no. And if I'm going to embrace the detective side of me – I might as well go all the way. But not like this, as a caricature of somebody's fictional creation. I take off the hat and the jacket and toss them to Ash.

Chloe squeaks in protest.

I turn to the camera and say, "A chocolate is announced." I can barely keep a straight face.

Chloe says, "The camera's not recording."

"See," I say. "I'm not sure why there even has to be a camera. We're riffing on a book opening where a murder was actually announced in the local newspaper, like a wedding or a church picnic. That was the gag. And it made sense. If we want to parallel the book, shouldn't we do something like that?"

"Nobody actually reads newspapers anymore, Mrs. Koerber!" Chloe protests.

Ash says, "She's right, Felicity. Some things just exist without the original context. And the idea of a murder mystery party riffing off of *A Murder is Announced* or *Murder on the Orient Express* is practically a trope. Every mystery TV series since *Moonlighting* has had a similar episode."

I frown at him. He makes a gesture for me to smooth my hair, which must have gotten rumpled by the hat. My hair is straight, brown and long. It's actually one of my best features. I run both hands through it, pulling it towards the back. I tell Ash, "And in every one of those shows, somebody dies for real. Which is why I'm reluctant to do this."

Chloe puts a hand on my shoulder. She's basically a kid, but she's looking at me like she's concerned for my sanity. "That's television, Mrs. Koerber. You understand the difference between fantasy and reality, don't you?"

I shrug her hand away. I tell her, "You don't understand."

Most people wouldn't. I'm nervous because I have a bad habit of collecting classic books, which then somehow lead to me getting involved with murders. I know it's not logical. But it keeps happening. The last time I'd been in contact with a Christie novel, I'd been on a cruise ship. I'd won a copy of *Murder on the Orient Express*, and I'd had to deal with a famous mystery writer getting murdered right beside my gift shop chocolate display. I don't actually have a copy of *A Murder is Announced* in my hand – but does re-enacting part of the plot get us close enough to count?

Ash tells Chloe, "Felicity's a little gun-shy. After all, she is a mega super mecha murder magnet." He steps over and puts the hat back on my head. He turns to Chloe and adds, "It's best just to humor her."

"At least Logan takes me seriously," I tell them, flashing the giant rock on my ring finger. Logan is my fiancé and business partner. He's also been my partner in solving unexpected murders. He's saved my life from a psychopathic killer – and I've saved his. I still shudder thinking about how he'd been seconds away from being electrocuted. What if I hadn't made it in time? There would be a hole in my life so huge it would be irreparable. I'd lost my first husband to a senseless accident. It had taken a lot for me to open up enough to love again. I'm not sure I could do that a second time.

Ash says, "I still think it's cool that Logan coughed up his grandmother's engagement ring – after you were the one who proposed."

"There was an upside to him going home to Minnesota," I agree. Logan's dad had been dealing with health issues, and Logan had gone to smooth things out. It had been good for him. He'd long had a difficult relationship with his father, and they'd taken some time to sort out the past. He's due back today. Any minute now, in fact. And his family is coming with him. He was here for the weekend two weeks ago, finalizing everything with his chocolate bars. But the thought that this time he's staying for good has me all happy-fizzy inside, in a way that not even this miserable video shoot can spoil.

I should just get it over with. I make a scrunchy face at Chloe. "Fine. Let's tempt fate."

Not that I am generally a superstitious person. I'd had a difficult time coming to terms with the book thing in the first place. And surely this is far enough removed from a first edition hardcover that everything will be fine.

Chloe scoots back behind the camera. "Smile, Mrs. Koerber. You can do this."

I take a deep breath and pretend I'm talking to Chloe, not the camera. "A chocolate is announced. Can you be in Galveston, Texas this weekend? If so, enter our contest for a murder mystery weekend including tours of my chocolate micro-factory and several historic homes, a visit to the farmer's market, and a bonfire on the beach in honor of our Mystery Flavor bars."

Ash sneezes, and I jump, startled. Chloe gives him a withering look. I glance away from the camera. I look back, freezing like the proverbial deer in headlights. I've completely forgotten the next line. I feel my mouth drop open, and a wordless sound comes out. Once it's clear I'm not going to continue, Chloe taps the camera, and it beeps, signaling it's stopped recording.

Ash produces a handkerchief from his pocket and wipes it across his nose. "Sorry, I think it's the flour."

"Never mind," Chloe says. "I have enough of a take to work with."

A lilting voice says, "Just in time, too. I know a man who's desperate to see your star, who's just out parking the car." Logan's sister Dawn strides into the room and wraps me in a hug. I've only met her a couple of times. She's tall and thin, and married to a guy who barely reaches her shoulder. He has followed her into the room, carrying a casserole dish. Fisher is a black guy who sports spiky short dreadlocks and favors nature-related graphic tees. Today, he's paired a maroon hoodie with a drab green tee with a picture of a monstera on it – and the caption reads, *Sometimes I wet my plants*. Incongruously, he's also wearing pink plaid oven mitts to hold the dish. Fisher always strikes me as rather a good sport. I guess he'd have to be, to make it work with Dawn.

Ash perks up. He's never met a casserole he didn't like. "What's that?" he asks.

Fisher says, "Macaroni and cheese. It's still hot from the warming oven. One of the benefits of marrying into a family that owns a number of private planes." He gives me a wink, obviously referencing my upcoming nuptials to Logan, who is a puddle jump pilot. Only Logan's largest plane, the one that can hold eight passengers, has space for such an oven. He sometimes uses it for tour groups who want a special occasion flight over the island. He loves to fly, and those island tours are one of his favorite things to do.

Dawn says, "Mac and cheese is Mom's specialty, dontcha know. She and Dad stopped off to see the beach. Dad wanted to take his shoes off and walk in the water. We're going to have to go back and pick them up later."

Chloe says, "They sound like a fun couple."

"They are," I say. And I mean it. Though Logan's dad tends to tell more jokes than actually open up about himself.

Dawn pulls me off to one side, out of earshot of the others. Her light brown hair is back in a ponytail, and she's wearing a blue Minnesota Timberwolves tee. It's a bit more casual than what she usually wears, but she probably wanted to be comfortable for the flight. We're behind the big potted fan palm that Ash had brought in for the party. It must have something to do with the plot of the mystery he is preparing to present. Otherwise, buying a mature tree is a big splash-out for the scale of the event we have planned, just for decoration.

Dawn's green eyes sparkle with mischief as she asks, "As host, you're not actually playing your murder mystery game, are you?"

I blink in surprise. I hadn't really thought about it. "I guess not. There should be at least one impartial observer. Though I think Imogen and Autumn may have me cast as Mrs. Marple."

"Good." Dawn gives a curt nod. "I want you to cast me as the killer. I want to prove I can outsmart both my dad and my brother."

"I'm not sure I can do that," I protest. "Ash is in charge of running the game. I think he already has someone in mind."

"Point me at this Ash." Dawn looks around the room.

Poor Ash is still sitting in his director's chair, having a conversation with Chloe. He has no idea what he's in for. Ash himself is usually a force to be reckoned with. But even he may not be able to stand up to tornado Dawn.

Logan breezes in, wearing his usual pilot's jacket, jeans and tee combo. He's usually clean-shaven, but it looks like he hasn't shaved in a couple of days. It's a good look for him. Of course, I may be biased, since he's mine. But I want to run my hands along his strong jaw and kiss him, deeply. I've missed him so much! And the sight of him, his intense green eyes, his well-muscled chest, makes me feel suddenly warm. But he's never been big on public displays of affection, so I have to settle for a hug and giving him a quick kiss on the cheek.

"Fee," he says, using his pet name for me, his hands still on my forearms, even after he has released the hug. "I have so much to tell you. Dad wants to buy us a house as a wedding gift. He even has one in mind."

I tense under his touch, sure that he's talking about cabin on Lake Superior, or a bungalow somewhere in the suburbs – but either way, in Minnesota. Logan has been nothing but supportive of my business, to the point that this launch party is celebrating him becoming an equal part of it. Surely he can't expect me to upend my life and move Greetings and Felicitations to a new city.

I start to ask him to clarify, but there's a crash in the office, off to the side of the lobby. "Aunt Naomi!" I shout as I turn to rush towards the office door. Logan follows right behind me.

I turn the knob and find Naomi sprawled on the floor. I gasp. She's not moving. "Oh my God!"

I knew it had been a bad idea to put myself in Mrs. Marple's octogenarian shoes. I just didn't think anything bad would happen to someone I care so much about. It's a weird thought, wrapped in shock and horror. Because this can't really be happening. My aunt can't be lying there, unconscious – or worse.

Aunt Naomi turns her head. "I'm okay." Although from her pinched face and tone of voice, clearly she's in pain. Still, I purse my lips and let out a slow breath of relief.

"What happened?" Logan asks, moving into the room and crouching down near Naomi. It's a relatively small space, with a big desk and a couple of chairs. There's a stack of building materials on the desk.

Naomi gestures at the stack and says, "I was replacing the ceiling tiles in here with the new copper-toned ones, and a spider fell out of the attic onto my face, and I freaked out and fell off the step ladder."

Belatedly, I register the ladder in question on its side on the floor behind her, and I look up and see the open gap in the ceiling.

I chide, "I thought you promised me you weren't going to do that until I could hold the ladder for you."

Aunt Naomi says, "I used to do these kinds of things by myself all the time, before you moved in with me. Your Uncle Greg is never home long enough for me to have gotten used to having help."

Greg's offshore schedule is complicated. He's actually going to be home this weekend, just in time for the mystery event. It's not the kind of thing I'd ever pictured him being into, but he sounded excited when we talked about it on the phone, saying he owed Naomi a date night.

Logan asks, "How do your neck and shoulders feel? Can you sit up?"

"That's easy," Aunt Naomi says, demonstrating by sitting up and rolling her shoulders. Then she gestures to her leg. "But I think I did something to my ankle."

I used to be a physical therapist, back before I became a chocolate maker, so my first instinct is to move forward to examine the injury. But Logan used to be a cop, before he'd put himself in self-imposed exile, so he's capable, too. I let him test out the extent of my aunt's injury without trying to interfere. What Logan and I have is new. After dancing around what we might mean to each other for far too long, I'd proposed – before we'd even had a proper date. I want to be careful not to make him feel like I don't trust his capabilities. He's had such a hard time getting his self-confidence back after the failed operation that had caused him to leave the police force, and the regrets over the tragedy that had come after, when he was doing private security.

Logan determines that Aunt Naomi merely has a sprain – actually more painful than a break. He helps her up off the floor, but she nearly falls again when she tries to put weight on the ankle, so he scoops her up and carries her out into the seating area in the lobby Aunt Naomi and I sometimes use as a makeshift living room. We often spend evenings down here, hanging out with my lop-eared bunny, Knightley and swapping stories about our days. I direct Logan towards the most comfortable spot for Naomi to sit.

Dawn, Fisher, Ash, and Chloe are all standing close to the door, watching with concern.

Fisher asks, "You need me to get some ice."

"I got it," I say.

Logan sets Aunt Naomi down on the pale leather sofa, and I turn towards the hallway leading into the cavernous dining room, and beyond it, the hotel-ready kitchen, which has our small two-person sized appliances clustered in one small area. The macaroni and cheese is already on the nearest counter, with several big spoonfuls taken out of it. I grab a noodle off the edge and pop it into my mouth as I head for the ice machine. Oh, wow. This is so good. There's multiple cheeses, probably a mozzarella and a parmesan – and maybe a Gruyere. And there are crunchy, buttery breadcrumbs baked on top.

If I wasn't on a mission to put together an ice pack, I would probably take some time to examine the dish further. As it is, I at least note that Logan probably got his ability to cook from his mom. I'm glad she's come to visit. She seems like such a sweet person, and I've been wanting to get to know her better. Only – I hope we don't wind up in a fight over Logan. Because I love him immensely, but I'm not moving to Minnesota, not with my grandmother here needing regular visits, not with all the close friends I've made. I'd left Galveston once, to be closer to my late husband's family, and when Kevin had passed away, I'd just felt lost. I know I could explain that to Logan, but if I force him to choose between me and the people he holds dear, I could well lose him.

I grab a dish towel and scoop some ice into it, and bring the bundle out to the lobby. Logan and his sister are sitting on the nearby settee, talking with Aunt Naomi. Ash and Fisher are standing behind Chloe, who is sitting at a table at the far side of the large space, working on a fluorescent pink laptop. They seem to be giving her conflicting advice about the contest setup.

I hand Naomi the ice pack. She wraps it as best she can around her ankle, which is propped up on several pillows on the sofa.

Dawn says, "I was just telling your aunt that I've always wanted to have a little sister."

"Aww," I say. I flush, unsure how to respond. My late husband had had several brothers, but I'd never thought of them as *my* brothers. But maybe this time, things could be different. I know I'm different, more open, less careless of other people's feelings. Yet, it seems weird to call her sister – maybe because I'm an only child.

Ash saves me from having to elaborate. "Koerber, come and see this. Your contest just went live a few seconds ago, and you've already got eleven entries."

"Okay," I turn and walk over to Chloe's laptop.

Chloe points at the screen. She says, "I set it up using my RaffleSchnaz account. People get entries for liking your website, following your Instagram, or re-posting the contest post. They get bonuses for following my social media accounts, or subscribing to Ash's podcast."

"Sounds pretty straightforward," I say. "And then in 48 hours, it chooses our winners?"

"Right," Chloe says. "Completely random. The more actions someone does, the greater their chance to win."

"I wonder who they will be," I muse.

"I hope they're all someone interesting," Ash grumbles. "The other side is getting video testimonials for your shop and the podcast."

Fisher says, "The kind of people who can drop everything on a three-day notice, who follow true crime and like chocolate are bound to be an interesting bunch."

Chapter Two
Friday

Two days later, Logan still hasn't brought up the idea of the house again. Neither have his parents. And neither have I. I don't want to ruin the great time everyone has been having. Even if it is causing me anxiety not knowing exactly what Logan had talked about with his parents, but not yet discussed with me. So when I find myself alone in the hotel's kitchen with my future-mother-in-law, I'm nervous.

Rosemary Hanlon is just over sixty, but she dyes her hair a dark blonde and wears it in a short cloud-like cut. She's wearing a silky knit blue top paired with velour jogging pants. She pours herself a cup of coffee from the giant urn we've prepared for all the people coming in today for the mystery weekend.

In addition to the contest winners, there will be a couple of my friends filling in the numbers. Most of the hotel rooms have been renovated and furnished with thrift-shop finds Aunt Naomi and my friend Tiff keep coming up with, so there's plenty of room. I love that everyone is going to get to stay. And I'm torn about the thought of Naomi flipping the place. I'm comfortable in my suite of rooms upstairs. And Knightley is completely settled.

As much as I can see Logan wanting the privacy of a house – I'm not sure I'm ready to leave here. I've always been bad at change. And I know, I'm the one who proposed to Logan, but we're taking things slow, so the extent of the changes to come hasn't really hit home until now. But what did I expect? That Logan would move in here, and run the hotel? It's ridiculous.

Logan's mom says, "This may be a bit forward, but I'd love for you to wear my pearls at the wedding. If they go with your dress, that is."

"I haven't chosen a dress yet," I admit. "It's my second wedding, so I don't want to go as over-the-top as I did the first time. I looked like an organza swan."

"But it's Logan's first," Rosemary points out. "And I may be a bit selfish here, but he's my last child to see get married. If it's a matter of money, I'd be happy to help out."

"Oh, no," I say. "Nothing like that."

Although, I am a bit on a budget, since I invested most of my free cash into helping Aunt Naomi buy the boutique hotel in the first place. We're tentatively planning a September wedding date, which is months and months away. Naomi will surely have flipped this place by then. I pour myself a cup of coffee and take a long, steadying sip.

Rosemary says, "I'm glad you and Logan are taking things slow. Traditional wedding nights are so much more special, don't you know. But we don't mind if you do a little cuddling while we're here. We're fairly hard to scandalize."

I choke on my coffee, and try to keep it from going up my nose. Exactly how much of our personal lives has Logan shared with his parents? If I wasn't so shocked, I'd probably be upset with him. Rosemary is nothing like my former mother-in-law. Janet had liked to pretend that me and Kevin were basically roommates, even after we'd been married for years. Except when she'd been saying that she would love a couple of grandchildren. I was never able to have kids, though, so she was disappointed on both counts.

"Yoo-hoo!" a lilting voice calls across the dining room. It's Patsy, someone else who started out as a rival but has become something of a friend. I peek out of the kitchen door. She and her boyfriend Arlo are crossing the room, hand in hand. Patsy is wearing a long black and white sun dress that matches Arlo's tie. He's wearing the same kind of clothes he wears for work, as a police detective.

I wonder if Logan's mom would be scandalized if she knew that until recently, I'd been in a love triangle, trying to choose between Logan, who had been my bodyguard after I'd gotten threats when dealing with that first murder case, and Arlo, who had been my high-school boyfriend. Or that Arlo had found a new girlfriend that looks a lot like me – same fair skin, same long brown hair and brown eyes. Patsy and Arlo had broken up for a while, and it's a complicated story, but I'd actually helped get them back together.

Looking at Arlo now, with his biceps that fill out his suit jacket, his thick dark hair, warm brown skin and generous, kissable lips, I still have to remind myself that it is no longer okay to kiss him. Even though it's been almost three months. Patsy's okay with us all being friends, but I'm sure she has some complicated feelings about it.

Arlo says, "You know you don't have to call the real police to investigate your fake murder."

"I know," I say. "But by now, it's a habit. Remember what you said when I found that body on the beach?"

Arlo laughs, looking embarrassed that he'd played it off that lightly. "I thought you were joking."

Patsy looks non-plussed, and it's suddenly awkward, since I'm sharing an in-joke she's excluded from with her boyfriend. How did life get this complicated?

Rosemary looks from Patsy to me and back again. I'm sure she's picking up on the awkward vibe. She may be the only person in her family who's not a cop, but you can't fault her investigative instincts. She extends a hand to Patsy and says, "Hi, I'm Logan's mom. So nice to meet one of Fee's friends."

Arlo flinches. He'd always called me Lis. It must still hurt him to hear me called by the pet name Logan gave me. I feel bad about hurting him, but he'd had to make a decision, too, and he and Patsy are good together.

Patsy introduces herself and Arlo, and they start making small talk.

Logan comes into the dining room, looking sleepy. Even in a rumpled tee-shirt with bed-head hair, he looks hot. He and Arlo exchange a nod in greeting, and then he asks his mom, "Dawn's not up yet, is she?"

"No," Rosemary says. "But Fisher went for a jog along the Seawall. He said she barely woke up when he left the room. You two stayed up way too late last night playing cards."

Logan looks abashed. "I was behind by 200 points. I couldn't just give up, could I?"

I had gone to bed before they'd even started playing cards last night. And now I feel like I'm the one on the outside of the conversation.

"Were you looking for Dawn for something?" I ask.

Logan shakes his head. "Just making sure I got up before she did."

He moves towards the coffee urn. This is a different side to Logan than I've seen before. The only person I've really seen him be competitive with is Arlo, and that was in part because of the whole romantic rivals thing.

Arlo tells me, "I didn't realize what a good actress you are until Patsy and I watched the contest video."

"What do you mean?" I ask. I hadn't actually watched the video. I'd felt like I must have done horribly, so I wasn't terribly excited to see how – well, terrible it was.

I pull up the video. I look better than I'd imagined in the frilly blouse, and I think the hat comes off as playful rather than frumpy. So, yay! I watch it until I get to the end of my lines. Ash sneezes off camera, and it sounds like a muffled gunshot. I look startled, and then turn away from the camera and then back again, looking scared. The expression was because I'd forgotten the line, but it looks like I was scared by the noise I'd heard, and whatever I'd seen behind me in the room. No wonder Chloe decided she had enough to work with in that one clip.

Logan, watching over my shoulder, looks impressed. The video continues, with information on the contest, and clips of the hotel, shot in a way that makes it look ominous. I feel a bit defensive on the hotel's behalf. It's actually lovely, after the work my aunt and my friend have put into it, when it's not shot at odd angles with the color saturation turned down. It has a view of the bay, and landscaping with palm trees and bromeliads that have to be covered when the island has the odd cold snap – as had obviously been the case the day someone shot the background video. It's all uncovered now, so Chloe must have collected the shots from someone – likely Ash. I can only imagine he'd been planning to use it for advertising his true crime podcast. Something about getting to see where the amateur sleuth lives, or some such nonsense.

Aunt Naomi comes in, hobbling on her sprained ankle. She says, "Felicity, your guests have already started arriving."

"I'll be right there," I say, hurrying over to her. "You should be sitting down, not greeting people."

Logan says, "Whoever it is, they're early. The emails we sent out clearly said that event check-in begins at four."

His mom says, "Honey, what have I told you about hospitality?"

He looks abashed again. He clearly cares more about his mom's opinion than I'd anticipated. But I don't have time to mull over what that means, in the context of the buying-us-a-house situation. I help Naomi into a chair at the nearest round banquet table and hand her my barely touched coffee.

Then I go down the hall and out into the lobby. There's a couple standing there with zebra-striped matching luggage. They look in their early fifties, white, but deeply tanned. The guy is wearing a polo shirt and has sunglasses perched in his thick blonde hair. The woman has a dark bobbed haircut and is holding an uncaged ferret. The ferret jumps out of her arms and runs straight towards me, making chittering noises as it moves. I take a few involuntary steps backwards. I am terrified of ferrets, ever since having been bitten by one as a child. Even though I love animals in general. I muffle a squeak as this one climbs up on my shoe and chitters up at me, holding up a paw in what looks for all the world like a greeting.

"Oh, look," the woman says. "She likes you."

I force myself to stay still, when I really want to shake the ferret off and move away. But I don't want to offend two of my contest winners. "Really?" I ask.

"You can hold her if you want," the woman prompts. Her bobbed black hair sways as she talks.

"But don't ferrets bite?" I protest.

"Only if they're not properly trained and socialized," the man says, sounding bored. "Sasha spends a lot of time with

Cheeseburger. As long as you pick her up without hurting her, you should be fine."

I don't like the way he said *should* there instead of *will*. But I force a smile, take a deep breath and bend down to pick up the ferret. I tell her, "Hi Cheeseburger. I like your name."

Cheeseburger squirms a bit in my hands, and once I've got her cradled in my arms, she shoves her head into my armpit. I gasp, so startled that I nearly drop her.

Sasha's bob moves again as she says, "See? That wasn't so bad. I'm Sasha Wimbleton, and this is my husband, Sebastian. He's my plus one, as per the event invite. I hope you don't mind that Cheeseburger is my plus two. The whole request was so last minute, we didn't have a chance to get a pet sitter."

"Of course not," I say, though inside I'm still panicking about the ferret in my arms. And not only on my own behalf. One of the few things I do know about ferrets is that they're not safe to have around rabbits. Even if, up close, they're not nearly as big as I remember, and Cheeseburger's masked face is actually cute.

Logan walks up to us, looking down at his phone. He tells Sasha and Sebastian, "The hotel isn't open in general, so there's no check in process. I just got the room list. It looks like you're in 307."

Which is only one floor down from my suite. Which does nothing to allay my panic towards my poor rabbit. Though the way the ferret is cuddling against me, I could almost swear she is trying to calm me down. Which is kind of sweet. I hand Sasha back her ferret, and Logan offers to help with the zebra-stripe luggage. The Wimbletons don't look exactly happy, and I'm not sure why. It's almost like they had expected something – more. But what can they expect when they're hours early?

As they're walking away, I hear Sebastian ask Logan, "Is there a conference room? I may need access to a computer while I'm here."

The minute they're all on the elevator, I whip out my phone and call Autumn.

She sounds distracted when she answers, and I hope I haven't interrupted her writing time, or her newlywed time. Still, I blurt, "I need you to come over right now and take Knightley home with you for the weekend."

"Well hello to you, too."

"I'm sorry," I say. And then I explain the ferret situation.

Autumn is on deadline for her new book, which is why she wasn't planning to be here for the mystery weekend. But Knightley is okay amusing himself, as long as Autumn makes sure there's nothing inappropriate he can chew.

"Calm down," Autumn says. "I'll be there in twenty minutes."

I hang up the phone and almost immediately, the elevator dings at the same time one of the front doors opens. Logan exits the elevator, looking bemused, just as a partly Asian guy with purple hair walks in, talking to his phone in a way that makes it obvious he's streaming the experience. His accent says Jersey. He shows off the entry to the hotel, then focus in on me and Logan. I wave at the camera.

The guy says, "Check it out, you guys, there she is! Can we get a little love for the mistress of mayhem, Felicity Koerber." Now that's a new one. I guess I shouldn't be surprised that a streamer won one of the contest spots, since it was a contest advertised mainly on social media. But I've heard about streamers getting in people's faces and being disrespectful. I hope he's not going to cause the other guests trouble. He turns the phone camera back at himself and says, "Gotta go. I'll let you all know later if I wind up solving the mystery. Buh-bye!" Then he pockets the phone and walks over to me and Logan. The way he approaches is intimidating. The guy has a thick, uneven scar running down the right side of his face. It looks like he was in a motorcycle accident or something, and scraped the pavement good and hard. He's wearing an oversized black hoodie zipped most of the way up, and there's a tattoo at the base of his neck that looks like a snake. But his ensuing easy smile belies the impression. "Sorry about that," he says, extending a hand to shake. "I wasn't expecting you to actually be here this early. I just got off a plane, and I didn't have anywhere else to go, so I wanted to use my time wisely. I promise not to stream during the party."

"That's a relief," Logan says.

"Though I'd like to take some video to post after, if that's okay."

Logan says, "You'll have to get all the guests to agree to that."

I know Ash is already planning to take some clips, but I don't really want to go into that. Instead, I ask the guy, "Plane from where?"

"Japan," he says. "I've been living there for the past four years. You may have seen my YouTube channel? TokyoGoGo? It's a pun, because gogo means afternoon in Japanese. And I go places my subscribers wish they could."

I chuckle politely. "Sounds like fun."

Logan asks, "What's your name? I need to find you on the rooming list."

"Hudson Nolan."

I ask, "And you seriously flew here from Japan just for this weekend? You must have left the second you got the email. Which is flattering. But why?"

Hudson says, "Are you kidding? I love Ash Diaz's podcast about you. And I have a sponsorship with an airline, so the flights are cheap."

I guess I never really thought about Ash having a following outside of Texas, let alone outside of the country.

Logan says, "You're on the second floor."

There are only four floors to the hotel. Logan's family is on the fourth floor, not far from my own suite. But we decided to scatter the guest on the various floors, so they don't feel crowded.

Hudson turns towards the elevator, but then he turns back and asks, "On the tour of the chocolate shop, are we going to get to see the murder books?"

I feel the hairs at the nape of my neck rising. I keep thinking I've come to terms with my shop's reputation. After all, I put the books that have helped me figure out clues to the mysteries I've solved in glass cases, on display. People sometimes come from out of state to see them, all rare editions of classic books. But it still irritates me the casual way Hudson calls them murder books, like it's just another landmark he wants to stream.

"You'll get to see everything tomorrow morning," Logan says quickly, before I can say anything defensive.

Hudson heads up to his room, and then it isn't long before Autumn arrives.

Autumn and I are the same age, and have been friends since middle school – though we lost touch for a while when I was living out of state. She is wearing a flowery sundress that accents her curves, and she has a red headband pushing back her afro. She's holding her hands at an odd angle away from her body.

When I go to hug her, I realize it's because she has wet nail polish.

"Were you at the salon?" I ask.

"Drake's mom got us a spa day as a wedding present. We finally decided to use it." She sounds a little guilty. Probably because she bailed on the mystery party because she's on deadline – and then she decided to go to the spa. Presumably, she wasn't planning on telling me, so as not to hurt my feelings. But how could I be hurt when she was willing to drop everything and come help me?

Fisher comes in, back from his run, carrying a bag with a logo on it from one of the tourist shops. Today, his tee-shirt reads, *I'd propagate that*. Mildly inappropriate humor, but he is a landscape architect, so it's at least logical.

Autumn gives a short laugh at the shirt, then gestures at the bag in Fisher's hand. "What'd you get?"

"Presents for Dawn and Mom," Fisher says, holding each object as he talks about it. "A silver sand dollar necklace for Dawn, since she loves the beach, and this pelican sign for Mom."

By which he means Dawn and Logan's mom. His own mother passed away, several years ago.

Autumn says, "That's thoughtful."

Fisher says, "I've been really enjoying visiting the area. People are so laid back, and the beach is great. I'm going back out to do a sand sculpting lesson later."

"Putting your architecture skills to good use," I say.

"Don't tell them," he says, as he turns towards the elevator. "I want them to just think I'm a genius."

"Come on," I say, gesturing Autumn towards the elevator while it's here. "Let's get Knightley, and then you can get back to Drake before they steam his pores for his facial."

Autumn laughs. "You joke, but that man likes being pampered even more than I do."

We take the elevator up to the fourth floor. Fisher goes into his and Dawn's room. I hear her mumbling sleepily as we continue on to my suite, which is at the end of the hall. When I open the door, Knightley is sitting I the middle of the rug, chewing on one of his toys, being his sweet lop-eared self. But when I move towards him, he starts snorting, a sure sign he's agitated, then he hops behind a chair. He must smell the ferret on my clothes, even though I'd only handled it for a short time. It did have a rather distinct odor. Still. He'd never reacted this way before when I'd petted, say, a dog.

Autumn gives me a sympathetic look. She has to realize that Knightley running away from me hurts my feelings. My bunny and I have been through so much together, and I know he trusts me. Autumn says, "I'll get him. I'm sure it will be fine once you change your clothes."

But it's not fine once Autumn leaves with Knightley and all his things, and my suite is quiet and empty. I tell myself that it's only for the weekend. And that there are only six guests left to arrive.

After I've been sitting on my sofa long enough to have gotten over the upsetting event, there's a knock on my door, and Logan is standing there. I let him into the living room, and he looks puzzled. "Where's Knightley's cage?"

I explain about the ferret, and Autumn's rushed trip over here.

Logan says, "Dawn and Fisher have challenged us to a sand volleyball game."

I say, "That sounds like fun, as long as you don't expect us to win."

Logan knows I'm not the most athletic person in the world.

He says, "That's fine," but the tightness in his jaw says he really wants to beat his sister.

Still, I change into one of my few tee-shirts and hop in Logan's car to head over to the nearest stretch of beach, leaving Aunt Naomi all the information for rooming at the hotel. Once we park and make our way down the steps, I can see Dawn waving at us. It's already crowded on the sand, even though it's just getting warm enough for good beach weather. The seagulls are everywhere, trying to grab snacks out of people's picnics, and kids are bouncing in the waves with colorful floats. I grew up here, and there are so many good memories of fun summers out here. But none of those memories involved playing volleyball.

Chapter Three
Friday

Logan and I lost three games in a row, and then Fisher drug us down to watch the sand sculpting. It was interesting, especially getting to see the finished sculptures already dotting the beach. There's a poignant one of a dog sleeping next to a pair of shoes. But that's simplistic, compared to the elaborate tableau of Jabba the Hut from Star Wars, or the dragon with the individually carved scales and hoard of sand-based "gold."

I give it a try for a few minutes myself, but I'm already hot and starting to sunburn, so we leave Fisher and Dawn and head back to the hotel.

The rest of the guests at least start showing up at the event arrival time, after I've had time to shower and change.

First, there's a Doctor Ted Durango, with a thriving cosmetic surgery practice in Houston. He has a wide face, and an equally wide plasticky smile. He has dark hair with mutton chops that accent his neat facial hair and brown skin – though when he tilts his head to look at the palm tree, there's an obvious bald spot in the back of his hair. He's probably older than he looks, and I wonder if maybe he's had a facelift. He doesn't say much as he's rolling his small black suitcase across the lobby.

He's heading for the elevator when a woman bearing a striking resemblance to the Doc, and wheeling a similar suitcase, comes in a moment or two behind him. Her hair is long and still thick, though there are some silver strands mixed in with the dark ones. She has crow's feet around her eyes, and deep smile lines. She is carrying a metal water bottle with some kind of filter at the top. She takes a long sip.

Logan says to the woman, "You must be Doctor Durango's plus one. Though I don't see him having marked one down here."

She blinks at him. "*I'm* Doctor Durango, PhD. Celtic Languages and Literature."

The elevator dings, but the original Doc Durango doesn't get on it. Instead he turns and blinks at the new Durango. "Elena?"

"Ted?" She sounds equally surprised.

"You know each other?" I ask.

"I should say so," Ted splutters. "Elena's my twin sister. Who hasn't spoken to me for the past six years."

Elena says, "I wouldn't be speaking to you now if you hadn't blindsided me." She turns to Logan and pokes him in the chest. "How dare you trick me into coming here?"

"Whoa. Wait a minute," Logan says, "We didn't have anything to do with this. You entered the contest, right?"

"Right," both Elena and Ted say at the same time.

Ted says, "I'm a huge fan of true-crime podcasts."

Elena makes a *weirdo* face at him, and says, "I love games. But more than that, I'm a huge fan of craft chocolate. We're going to get to tour your chocolate shop, aren't we?"

"Well, yeah. Tomorrow," I say. It's a bit odd that she just asked the same question as Hudson.

This whole interaction feels a bit odd, in fact. The contest was supposed to be entirely random. What are the odds of it having picked two people who are related? And not only that – they're twins. Which is a big thing in *A Murder is Announced*. Suddenly, I feel incredibly uncomfortable. What might I have put in motion?

Aunt Naomi comes hobbling up the hallway from the dining room. She must have heard the surprised voices and come to check things out. I give her a stern look. She really should be resting that ankle. Yet she's not looking at me. She's heading for the front door, and when it opens, Uncle Greg is standing there. He has dark hair, with hints of gray at the temples, and hazel eyes. He's wearing a tee and jeans and black steel-toed boots. Because he works offshore, they don't get to spend as much time together as either would like, and they aren't shy about sharing a deep kiss right there in the doorway. When they finally break apart, Naomi's lipstick is smeared all over Greg's mouth. She says something, and he wipes at his face with his sleeve.

Ted abandons his suitcase and steps towards them. He tuts, then says, "Naomi Lavergne, is that really you?"

Naomi gasps. She shrinks back towards Uncle Greg, grabbing for his hand. "Ted. What are you doing here."

"You guys know each other, too?" Logan asks.

It's obvious that they do – and that my Aunt Naomi isn't happy to see Ted again. She looks more skittish around him than I had been around Cheeseburger the ferret.

Greg squeezes Naomi's hand. He says, "I'm Naomi's husband, Greg. She's Naomi Thibodeaux now."

"That's a shame," Ted says. "I wouldn't have minded another chance at trying to make her Naomi Durango. We came pretty close, didn't we Naomi?"

Naomi is squeezing Greg's hand so hard her knuckles have gone white, but she doesn't say anything. She may be trying to keep her composure, so as not to disrupt my event – but I'd be happy to kick this guy out of here if she needs me to.

Elena slaps Ted's shoulder with her envelope purse and says under her breath, "Read the room, you jerk." She offers Naomi a tense smile. "I'm so sorry. You'll have to excuse my brother. He only has two brain cells to rub together, and no idea how to live in the present. I'm sure you don't want him around all weekend, so I can help him with his luggage back into his overpriced car." She turns to Ted. "I assume that was your Bentley out front?"

Naomi lets go of Greg's hand and takes a step forward. Her hands are trembling, but she says, "That won't be necessary. We're all adults here, and Ash already has all the roles for the mystery cast. I'm sure we can survive a weekend together."

Ted smirks at Elena and tells her, "See how you're always over-reacting. Just like about Mom."

Elena gives him a poison look. "You got her power of attorney and sold her house. Now she lives in what used to be my home office. How is that over-reacting?"

"It's been six years, El."

As they're discussing this, Greg helps Naomi hobble out the door, presumably heading for one of the wrought iron tables in the little patio area.

Ash and Imogen come in that same door, dressed like they belong at a British Country Fete. Ash is still wearing his trademark square glasses, and Imogen has her long blond hair held back with a glittery scrunchie, so it's not a perfectly costumed look. But it's enough for this party. Ash is holding a box with manila envelopes lined up vertically inside. Imogen has a big whiteboard that keeps threatening to slip from her grasp. I turn to help her, leaving Ted and Elena to their fight. We get the supplies into the dining room.

I can hear Carmen, my pastry chef at Greetings and Felicitations, humming in the hotel's kitchen. She and Enrique are handling the catering this weekend. Carmen is bringing us her breads and desserts, while Enrique, a chef who does pop-ups and catering, is handling the savory foods. We've worked with him before – most notably at Autumn's wedding. They must have come in the kitchen entrance – which Aunt Naomi had only recently gotten around to uncovering and restoring, since it had been previously been boarded up. Another reminder about how close this place is to being ready to sell.

My chest feels heavy. It feels like Aunt Naomi needs me right now. I really can't move far away.

And what's up with her and this Ted guy anyway? I really don't remember her dating anybody except Greg, back when I'd been a kid. I mean, she probably did have other boyfriends before that, but wouldn't I have met someone she was that serious about? Unless it was before I was born. In which case, we're talking about a guy who's been holding a torch for over 30 years, but never bothered to get in touch. And Naomi would have to have been extremely young.

It's very odd. And I don't like the fact that he's going to be staying in the hotel.

"Chin up, Koerber," Ash says. "This time, there's not really a murder. All you have to do is play host, which you're great at."

"Sure, right," I say. It's about time I get to have a party where nothing serious goes wrong. The universe owes me that. And if Aunt Naomi can suffer through the presence of her old flame, so can I.

Imogen says, "I had so much fun working with Autumn to write this thing. You know she offered to look at my novel? I know what a huge imposition that is, so I never would have asked. But I was telling her how much I love her new series, with the chef and the ghost kitchen, and we got to talking about how I've been trying to get published writing romance, but I had an idea for a romantic suspense." She giggles. "Sorry. I'm babbling. I'm just nervous to see how well the game goes over."

"It's fine." I give her a brief hug. "You know, I know someone who writes romance." Though I have been sworn to secrecy as to the real identity behind the author's pen name. "I can ask if there's any openings in her writers' group."

"You would do that?" Imogen practically gapes.

"Of course." I feel a connection to Imogen. After all, not only have we both suffered a tragedy in our lives, but we're both engaged at the same time, to guys in the same friend's group. She and Ash are getting married a few months before Logan and me. Isn't it weird how often one person – in this case Autumn – gets married, and then it seems like everybody else is following suit? If you'd asked me a few months ago, I wouldn't have been sure I'd ever be ready to get remarried. Let alone that I'd be the one to propose. But I had, and I feel like I'm finally on the right path.

There's a clatter out in the lobby. Oh, no! Could Aunt Naomi have fallen again? I rush down the hall, but Naomi and Greg are still gone. There's a middle-aged black guy leaning over the sofa from the back, trying to right the end table. He's thin and in relatively good shape, showing off thick biceps as he grasps at the table. The guy is moving like he's drunk, which is entirely possible, since it would be much easier to move around the sofa than to try and grab the edge of the end table on tip-toes over an obstacle.

I look at Logan, who grimaces and nods. This must be one of our guests. Toasted, and it's not even one in the afternoon.

"Hi," I say, forcing a smile. "I'm Felicity."

The guy gives up in the coffee table and straightens up, squaring his shoulders. "I'm Jordan. Is there going to be an open bar at this thing?"

"Sadly, no," Logan says, sounding like he'd like a drink at this point himself. After all, we are in for a doozie of a weekend with the assembly of party guests we've had so far.

Jordan says, "I guess you can't have everything. We get to tour the chocolate shop, though, right?"

Why does everyone keep asking that? "Yes, of course, tomorrow."

Jordan nods. "Good. I've heard you do boozy truffles there."

What is it about this guy that feels so one-note? It's almost like he's pretending to be obsessed with alcohol. I don't know. There's just something fake about him.

Logan asks Jordan, "Would you like me to help you to your room? There's about an hour before everyone is supposed to meet in the dining room for Friday night dinner and orientation. Maybe you want to freshen up a bit."

Jordan looks at Logan like he can't decide whether he ought to be offended. But then he says, "Maybe I can take a nap, then you can recap orientation."

Logan scowls, but doesn't comment. I get it. If the guy bothered coming here, he should at least participate. Logan picks up a duffle bag off the floor—obviously the object that had knocked over the end table—and hefts it. He says, "What have you got in here? Rocks?"

"Close," Jordan says. "Gold." He doesn't elaborate.

Logan and I exchange a skeptical look. It feels like Jordan is trying to create his own character for the weekend. Some kind of gold miner or bank robber or something.

Logan suddenly chokes back a laugh. He's looking at the front doors. I follow his gaze. There's a woman in her thirties just reaching for the front door. She has curly black hair — and she's wearing a burgundy jacket, khaki slacks and a gold-trimmed pillbox hat. Talk about coming in character. She's dressed as the singing telegram girl from the movie Clue. Once she enters the lobby, it's clear that she's wearing tap shoes. There's a series of sharp clicks as she walks across the lobby.

When she is standing ten feet in front of me, she goes into a little tap routines and sings, "Thanks for inviting me, to your fun mystery. And for the chocolate, it will be great I bet. Signed Ireeeeeene."

"Wow!" I say. "You put a lot of work into to this." I feel bad for having to add, "But the invitation instructions clearly stated modern setting, with pre-created roles for all of you. I don't think any of them is as a singing telegram girl."

"That's okay," Irene says, gesturing at her hat. "I'll just wear this to orientation. See who gets a kick out of it. I have other clothes in the car."

Jordan, who never made it onto the elevator, says, "That's great." He's grinning at Irene in a way that makes him look totally smitten. She returns a flirtatious smile. He asks her, "What do you do when you're not cosplaying?"

Irene taps in a little circle, moving her hands dramatically. When she stops, she sings, "I'm a tra-a-a-vel agent."

Jordan claps his hands. "That's great. I'm a theater teacher. And a film reviewer. And I think you have a lot there to work with."

"Really?" Irene blushes.

Jordan turns to Logan and says, "I think I'm going to need a couple of strong cups of coffee and a shower. Do you think someone could bring a pot up to my room?"

"That can be arranged," Logan says. He sounds as relieved as I am that Jordan seems to have found a reason to focus on what's actually happening this weekend.

My friend Bea shows up next. She's a canine unit dog trainer, who is accompanied by Satchmo the Beagle. I appraise her of the presence of a ferret in the hotel. Bea is concerned, since dogs can consider ferrets as prey animals, but she has Satchmo leashed, and he is a trained—albeit retired—police dog.

We're standing together chatting, when the door opens again and a tall heavyset man with a luxurious beard and mustache walks through it and says, "My, what a lovely dog. Top of the morning to ya."

His cockney accent is thick, to the point it's almost indecipherable. He's wearing a beige suit with a wide gold tie that looks ten years out of date.

Logan appraises the guy and says, "Actually, it's afternoon."

The guy looks taken aback. "Well, top of the afternoon then. I'm Colin Lipscombe." Colin leans down to pet Satchmo. The beagle licks the back of his hand. "As luck would have it, I'm a dog trainer."

Bea says, "There's no need for that. Satchmo is a retired police dog."

Colin flinches, no doubt rebuffed by her brusk decline of his services. "You don't say."

Logan says, "You're on the third floor. I can help you find your room."

"I'd be mighty obliged." Colin has all his luggage in a backpack, so there isn't much for Logan to do.

Logan returns shortly and is back talking to Bea about the best way to condition a dog's coat – now that his mom has decided to keep Cindy, the little dog he was fostering. I know Logan had gotten attached to Cindy, so I'm not sure why he decided to give her up. Maybe his mom needed some cheering up, dealing with his dad's medical issues. Who knows? Maybe he just doesn't mind because he plans to move closer to them. At any rate, Cindy is still in Minnesota, with Logan's mom's friend.

Bea and Logan's conversation breaks off as a white woman in her late twenties, wearing a long beige sweater over a long brown skirt, walks in. She introduces herself as Cynthia Reed. She doesn't say much else. I can't tell if she's shy or disinterested in the whole event. Maybe she just entered the contest for the free hotel stay.

At least now all the contest winners are here.

The orientation session goes off without a hitch. Carmen and Enrique's catering is delicious, starting with a lemon chicken and orzo soup and a goat cheese and pear salad, followed by enchiladas and skirt steak.

The room has twenty large round tables, and an area on one side with two banquet-length tables on an elevated stage. The tablecloths are all stark white, and the walls have gold accents – another recent addition – against dark beige paint. Obviously, we're not using all the space, and we are encouraging the guests to sit close to the stage.

About half of us have changed clothes for dinner, to look a bit dressed up for the game. Logan's set aside his usual pilot's jacket for a long-sleeve button up shirt and tie. The tie has tiny planes all over it. It's not his usual style, but it was a recent gift from his mother. I've switched to a sundress with big sunflowers on it.

Thankfully, Sasha leaves Cheeseburger the ferret in her room, and her husband Sebastian seems too occupied by something on his phone to be snide. Cynthia, the carefully nondescript woman is still wearing a long sweater over a different long skirt. She is sitting next to Sasha, attempting to show her pictures of a cat. Colin, the big guy with the heavy beard, is sitting at the other side of the table, studying the room.

Elena and Ted, the feuding twin brother and sister, have chosen tables as far as possible from each other in the dining room. Jordan no longer appears drunk. He has showered and changed into fresh clothes – before seating himself next to Irene, who is still dressed as the singing telegram girl. Hudson, his purple hair now spiked up with very solid looking gel, has ditched his hoodie in favor of a brown corduroy jacket with elbow patches. He sits down on the other side of Irene, and asks permission to film her singing telegram outfit. She gets up and does a whole dance routine she's obviously practiced for the occasion. Jordan looks a little annoyed at the interruption, but he still smiles when the camera is turned his way. He did say he was a theater teacher, after all.

Sasha, turning around from her own table, asks Hudson, "Have you ever considered reconstructive surgery on your face? I know a guy out in LA. He's very good."

Is she saying she's had work done? If so, I can't tell.

Hudson says, "I've made my peace with the way I look."

"Oh," Sasha says, and I can see the curiosity burning in her eyes, though she doesn't quite dare ask him what happened to cause the extensive scarring.

Hudson says, "It's okay. You can ask. About eight years ago, I skied into a tree."

"You poor baby," Sasha coos. "You could have been killed. How did your mother take it?"

Hudson waves a dismissive hand. "She wasn't that worried. This is a lot more superficial than it looks."

Sebastian taps Sasha on the shoulder and asks her something quietly. Sasha turns back to the conversation at her own table, but she keeps glancing back, giving Hudson encouraging looks.

My friends all wind up clustered around one big table. Bea has brought Satchmo down with her, and the beagle has moved over to sit on my feet. I love this dog. Patsy and Arlo are holding hands on the table, which is sickeningly cute. So are Aunt Naomi and Uncle Greg – which is just cute.

Logan takes my hand unselfconsciously, rubbing his thumb across my knuckles, sending giddy loving warmth through me. We really do fit together perfectly, right here. Logan's parents and sister, and her husband, are at the table with Hudson, Jordan and Irene, but they're on the other side and seem to be absorbed in something they're debating amongst themselves. Fisher is wearing a sweater vest over a dress shirt, and Dawn has her hair down, hitting her shoulder in a puffy sleeved red dress. Logan's mom opted for a sequined top and black pants, and his dad has added a jacket to what he was already wearing. Fisher hands a piece of paper to Dawn, and she shows it to her parents, who both start laughing. It's hard to see how close they are, with little room to fit an extra person in. And the fact that they might want to pull

Logan away from this table, all the way back to Minnesota, hits a sour note.

Ash passes out the packets for everyone's characters. I don't get one. Everyone else does — including Aunt Naomi and Uncle Greg.

Once we're dismissed from the table, Logan shows me his character sheet. He asks, "What am I supposed to do with this?"

I say, "You pretend to be whoever is on the page during the scheduled mystery-solving sessions. You can be yourself the rest of the time."

Logan gives a dismissive wave. "I *know* that. I mean, what am I supposed to do with this character? I'll feel stupid."

Ash has given him Paisley Vain, an arrogant aristocrat with a heart full of greed. Which is so not Logan. Ash probably thinks this is hilarious, considering Logan is a tough-guy, ex-bodyguard, ex-cop, with a tortured, tragic past.

Logan doesn't look amused, but I convince him to be a good sport. After all, this event is in his honor. It's a testament to his personal growth over the course of the time that I've known him that he can at least attempt to be silly.

In character now, Ash gathers us in the lobby.

Several people sit on the sofa in front of the fireplace. Imogen lets out a startled, "Oof." She reaches underneath herself and pulls out the sheathed knife she sat on. She places it on the coffee table, saying, "Oh my, who could have left that here?"

She looks conspiratorially at Ash, but he looks a bit confused.

It must be a prop knife, and maybe there had been some miscommunication on where it had been left. Or maybe the game's killer or victim was already supposed to have it.

But that sheathed blade, easily a foot long, looks so ominous sitting on the table. It looks so real – like we've genuinely invited violence into the room.

Ash puts on a fedora and gestures to Imogen, who is fastening a glittery peacock fascinator to her hair. Ash says, "Mrs. Iwanna Besomebody and I are grateful to you all for coming tonight, as we celebrate our good friend Paisley Vain and his new chocolate bars – along with his engagement to the enigmatic chocolate maker, Nawu Seeme."

I realize he's looking at me. But I don't have a character sheet. Does that mean I'm the victim? Or maybe that I disappear, to be myself as host, or to check on the chocolate shop. Tracie and Miles, my two most responsible employees are running it, along with a couple of new folks I've hired, since both Tracie and Miles have college classes to work around. And tomorrow we'll be heading there for a tour. But right now, I have no idea what to say, and embarrassed heat comes to my face.

Logan saves me. He sniffs dramatically and says, "Thank you, Ivan."

I stifle a giggle when I realize Ash has named his own character Ivan Besomebody. Somehow, that suits him.

Logan takes my hand and says, "Focus, Miss Nawu. This evening is all about me – I mean us. Don't go looking at our host with eyes meant for me." Man, Logan's a better actor than I gave him credit for. I'm getting to see lots of new sides to him this weekend.

I giggle louder, and try to improvise. "You know I only have eyes for you."

Logan says, "Now tell everyone how great I am." His lip is quirked up on one side, a sign he's joking, but there's challenge in his eyes for me to play along.

I say, "Paisley's great, y'all. If you ever need a shoe repaired, or a five-course dinner cooked, or a greenhouse built – he'll know just who to call to get the work ordered."

Logan bites back a laugh. In real life, he's genuinely a good cook and a decent carpenter. No idea if he's a good cobbler or not, though.

Ash says, "That's all true. Paisley even still has his first Rolodex, from 1993, to prove it. But Paisley is genuinely an excellent chocolate maker. So don't be afraid to try the samples you'll receive throughout this weekend."

Irene waves her hand and when Ash acknowledges her, she asks, "What's a Rolodex?"

I know Rolodexes are antiques now, but has she seriously never watched an old enough movie or TV show to have seen reference to one? I have seen plenty, and I'm not that much older than she is. I glance across the group, to Aunt Naomi, who mouthes back at me, *I had one.*

I guess I just assumed that Irene, as a Clue fan would have a bit more '80's nostalgia in her wheelhouse. But maybe – is she talking as herself or in character?

Ash says, "As the youngest one here at only sixteen years old, I guess we'll have to cut you some slack, Miss Pikkit." Okay. It makes sense, since her character is a kid. "But since you are Paisley's ward and heir, maybe you should get him to explain it later, since it may be part of your inheritance. Unless, of course, Miss Nawu swoops in and snaps it up first."

I arch an eyebrow at Ash. Am I supposed to be the victim in this scenario? It would have been nice for him to give me a heads up.

Logan turns towards Irene. "Now Nose."

"It's No-zay," Irene says. "No-zay Pikkit. You of all people should know that."

Ash splutters, trying to hide his reaction that Irene has turned his juvenile name joke back on him. Nose Pikkit indeed.

Imogen is over in the corner, looking pleased. She did write the script for this, after all.

"Say, Nose," Logan's sister says.

"It's No-zay." Irene chose the bit, and now she's going to have to commit to it.

"Okay, Nose," Dawn repeats. "When you're rich you won't leave your old violin teacher, Mrs. Stratovarius living in a shack in the mountains with her husband and twenty poodles, will you?" She smiles a big cheesy smile at Irene and then gives a challenging look at Ash – very much like the look her brother had given me.

I glance at Ash. He obviously gave Dawn and Fisher the characters with the weird complicated backstory on purpose, probably after she tried to steamroll him into letting her be the killer. That doesn't mean he told her no, since embarrassing her and then giving her what she wants would be a very Ash thing to do. It doesn't mean he told her yes, either.

Colin stands up. In his thick cockneyed accent, he says, "I object. No-zay is an absolutely charming woman." He turns to Irene. "How'd you like to go on a date with old Cecil Flirty? Get away from all this riff-raff and really see the island?"

Logan says, "No, I object. As her guardian, I demand you leave her alone."

"Fine. Well anyway, top of the morning to y'all." Colin looks around, as though expecting someone to continue the skit.

Logan whispers, "He's been saying that to everyone all night. I'm beginning to wonder if something is wrong with him. Or maybe he doesn't really speak English."

That doesn't make sense. How could a man with that thick of a British accent not speak English?

The lights flicker, which I assume is Chloe's doing, since she's here somewhere setting up effects. I'm surprised she wasn't at dinner, but she's probably trying to keep the illusion intact that there's nobody else at the hotel. I'm sure Carmen made sure she got fed.

But then the lights go out, and I feel a shiver of fear. I've worked myself up, convinced I'm the victim, and that bad things will happen in the dark. That that knife – showing up so unexpectedly – will somehow come into play. There's a scream, and confusing sounds of movement, but when the lights come back on, there's Chloe, lying in the middle of the floor.

I move towards her, my heart thudding. Is it still the game? Or has something really happened to her? She's still a minor – her mother would never forgive me, if I set all this up and something happened to her a la *A Murder is Announced*.

But then Chloe sneezes. Repeatedly. "Sorry," she stage whispers, "But somebody needs to dust under this credenza."

Strangely, Chloe doesn't have the knife. Shouldn't she, if that's how she was supposedly killed? Logan notices me looking over at the table. He moves over and picks up the knife. He asks me, "Think I should lock this away for safekeeping?"

I nod. We can figure out how it got there later.

Chloe sneezes again, bringing all the attention back on her.

Imogen says, "I think I detect a voice from the great beyond. What are your sneezes trying to tell us, Clementine Vanderclump? Do you know who murdered you?"

"No," Choe stage-whispers from the floor, deciding to just go with it. "But I read the character sheets, and I strongly suspect my secret brother Paisley, or my boyfriend, Walt Wishman."

"Me?" Ted says, and the group turns to look at him.

"Sounds about right," Sebastian tells Sasha, and there's such vehemence in his voice, I don't think he's acting.

Ted starts to say something, but then realizes we're all watching and settles for giving Sebastian a pleading look instead. Sebastian pointedly looks away. I have no idea what that's about. But clearly, the two know each other. Which is another weird coincidence for this contest.

Ted stands up, seeming to regain his composure. He says awkwardly, "I, Walt Wishman, just want to state that I only had love and respect for Clementine."

Elena – Ted's own sister – laughs and says, "You've never had respect for anyone in your life." She gestures towards Irene. "That one should know that better than anyone."

Irene hisses, "You're supposed to stay in character."

Elena says, "Fine. As Rhonda Vanderclump, I accuse Walt of killing my adopted sister, Clementine. That okay with you, Clem?" She gestures down at Chloe, but Chloe's done talking, and is doing a slightly more convincing job of being a dead body. The main giveaway is her smile and the slight movement of her head in time to whatever she's now listening to on her headphones.

Chloe sneezes again.

Elena nods. "See? It's fine."

Ash says, "You can accuse whoever you want, and make any speculations you choose. But you won't get the opportunity to officially vote for who you think the killer is until Sunday morning. But don't narrow your pool of suspects too soon. People often have secrets, and what you learn about the other suspects may surprise you."

People start breaking into groups, asking each other preliminary questions. I scan the room for Aunt Naomi and Uncle Greg, but they're gone.

I go outside and find both of them sitting at a patio table, talking softly. This landscaping is all new, as are the tables with their jaunty umbrellas and the gas fireplace for use in winter. Uncle Greg loves plants, so Aunt Naomi has started work on a small garden off to one side of the hotel, as a surprise for him coming home. They're sitting with their backs to it now, though.

I walk over and ask, "Is everything okay?"

Aunt Naomi says, "Yes," at the same time Uncle Greg says, "No."

I just stand there and wait for one of them to clarify.

Greg says, "I'm not comfortable subjecting my wife to bad memories from the past. Ted's a classic narcissist – manipulative and emotionally abusive. He isolated your aunt from her friends, damaged her self-esteem." Greg puts a hand on Naomi's, both palm down on the table. "Nobody should have the power to damage another person like that."

"It was a long time ago, Babe," Naomi tells him. "And I got out of the situation before things went too far. We hadn't been dating that long when he proposed. It felt like he was trying to trap me into something, which woke me up to the reality of the whole situation. This weekend – seeing him again – I'm not the same naive girl, and everything that happened seems ridiculous now that I have more self-worth. Throwing Ted out now means he still won. Instead, I can prove to myself that I have truly healed and put my regrets to rest."

I leave them to their discussion. Aunt Naomi has always seemed confident to me, and she's pushed for me to be happy and fulfilled my whole life. Even her attempts to get me out of my grief after Kevin's death – including her attempts to get me to try dating again – had come from a place of love, and didn't seem like something someone with a fear of relationships would have done. So maybe she wasn't permanently scarred by the ordeal – the way someone who hadn't been able to see the warning signs and walk away might have been.

When I get back inside the hotel, Ted is waiting for me at the door, though the others seem to have moved to different parts of the ground floor. His arms are crossed over his chest, and he looks none too pleased. He says, "I'm not sure why Naomi went through all this trouble to get me here with people who have a grudge against me. And after all this time – tell her I'm flattered I made such a big impression."

I say, "Naomi had nothing to do with the contest, or with who got chosen as winners. I assure you, they were all chosen randomly using Chloe's RaffleSchnaz account."

"Yeah, right," he says. "Maybe you should talk to your little Clementine and see if she and Naomi planned this together."

That seems a little bit of a stretch, but I don't see Chloe anywhere to defend herself. She's probably either gone home, or headed off somewhere to prepare for tomorrow. Honestly, I wish I could do the same. But I still have to play host, and right now I need to hand out the samples of the first of Logan's new chocolate bars. This one has a dragon fruit swirl running through it. The first person to correctly guess the flavor will win a prize. So I shake away the ickiness of talking to Ted, and try to remember that this is for Logan. I bet Sasha will win the prize. After all, in addition to being a fancier of ferrets, she's also a restaurant critic, according to Enrique. The fact that he knows her feels like just one more coincidence.

I head through the lobby and down the hall towards the dining room, intent on getting a snack. We haven't even done the cocktails yet, and there's no more real food coming tonight. I deserve a treat, after everything I dealt with today, and that soup Enrique made is calling my name. But before I go into the dining room, I hear voices coming from around the corner. I recognize Logan's voice. It sounds like he's at a table nearby, just inside the dining room. I start to go into the room and join him, when I hear him say, "This has nothing to do with Felicity."

I freeze. What has nothing to do with me? He sounds upset.

I scoot closer to better hear around the corner, without being seen. It may be bad form to eavesdrop on my fiancé, but this sounds like something I really need to know.

I hear Dawn's voice. She's saying, "Uff-da! All I'm saying is think about it. You could be doing important work. You have enough connections in high places, you'd have no problem getting back on the force, or joining whatever agency you wanted. You can't be happy wasting your life flitting around in airplanes."

"I happen to like airplanes," Logan says. "And I like my life a lot more now. I can be of service to others without constantly putting mine – and other people's – lives at risk."

Dawn lets out a frustrated grumbly noise. "This is still about the mistakes you made in the past. Yes, people did die. And yes, you were disgraced. But you can get over it."

Logan says, "I made my peace with all of that. Felicity's the one who helped me do it."

Dawn says, "And yet you have no qualms putting her life in danger, letting her act without training as an armchair sleuth. How many times has she almost died? And how many times have you?"

Logan is quiet for a long time. Finally, he says, "What Felicity does is her choice. I'm doing my best to support her decisions, and honestly, she's a good detective. But these are all cases she's gotten caught up in because of circumstances out of her control."

Dawn says, "Has she thought about getting training? Applying for a PI license? You two could work together, do something more meaningful than making candy."

Logan sounds frustrated, "Look, Dawn. I happen to like making chocolate, too."

Dawn says, "I kind of get the airplane thing. Flying was always Mom's passion, and I know you two were especially close because of all the hours spent in the air when she was teaching you to fly. But making chocolate bars? You can just buy chocolate at the store."

"But it's not the same quality as the bars Felicity and I make. And have you ever thought that maybe I want to spend time doing things my fiancé enjoys? That I like the work more because she's there? You know what? I have to go make cocktails for people who are actually excited about my silly little chocolate bars."

Oh no. I'm in the hallway, and he's definitely going to see me eavesdropping. I try to scramble backwards, but Logan turns the corner and sees me. He steps quickly over to me and takes my hand in his. He whispers, "How much of that did you hear?"

I say, "Enough. But not on purpose. I really just came down here for some soup."

"That sounds good, actually." Still holding my hand, he draws me into the dining room where Dawn looks both startled and chagrined.

We cross through the tables and into the kitchen, and Logan puts a hand on my back while we stand waiting for the soup to heat.

He says, "Sorry about Dawn. She can come on a little strong, but she means well."

"Yeah," I say. I'm sure she does – but is she drawing him away from me?

Chapter Four
Friday

The guests and my friends spend the rest of the evening chatting, some in character, some not, as we prepare the cocktails and then a late round of chocolate desserts. Carmen's pastry work is on point. Among other things, she's made chocolate-dipped alfajores, which are melt-in-your mouth sandwich cookies filled with dulce de leche. They're rich and crumbly, and she's used our earthy Chiapas chocolate to counterpoint something that otherwise might have been too sweet. That's one thing I love about working with Carmen. She understands the effort and care that goes into finding farms and collectives to buy beans from, in different regions of the world. Cacao beans are like wine grapes, in that the soil they're grown in, and the growing conditions have a big effect on the finished chocolate. The local varieties of cacao trees also produce slightly different fruit. That's why you can taste a two-ingredient chocolate bar – containing only cacao and sugar – that you'd swear had added cherries and raisins, or a different one that seems to have citrus, or even flavor notes like smoke and leather. They're a lot more than silly little chocolate bars, thank you very much, Dawn.

I know I'm a contradiction. Even though I don't like change, I love travel. I love flying to origin and meeting the people who grow the materials I work with. I love spending time talking to people about their passions, and eating new unfamiliar foods. I just want all of that on my own terms, knowing I have a safe place to return to. Which is probably why Logan wants a house – something permanent to call home.

I go back to my suite exhausted, planning to sleep the satisfying sleep of the successful hostess. Despite my paranoia, and the odd coincidences among the guests, and even the lights going out as part of the game, nothing bad had happened. I sit on the edge of my bed, putting moisturizer on my face, and I still feel anxious. It's almost anticlimactic that no one got killed. Which is a stupid way to feel, right? Like something is missing, no game afoot. Am I that twisted of a person that I tempted fate on purpose, half expecting bad things to happen? I refuse to believe that about myself. It isn't fair that so many murders have happened in my life that I've stopped telling myself that something like that won't happen again, and instead bracing myself for when it does.

My room is very quiet, and I'm extra alone without Knightley, even if Logan is sleeping just a few doors down the hall. But I don't think I'll lie awake thinking about him – this time. I'm way too tired.

Only, when my head hits the pillow, it is with a thump. There's a hard object underneath. I turn on the light, then I move the pillow. There, in my bed, is a vintage copy of *Frankenstein*. It looks like it could be an original edition.

My legs go all shaky when I try to stand up, as my heartbeat starts thudding in my ears. Oh no. Oh no. There's only one reason this book could be here. The guests at this mystery weekend are all fans of Ash's podcast. They all know about my connection to the vintage books. One of them has just announced the intention to commit a murder.

See? I hadn't been waiting for this to happen – I'd been dreading it.

I scramble across the room and into the hallway, heading for Logan's room. We have to get everyone out of their rooms, and find Arlo to notify him *before* the murder happens, for once. But before I reach Logan's door, behind me, from somewhere down the hallway, a gunshot rings out. I turn, but there's no one in the hallway. The shot has to have come from inside one of the rooms. But which one?

In a panic, I try to remember where everyone is supposed to be. Relief floods through me that Logan's family is all on this end of the corridor.

But that's tempered by dread. Something horrible has just happened, presumably to someone I just spent the evening with. The only two occupied rooms on the end of the hall the shot had come from belong to Ted the medical doctor and Irene the singing telegram travel agent.

I finish my mad dash to Logan's door. He's already opening it — shirtless, I might add — to enter the hallway and investigate the noise. He's built, and I can't help admiring his torso, before making eye contact, and telegraphing the worry in his alert green eyes.

"Fee," he says, crushing me to him. "You're safe. My heart can start beating again."

"I'm okay," I say softly, though my voice sounds weak. I want to just melt there, against his chest, but there's no time. Someone could be hurt – or worse. So I pull back and say, "That was a gunshot, wasn't it?"

"It sounded like one."

There's no way to know which of the occupied rooms might contain someone dangerous. But I'd been in the hallway when the shot was fired. And we're on the fourth floor, which doesn't have windows at the end of the halls, like the ones on the second and third floors, or easily climbable routes between the balconies and the smaller ones on the floors below. So it's unlikely that whoever left that copy of *Frankenstein* on my pillow has had a chance to escape.

I whisper to Logan, "Irene's in 406, and Ted's in 402."

Logan says softly, "Stay here and call Arlo. I'm going to see if I can hear anything through either of those doors."

I follow Logan partway up the hall, getting a good vantage point, right where I can tuck into the space where the corridor T's into the landing for the elevator if something dangerous happens and I need to get out of the way. Logan has a gun in his hand, and he's moving like the cop he used to be.

I step around the corner and call Arlo.

He says, "This better be important, Lis. Patsy and I are about to settle a bet."

He sounds like he's flirting with Patsy, while talking to me. Eww. I don't want to know what they're up to. I stare down at the blue patterned carpet.

I tell him, "Believe me, the last thing I want to do is interrupt your date. Both Logan and I believe we heard a gunshot on the fourth floor of the hotel. Where are you?"

"Down by the beach," Arlo says. "I can be up there in five."

I move back into the hallway, getting close enough to Logan to stage whisper, "Five minutes."

He shakes his head. "Can't wait that long."

There's a soft popping noise, like a soda can opening, coming from inside 406. Logan looks at me, and I take two steps back. I guess he figures that's about as good a compromise as he's going to get, because he sighs loudly and gives me an exasperated look, then he kicks in the door.

There's a startled – yet masculine – squeak. Hudson – the vlogger who'd taken the video of Irene – is sitting at the small desk. He has headphones covering his ears and putting a dent in his purple hair. His eyes are wide as he stares at the gun in Logan's hand.

Hudson slowly raises both his hands in surrender.

Logan asks, "Where's Irene?"

Hudson blinks. Obviously, he can't hear a word Logan's said. He slowly lowers his hands enough to take off the headphones. He's trembling.

Logan repeats, "Where's Irene?"

"I don't know, dude." Hudson licks nervously at his lips. "She said something about seeing if there's a bar. But that was like an hour ago."

Logan gestures for me to keep an eye on the other occupied room across the hall, while he checks the bathroom and closets and under the bed. The curtains are open, and there's clearly no one on the balcony. He tells me, "He's right. She's not here."

"But what are you doing here?" I ask Hudson. Tension is flooding out of me that we found him alive. Maybe there's a reasonable explanation for the noise – one that has nothing to do with that copy of *Frankenstein* showing up in my room. Maybe I'm not really a murder magnet after all.

Hudson gestures to the laptop computer on the desk. "I'm helping Irene with her website for her travel agency. She told me she'd give me a hundred bucks. Plus, it's driving Jordan crazy that I'm in here."

I feel a twinge of disappointment. "So no action scenes, or anything that might have sounded like a loud bang?"

"Not really," Hudson says. "And I had the audio feeding into my headphones, so nobody else would have heard it, even if there was."

Which means the gunshot was real – and the other room it could have come from is Ted's – the guy nobody liked. And that thought fills me with dread.

"Stay here," Logan tells Hudson. "And keep the door closed."

"What's going on?" Hudson asks, but Logan's already moving out in the hallway, closing the door behind him as best he can with the busted lock.

Logan says, "Well, any element of surprise we had is gone." He moves over to 402 and tries to turn the handle. It's locked. He sighs before he kicks that door too. Only, it doesn't budge. Logan gives me a confused look, and tries pushing the door with his shoulder. It seems to bounce a bit, but not really open. He shrugs and kicks it again, and this time it flies open.

And any hope I'd had that I was overreacting, that that book hadn't actually been a message from a murderer, vanishes. "Oh no," I say to the silent room wishing I could summon up more of a panic. I'd been panicked before, when I thought there might be a chance to save the victim. Now I'm just sad, overtaken with empathy.

Ted is at the desk in his room, too, but he's slumped back in his chair. There's a laptop in front of him, but the screen is solid blue, like it had crashed at the same time as its owner. Ted is clearly dead, shot in the chest, but I move carefully over to check his vital signs anyway. Nope. Zero pulse.

I let out a long sigh. Ted was obviously unlikeable. He hurt people, made them keep grudges. But even he didn't deserve to die.

Logan clears the room. There's no killer in the bathroom or the closet, or hiding under the bed. And the patio doors in this room are still completely painted shut. He says, "No one could have disappeared down the hallway while we were still in it. So you know what this is."

Arlo appears in the open doorway. "It's a locked room murder." He half grins, despite the scene in front of us. "Sorry, it's just that I've always wanted to say that. Most homicides are pretty mundane."

I gesture vaguely in Ted's direction. "Well, this one's not. I mean, how'd the guy get shot in the chest while he was facing the laptop set on a desk against the wall?"

"That's what we have to figure out," Arlo says. "A lot of locked room mysteries hinge on some sort of trick. It's possible that Ted was killed somewhere else and then posed here."

Logan says, "So you're saying that the bang we heard was a misdirect?"

"Not necessarily," Arlo says. "Honestly, we know very little at this point."

"Ted's body is still warm," I point out. "I don't think this happened more than a few minutes ago."

Arlo nods. "Then the shot you heard may well have been the real one. Look for anything out of the ordinary. But please, don't touch the evidence. It's going to be hard enough explaining how you two just happened to find yet another body."

"It's not on purpose," I say, glancing back at Ted's still form. He's obviously not the first dead guy I've seen, but his quiet presence still makes me shudder. "Trust me."

"So you think this is yet another coincidence?" Arlo asks.

"No," I say. "I think this was all carefully orchestrated. There's another killer calling me out."

Logan sucks in a sharp breath. He had nearly died the first time a killer had sent me a rare book as a challenge. He says, "Fee, we should get you out of here. If another sick mind has fixated on you, we need to take away the challenge."

I say, "I feel responsible, for bringing all these people here. And there are some things that don't make sense." I explain finding the copy of *Frankenstein* under my pillow. I say, "We created a mystery weekend spoofing *A Murder is Announced*. So why not just follow that? Have the lights go out at dinner tonight, before Ash has a chance to shut them off during the game, and then leave me a copy of Christie? How does *Frankenstein* play into this? It's not crime fiction, and there's certainly not a locked room."

Arlo says, "Obviously, somebody considered Ted a monster."

My aunt certainly seemed to feel that way. But I know she's not a killer. And neither is my uncle Greg, no matter how protective he might feel right now. That's the real reason I need to stay – to make sure they don't wind up getting blamed for this. After all, Aunt Naomi had been the one to offer up the hotel for the party. And now she's going to be stuck flipping a hotel where a murder happened. Though, to the right person, that might be a plus, since certain groups of people flock to hotels with sordid histories out of morbid curiosity. Especially in places like Galveston.

It feels callous even thinking that, with Ted's body still in the room.

Logan asks, "Were those scratches always there?" He's pointing at the floor near the door, where there are several long scratch marks.

"I'm not sure," I say. "I think Naomi redid the floors already in these rooms." I look around, trying to see what could have caused scratches. "Or maybe she didn't get to this one." I gesture over at the floor vent on the other side of the room, which is currently missing its cover. "You'd have to ask her."

I vaguely hear the elevator ding in the distance. Someone giggles as two people move down the hallway.

I hear Jordan say, "I just want to drop you at your door, to make sure you made it back safe."

Irene giggles again. She says, "You just want to punch Hudson in the teeth for being in there."

"Can you blame me?" Jordan asks.

Irene says, "I told you, he's working on a project for me."

"So you say," Jordan says petulantly.

Irene says, "Look Jo-Jo, you're the one who wanted to play this off like we just met. I would-" Her voice cuts off suddenly as she notices the open door. She clears her throat. "Good evening, Felicity. I hope we didn't disturb you rehearsing the script Jordan just gave me."

She's stiff and awkward, and quite a terrible liar. These two know each other, and are terrible at hiding that fact. But why hide it? Why would we even care? Especially now that we have more important things to worry about.

Irene looks past me, sees the scene inside the room and gasps. She says, "Is this all part of the mystery? I'm sorry we came early and ruined the fun. But it all looks so *real*."

"It is real, Ms. Laslow," Arlo says. "And I'll ask you to step back until we have secured the crime scene."

"Come on, Irene," Jordan says, taking her arm and leading her down the hallway towards her room.

"It can't be." The shock and dismay on her face as she glances back looks genuine.

"You too had better go downstairs," Arlo says to me and Logan. "My CSI guy should be here soon."

"Fisk?" I say, somewhat cheerfully. He's a nice guy, who always appreciates a good pastry. And we have plenty of leftovers. "I better put on a fresh pot of coffee."

In the meantime, Arlo secures the scene while Logan knocks on doors, waking people up to herd them back into the dining room to await questioning. There are some folks missing. Elena is nowhere to be found. Bea is walking Satchmo, so he can take a quick potty break. And before the body was discovered, Chloe told Aunt Naomi that she was going for a moonlit walk down on the beach. Dawn and Logan's dad, the two cops in Logan's family, have the guests separated at different tables on one side of the room, waiting for the local cops to get organized enough to be ready to collect statements.

Dawn keeps looking at me, like maybe she wants to say something about earlier. But I'm not ready to talk to her. She said she thinks of me as a sister already. Well, a sister who doesn't respect me isn't something I need.

Bea walks back into the room and stands next to me, Satchmo heeling perfectly at her side. The beagle looks up at me, hoping I'll pet him.

On the far side of the room, Sasha has her ferret in her arms. Cheeseburger starts making upset noises at the sight of the dog.

Satchmo looks over, curiosity peaked, but he doesn't move away from me and Bea. Satchmo's training as a former police dog is probably part of what has him in check.

I notice Sasha has a harness and a leash on the ferret, unlike earlier. Sasha sees me studying the red rhinestone leash and says, "This hotel has so many nooks and crevices. I thought I lost Cheeseburger for a while, earlier, only to find her stuck in a drawer in the dresser."

Satchmo barks at the ferret, and Bea makes a scolding noise. Then Satchmo turns, his attention caught by noise in the hallway, as more people start moving into the dining room. Satchmo barks again, this time a happy sound, and he trots over to the door. Fisk leans down and pets the dog, his messy sandy-blonde hair flopping into his eyes. They've gotten to know each other, since Satchmo has actually helped sniff out clues in several murder cases since his official retirement.

In addition to Fisk, the whole crime scene crew comes through for coffee, and the guests sit gawking on the far side of the room as I hand out some of Carmen's alfajores, and the mini-chocolate chip cannoli, and egg tarts to the cops. It feels like I've been here before, too many times. I've admitted that I do like the puzzle aspect of solving a crime. But the shell-shocked look on people's faces after being touched by violence and depravity. That's something I will never get used to. That and the lasting effect on the family and friends that a death touches. Having suffered a loss myself, I know what it feels like to be going along one day, thinking you have your life and your tiny speck of the world figured out, only to have everything upended.

Poor Elena. She doesn't know it yet, but her brother is dead, and the last words she said to him were in anger. I don't know how to make it better. Empty platitudes are meaningless. And so I do what I always do. I feed people, nourishing the body to salve the raw emotions.

I go back into the kitchen and start pulling coffee from the oversized urn into cups for the guests. I have a smaller pot of decaf, so I put some of that into differently patterned cups. I go back out with a tray of coffee. Bea and Fisk are talking in the hallway, barely visible as I head for the tables. But Bea's cheeks are crimson, and there's a bemused expression on her face. Dare I say that Bea has a crush? Good for her. It's the first time she's expressed interest in someone since moving to Texas.

I start asking full caf or decaf, and then placing the appropriate cups in front of everyone. Sasha declines entirely.

Ash, who is on the other side of the same table, says, "I'll take hers."

Of course he will. Ash has never turned down food in his life.

When I move to the next table, Sebastian says, "I don't understand why we all have to stay here. It's obvious that your aunt killed Dr. Durango."

I look around to make sure my aunt didn't hear him say that. Naomi is missing from the room, but Greg is sitting alone, looking nervous. Presumably, that means Naomi is being questioned by the police. The thought sends a jolt of panic through me. Why is it taking so long?

"Be more sensitive, honey," Sasha tells her husband. "This has to be really hard on Felicity." She turns towards me and adds, in a confidential tone, "Sebastian's a therapist, so he's a student of human nature and psychology. And he's really patient when he's in a session. But it's way past his bedtime, and he gets cranky when he's tired."

Sebastian snaps, "Anyone would be a bit upset under the circumstances. I've never seen a dead body before. Have you?"

"Technically, you didn't even see the body," Sasha points out. "But it is very strange. Us being here when it happened."

Sebastian nods tersely. "Poetic justice, Sweetness. But it's still incredibly creepy being under the same roof with a corpse. It's like Brad is reaching out for revenge."

"Who's Brad?" I ask.

Sasha looks down at Cheeseburger, cupping the ferret's face in her hand. At first I think she's ignoring the question. Then she says, "Brad was our son."

Was. I'd gotten the impression of the Wimbletons as shallow and a bit arrogant, an irritable therapist and an eccentric food critic moving through the world as an unstoppable force. But how much of that is bluster, to cover the raw grief over their loss? There's a depth of empathy and understanding between us that would have been unimaginable a few moments ago. Sebastian isn't complaining about being here just because it's an inconvenience. This is bringing up some uncomfortable feelings, and he does honestly look a little scared. But what connection could there be between their lost son and Ted? Why had Sebastian used the word revenge?

Sasha says, "Before Ted became a fly-by-night plastic surgeon, he was a real doctor. Brad went in for a sports injury. Seventeen years old, a year from graduating high school, it's supposed to be routine surgery. Only – Brad doesn't make it out. There were accusations of negligence, and we had to take our comfort in the fact that the doctor responsible had lost his license. It was upsetting to find him here, at the same party, and to learn that he was operating on people again."

"Not upsetting enough to kill him," Sebastian says quickly. "We aren't that kind of people."

"Of course not," Sasha says. She looks down again and ruffles the ferret's fur. "Are we shnookums?" The ferret chitters, almost in agreement. "And we don't believe in ghosts, do we?"

"Neither do I," I say. "There is a logical explanation for what happened to Dr. Durango." Though at this point, I'll be danged if I know what it is. Not only is there the mysterious circumstance of the locked room murder, where it basically looks like someone shot the good doctor through his laptop screen, but the wild coincidences of this whole weekend. The Wimbletons being here, blaming Ted for their son's death – that's just one coincidence too many. I have to figure this out. I ask, "Why did you enter this contest in the first place? You don't strike me as the usual fans for Ash's podcast."

Sasha blinks at me curiously. "We didn't enter any contest. I received an email asking me to evaluate the hotel restaurant during a gourmet murder mystery weekend. Only, I got here to find that not only was I not a special guest, but the hotel restaurant in question isn't even open. I have heard about the young man doing the catering, because of his pop-up dinners, and I was intrigued. And the game aspect sounded fun. So we decided to just roll with it."

There's a weight sinking into the pit of my stomach. Someone had intentionally lured this couple here, knowing that they would recognize Ted.

I ask, "So you're not fans of my chocolate shop either?"

"I've never heard of it before," Sasha says reluctantly. "But after tomorrow's tour, and the year of chocolate certificates, I'll get a full chance to evaluate that too. Don't worry – if I like it, I'll still talk it up."

From one of the nearby tables, Jordan asks, "Are we still having the tour, considering there's been a murder? I assumed the whole weekend was off."

I'm still trying to figure out what Sasha meant by a year of chocolate. That hadn't been part of the contest – to my knowledge – but nobody else seems surprised. It explains why everyone seems so excited about the chocolate shop tour, though. Maybe Logan added it? I'll have to talk to him later.

Arlo walks into the room, trailed by Logan, who is supporting Aunt Naomi as she hobbles on her twisted ankle. Arlo says, "I'm taking lead on handling this case. We've set up a room where I can do the statement interviews. I'll start taking you one by one."

Does that mean Naomi was helping with that – or being interviewed? Surely they realize that with her hurt ankle, she couldn't have done the gymnastics to have disappeared out of a locked fourth floor room.

"Wait," Jordan says. "I thought you were just another guest, with the role of the bumbling detective for the mystery game. Sherrif Mitch McCowboybritches is a real cop?"

Arlo casts a sour look in Ash's direction.

Ash points at Imogen, who is sitting next to him. "Don't look at me. She came up with all the names."

Imogen pokes him in the shoulder. "Yeah, but you're the one who cast everybody."

Suddenly, there's an air of suspicion in the room, directed at Ash.

Hudson stands up and says, "You do seem to be orchestrating a lot of what's been going on tonight. How do we know you didn't set up the murder, too?"

Dawn stands up too and says, "This isn't going to turn into a lynch mob on my watch. I need you to sit down, take a cup of coffee and eat another cannoli, while you let the police handle this in an orderly fashion."

Hudson sits, but he doesn't look happy about it. He stares at his phone, which is sitting on the table in front of him, even though Dawn expressly forbade him to stream anything about the murder. You can practically see his fingers itching to share his news in a YouTube video.

I finish handing out coffee, then I move over to Logan. I ask, "Should we cancel? Send everyone home?"

He starts to say something, but then Elena enters the room. She's moving quickly, but she seems unsure on her feet. Safe to say, she's been drinking. She says, "I got a text on my phone that there's been an emergency. Is my mom okay? I told her she needs one of those slip and fall emergency devices."

Arlo steps forward. "As far as we know your mother is fine. But I regret to inform you that your brother was found dead tonight."

"Oh," Elena says. "Good." Then she seems to register the horrified silence around her. "I don't mean, good, like I'm happy he's dead. I just mean that I'm glad the emergency isn't about my mother. It's a lot more logical for something to have happened to

Ted. It wasn't an accident, was it? I assume somebody finally had enough of him and just killed him."

Irene gasps and says, "What a horrible thing to say."

Elena scoffs. "Even after everything, you always did have a soft spot for him, didn't you?"

Irene's face goes an angry crimson, and she balls her fists up on the table. "Ted may have been a horrible human being, but he was still a human being. Sometimes I wonder if you're the reason he was the way he was. I was never afraid of Ted as much as I was afraid of you."

"Why you!" Elena says, moving forward, a hand raised towards Irene.

Arlo intercepts her. "I think I just found the first person who needs to give me a statement tonight."

Elena wrenches away from him. "Get your hands off me, Stupid McCowboybritches."

"Actually," Arlo says, "It's Detective Romero. I have a real badge and everything." He takes it out of his jacket pocket to prove it.

Elena's mouth drops open and she lets out a squeak. Then she says, "Sorry. Of course, I'll cooperate in helping you identify whoever caused this horrible tragedy." She follows Arlo out of the room, looking back at me like, *you could have told me he's a cop*.

"That's it," Jordan says. "In the morning, I'm leaving."

"Why not right now?" Hudson asks. "I'll go next giving my statement, then I'm out of here. I'm not spending another night in the same hotel as a killer."

"You don't know it was one of us," Patsy points out. "It's not like this hotel is isolated from the rest of the island."

Hudson splutters out a laugh. "You think some random person off the street just stumbled in here and randomly killed the least likeable person on the premises?"

"You said random twice," Jordon points out.

"That's how random it is!" Hudson runs his hands through his purple hair. "Have none of you ever seen a mystery movie? There's always a second murder, to prove things are serious. I've already had a gun pointed at me once tonight."

Ash says, "Just because we were playing a mystery game doesn't mean things are going to happen like in a game – or a film."

All of the phones in the room start buzzing as a text message comes in to everyone's numbers. Even mine.

Hudson jumps like he's been stung. Everyone else responds something between curious and wary.

I check my messages, and there's a new one from GuessWho? – which isn't an extremely creative handle for a killer. And there's no question that's who this message is from. It says, *Pretend we are all locked in, in an isolated spot. No one is allowed to leave the hotel until noon, Sunday, except the caterers and the police – and Felicity, Logan, Dawn and Arlo, of course. If anyone else leaves the hotel doors, two more people will die. In the meantime, it's time to uncover all the secrets and clear the air.*

Everyone starts looking at each other, trying to figure out who could have sent the message. It seems to mirror the conversation we've been having, so it feels like it must be someone who's here. But I didn't notice anyone playing with their phones. It's like a magic trick, just like the setup of Ted's murder scene.

The vibe in the room has turned anxious.

Hudson says, "This is stupid. There's no way the killer would follow through with that. I'm out of here. Tell McCowboybritches that I'll email him a statement."

He tries to leave, but both Logan and Dawn rush to stop him. They get in each other's way, and Dawn winds up tripping Logan as Hudson nimbly dances around them and heads for the hall – where Bea – who's still there talking to Fisk – tackles him, using a technique that involves hitting at the back of the knees to pull down her much larger opponent. Satchmo barks, then growls. I follow Logan and Dawn towards the hallway. When I get closer, I can see the beagle has Hudson's tee-shirt sleeve in his mouth and is shaking it as he watches for signs Hudson is getting up.

"Fine," Hudson says. "If you insist I stay, I demand the right to talk to my audience, and at least tell them why I'm trapped here. Also, I want another caramel cookie. And a better lock for my flimsy door." He looks skeptically at Logan's shoes.

Logan turns to Irene and says, "Sorry about your lock. We'll get your things moved to a different room."

Once Logan gets Hudson back into a chair in the middle of the room, I wave for everyone's attention.

I ask, "Who here actually entered the contest off Ash's podcast or my social media?"

Except for Sebastian and Sasha, they all raise their hands.

Jordan says, "Although, I only heard about the podcast because of an ad that showed up on my socials last week."

Irene says, "I got that same ad."

Hudson says, "I'm a long-time fan of both Ash and Felicity. I entered multiple times."

Cynthia says, "I think I entered. I enter so many contests on social media, I couldn't say for sure."

"Me too," Colin says.

So, clearly, something happened to my contest. And I must have been specifically targeted because of Aunt Naomi's connection to Ted. But the contest was Autumn's idea – and I trust both Ash and Imogen, who are the ones who put the script together. So something happened between the steps where the idea was created, and the RaffleSchnaz. Which means I need to talk to Chloe – only she's still not back from her walk on the beach.

Logan asks, "And are you all saying you were promised a year of chocolate?"

"Absolutely," Hudson says. He holds out his phone, showing Logan an acceptance email.

Logan looks at me. "This doesn't define what giving them a year of chocolate actually means. You okay with giving them each a box of filled chocolates every month for a year?"

"That sounds reasonable to me," I say. Though honestly, I'm surprised that any of the guests would hold us to that, considering so much about the contest was obviously faked. But it just goes to show – chocolate really can be important. And I don't want to upset these people any more than they already are.

I tell Logan, "I'm going outside to look for Chloe."

He insists on going with me.

I ask, "What about this whole roomful of people? It seems like this could easily get out of hand."

Logan laughs and waves a dismissive hand at Dawn. He says, "I believe my sister can keep things well in hand. And if not there's my dad. Or Bea."

Chapter Six
Friday

The hotel is on the bay side of the island, But Galveston is a barrier island, which means it is long and skinny, part of a chain of such islands running along the Texas coast. So it won't take too long to get to a decent beach on the other side.

Logan and I take his classic Mustang, and even though there isn't a ton of time, I do a Google search for Ted Durango. There's the basics, with his website for his cosmetic surgery practice – which looks sketchy, even in website form, and a few interviews. He doesn't seem to have social media, but he does show up in other places. There's a picture of him at a coin show, holding up a rare dime that he bought for a record amount of money. And one of him with a ski boat that just pops up as an image, without context. There's a serious headshot of Ted in a blue suit with a wide navy tie, scowling at the camera. The caption says something about a law suit. That's to be expected, given the negligence allegations the Wimbletons had talked about.

The dime is actually one of the more unique things about Ted, so I go back and read the article, which talks about how

Ted's childhood hobby had actually financed his first year of medical school.

I tell Logan, "I think Ted had a thing for coin collecting."

Logan says, "I doubt he was killed over a couple of rare pennies."

"It was a lot more than that," I say. "Maybe the coins were a way of hiding how much money he really had. I wonder who inherits?"

"Arlo says they haven't found a will," Logan says. "He was no longer married and he had no children, so figuring out what happens to his assets is going to be a mess without one. They're going to try to contact his lawyer in the morning."

Logan turns the corner, and we start driving up the road along the Seawall, looking for Chloe's car. We're starting at about the same place we played volleyball earlier.

It's about one in the morning, on a weekend. A few of the businesses are open, mainly bars, but there aren't a lot of cars along the Seawall. It isn't hard to spot Chloe's pink VW Bug, which she drove to the island in from her home in Austin. We get out. There's no sign of Chloe in her car or on the beach. Logan and I still go down the steps to check out the area near the wall and farther out in the surf. Though if Chloe was either of those places, it would mean she was injured – or worse.

Thankfully, Chloe isn't here. But that only makes me more anxious for her safety. She's seventeen. Anything could have happened.

Logan catches my hand. We're down on the sand, not far from the water and there's the rhythmic sound of waves crashing, with the moon bright in the sky. It's a perfect, romantic spot. And a perfect moment. I look up at him, overwhelmed by how deeply I've fallen in love with this man. He kisses me, deeply, and I reach up to run my fingers through his hair. We've been through so much together, come so far from our respective broken places, and now we're supposed to get our happily ever after – if his family doesn't pull him away from me.

Logan breaks the kiss, and I come away breathing heavier. But he looks troubled. He says, "I'm sorry. I know you're worried about Chloe. I just couldn't help kissing you when you look so beautiful in the moonlight."

"I'm glad you did," I say, feeling giddy. He thinks I'm beautiful.

"Really?" He looks even more troubled. "You didn't really seem to be into it. Like you were distracted or something. You've seemed a bit distant over the past couple of days, and I'm worried I did something wrong."

"You didn't do anything wrong," I reassure him. "Not exactly."

He takes both of my hands. He says, "I've had to fight for my relationship with you, and that makes me feel like I've never been on equal footing. So if I'm losing you, be honest."

I suck in a gasp of salty sea air. He feels insecure? What about me? I blurt, "I'm just afraid-"

Then I stop myself. How can I tell him what I'm afraid of? If I confront him about the house, what if *I* lose *him*?

"What are you afraid of, Fee? You're one of the bravest people I know." He gives me that challenging look again.

Fine. I'll be brave. Logan has never been anything but honest with me. He deserves for me to be honest with him. I try to loosen the tension in my shoulders and keep my hands from balling into fists. I tell him, "I don't want to move to Minnesota."

He blinks, and a sudden frown makes his face look craggy in the moonlight. "Why would I think you wanted to move to Minnesota?"

Less sure of myself, I say, "You said your parents want to buy us a house."

"Yeah," Logan says. "Here, on the island. With my dad retiring, and all his health issues, they thought it would be good to have a place to get away from the Minnesota winters, so they looked on line and found an old Victorian home with a carriage house. Dad wants to convert the carriage house into a guest house, so he and Mom can stay when they want without being underfoot of us in the main house as newlyweds. Besides, he needs something that's one-story. I thought maybe you could talk Naomi into helping with the renovations in both spaces. Maybe get your dad to design the carriage house interior."

"Oh," I say. "Why didn't you tell me any of that before?"

He sighs. "Every time I even tried to bring it up, you suddenly seemed very busy doing something else."

He isn't wrong. Feeling a bit sheepish, I say, "I'm sorry I made so many assumptions."

Logans says, "And I'm sorry I made it sound like a done deal before talking to you. Where did you imagine we are going to live?"

Logan currently has an upscale apartment, also with a view of the bay. It would be reasonably easy for me to move in there. After all, he's already rabbit proofed it from the time Knightley and Aunt Naomi stayed there. But I've fallen in love with the hotel. Or maybe I just see it as safe. I shrug, like it's no big deal. I say, "I imagined that you'd move into the hotel. We could even knock out a wall to expand the suite."

"Fee," Logan says. "Naomi is going to have to flip the hotel. There's too much money tied up in it – both hers and yours."

"On one level, I know that. But I love having the place, with room to have events like this. I keep thinking there must be some way we can work it out." I give him a hopeful smile he probably can't clearly see in the moonlight.

Logan says, "I thought you wanted to work on expanding the production at the chocolate shop. We've talked about buying one of the depositor machines that drops chocolate chips on a conveyer system. Remember? We're getting enough orders now to justify it. And you wanted to take a couple of international sourcing trips. Even using one of my planes, those trips won't come cheap. I don't mind investing the money for a big chunk of it, but I can't afford all that, plus everything that would go into running a hotel."

Logan and I haven't really discussed much about how we're going to combine our finances. Kevin and I had had a joint account, and I had assumed Logan and I would do the same, but he's still talking like it's going to be my money and his money, and that I'm going to have to come up with some funds to keep my business running. I'm realizing that while we've talked about the big picture of what we want for our lives, there's a lot of small things we need to discuss. I tell him, "I think the chip machine can wait."

Logan says, "Now I've said something wrong again."

I shrug. "Just me assuming again. This time I assumed joint accounting."

"Really?" Even by moonlight, he looks surprised. "I assumed you'd want to have your own accounts. Isn't that the way couples today do things?" After a pause, he adds, "Though one set of books would make it easier to keep up with both of our businesses plus the household expenses."

I laugh and tell him, "I can't believe we're discussing household expenses on a beach in the moonlight, on a night when there's been a murder."

Logan shrugs. "We're getting married. We're going to be discussing a lot of mundane things. But we have to talk about the important stuff, too. Is there anything else bothering you?"

I've opened up this far, and it's gone well. I might as well be honest all the way. I say, "I'm still afraid of your family pulling you away from me."

Logan laughs. "Impossible. My mother loves you. She's always wanted a daughter-in-law who likes good food."

The giddy feeling is back, a bit. I've made a good impression on his mom. But I say, "Your sister doesn't. She finds me somewhere between incompetent and frivolous."

Logan says, "Then let's prove her wrong by solving Ted's murder."

I tell him, "I love how much confidence you have in me."

And he says, "I love how your lips taste like strawberry lip gloss in the dark."

His hands come around my waist, and he draws me to him, and we share a longer, less troubled kiss. But we finally have to break apart again and go back up those Seawall steps to go figure out what happened to Chloe. I use the light on my phone to get a better view as I peer into the back window of Chloe's car. Logan's looking at his phone, instead. Maybe he's looking at some kind of tracking database. He's been known to find obscure data like that using the connections in high places his sister had commented on.

But when Logan turns his phone to me, he's pulled up the Greetings and Felicitations Instagram account. And there in the feed is Chloe, taking a selfie in front of a bar that does axe throwing. "There she is."

Behind Logan, on the other side of the street, is the very bar I'm looking at in the picture.

I say, "Well, what are we waiting for?"

We leave our car parked where it is and carefully cross the street. I wouldn't willingly cross Seawall Boulevard during the day, when the traffic is heavy and unpredictable, unless I was at a crosswalk with a green light, but there's no traffic on the street at the moment. We quickly reach the bar and open the door to a blast of loud country music. I'm not opposed to country, but it hardly seems like Chloe's scene. There's the thud of someone throwing an axe into something wooden. We follow the sound past a number of tall wooden booths into an area at the back. There are a couple of guys with axes standing about twelve feet away from a wall with wooden targets. One of them is wearing a polo shirt with the bar's logo on it.

Logan holds up his phone and asks, "Is this girl still here?"

The employee looks Logan up and down and then turns to me. "Is she in trouble?"

I say, "We're friends. But there's been an emergency, and the ringer must be off on her phone."

The guy looks skeptical, but he gestures over to a corner stuffed with beanbag chairs. We walk over and find Chloe sitting in a big purple one that looks like it's made of alien fur. She's curled up with her laptop, a pair of earbuds and a glass full of peach slush. She sees us and takes the earbuds out. In the same motion, she closes the laptop.

Logan nods his chin at her glass. "That better not be booze."

She says, "It's just blended fruit and ginger ale. You can check with the server."

"We trust you," I say, feeling surreal that I'm having a parenty discussion on underage drinking as a lead in to questioning her about a murder. Honestly, I don't think Chloe could have murdered anybody. But I can't let her age blind me to the fact that she's the only one in the position to have rigged the contest to draw in specific people. I try to think how to put this diplomatically. I start vague. "We were worried when you didn't come back to the hotel when you said you were just going for a walk on the beach."

"I did take a walk on the beach," she insists.

"She did," Logan says, showing me another shot from Chloe's Instagram feed, capturing the moon in the background of a night shot of white-topped waves heading for the sand. It's actually a beautiful shot, showing that despite her youth, Chloe has real talent.

I ask Chloe, "What time did you take that photo?"

Without asking why, Chloe pulls up the shot on her phone and shows me the timestamp information. It's about twenty minutes after that gunshot had shattered the night at the hotel. It would be a tight window for getting to the beach after somehow escaping from a fourth-floor room – but it could be done, so the photo doesn't serve as an alibi.

Logan asks, "Why did you come in here? I thought you were staying at the hotel."

Chloe scrunches up her nose. "I just wanted to talk to a few friends and verify something. I was right. That Dr. Durango? He's the same guy who got a number of YouTubers involved in hyping some skin care products that turned out to be dangerous. You guys really shouldn't trust him."

Logan and I look at each other. Surely, that's not a motive for murder. It doesn't even sound like Chloe was personally involved.

Logan says, "I don't think that's going to be a problem."

It's almost a quip, but Chloe can't know that. Instead, she nods and says, "Good. I knew you had good instincts about people Mr. Hanlon."

He says, "I think I have pretty good instincts about you. You're a good kid."

I say, "Did you not realize who Dr. Durango was when the app drew his name for the contest?"

Chloe shakes her head. She says, "He was going by a different name when he was selling the skin care line. Falsely claiming he was a dermatologist and everything. I did think it was a bit weird when the app sent me a list with two people with the same uncommon last name but different mailing addresses on it. But I figured it might be family that all liked to talk about the same true crime podcasts."

I say, "So you didn't get to see all the entries that got made, just the final list?"

"Yeah. I told you Mrs. Koerber, that's how it works. I think you can pull reports and stuff if you want to, but the whole point is to get people to follow your social media accounts and share whatever event or product you're advertising with your friends. You see the contest entries in real time, as likes and reposts and subscribes."

I ask, "Were the Wimbletons on the list when you got it?"

"Of course," Chloe says. "Otherwise I would have told you there'd been a mistake."

"Fair enough," Logan says.

I ask, "So you're saying you sent them the exact same email text you sent everybody else?"

"Why would I have sent them anything different?" Chloe looks from me to Logan and back again. "Will one of you please tell me what's going on?"

Logan says, "There's been a murder at the hotel. Dr. Durango is dead. And the killer has said that if anyone other than four specific sleuths leaves the hotel, more people will be killed. You're already not at the hotel, so I don't want you going back there and putting yourself into more danger. I'll give you some money to stay somewhere else, and to buy a toothbrush and clothes, or whatever you need."

"You don't have to do that, Mr. Hanlon," she says, but she still takes the money when he pulls it out of his wallet and hands it to her. But then she tries to give it back to him. "Are you sure the killer exempted me? I don't want anyone else to die just because I'm too scared to show up."

I say, "We can't honestly promise you that. After all, you knew Dr. Durango, at least in some context. And it sounds like at least half of the people who got invited to this event knew him too, and had been wronged by him in some way."

"But that's statistically impossible." Chloe gestures with her phone. "Somebody must have hacked the list."

Logan says, "And that same person sent the Wimbletons a different email, inviting Mrs. Wimbleton to come to the hotel in her role as a food critic. So the list you got also contained fake emails for them. You must have sent the congratulations letters to someone else, and that person sent the critic request as you."

Chloe takes a beat to absorb this. She says, "That sounds so unlikely. I'm a suspect in this murder, aren't I?"

"Officially?" Logan says, "Not yet. But keep the ringer on. The police are definitely going to want to talk to you."

She nods, solemnly. "I promise not to leave town, or talk about the case, or anything else. And I won't livestream about it, either."

"Good girl," Logan says, and we leave Chloe nursing her ginger peach slush and putting her AirPods back in her ears.

We get back in the Mustang and Logan starts it. He says, "What about you? The killer said you could leave – not that you had to go back. Want to stay somewhere safer tonight?"

It's tempting. Of course it is. But I shake my head. "I doubt that was the intent of that text. We're supposed to be trying to catch the killer, and if we disappear, who know what other measures they might resort to."

"Okay," Logan says, though I can tell he would rather argue with me on this.

We get back to the hotel, where everything is quiet, as even when tragedies happen, people still have to sleep. When we get to the fourth floor, Dawn is outside her room, leaned back in a chair propped against the door. She wakes as we walk towards her.

Dawn whispers, "I had to find a way to keep an eye on Hudson. There's no way down outside, and my chair will fall if he opens the door."

"Good call," Logan says.

"Where's Fisher?" I ask.

Dawn says, "He's sleeping on the sofa, which we moved to block the patio."

"Poor guy," I say.

Dawn says, "Don't you mean poor me? At least he got a pillow."

The elevator starts moving again. I go back to look and it's headed for the first floor. Somebody was in the lobby after all – or. Oh, no. I rush into my suite and out onto the balcony. There, in the parking lot is Chloe's pink VW Bug. Which means she's back in the hotel. And now she has to stay.

It's honorable of her to not want to risk the killer's ire being directed at others.

Logan shows up on the balcony beside me. He says, "I'd rather die than have a kid risk death to ensure my safety."

Logan and I may have to discuss a lot of conflict-driven things, but that's one thing we can agree on.

Chapter Seven
Saturday

The next morning is chaotic. I know Carmen will be up early, baking, so the first thing I do is call her to appraise her of the situation. I tell her, "Given the circumstances, everyone will understand if you cancel. The police can bring in take-out pizza."

Carmen says, "Don't worry. We'll be there. You can't do a proper investigation fueled by takeout."

I say, "You can't just speak for Enrique too. You have to make sure he knows what he's getting into."

"Oh, I'll tell him," Carmen insists. "But he'll still be in. He wants to cook for Sasha Wimbleton so bad, he'd walk on hot coals to do it."

I ask, "Even if Sasha has the strongest motive to have committed the murder out of anyone here? Ted is responsible for her son's death."

Carmen says, "Even if she's guilty, a nod from her about his food would mean a lot. He's gone all out this morning, creating a Salvadorian breakfast buffet to celebrate his roots.

Remember those pupusas he made for the tea party at Wobble House? He's made those again – but full sized and stuffed with chicken seasoned with chile de arbol. And his atol de elote is to die for."

"Maybe don't use that phrase with the guests," I say.

Carmen says, "So is the plan then to cancel the tour of Greetings and Felicitations?"

"Not exactly. Tracie's going to do a virtual tour. She found a service that offers drone delivery to send over samples of all the bars. They claim to be the world's first party in a drone."

Carmen laughs. "There's no need for that. Enrique and I are using the kitchen here at the shop. I can just pick up samples on my way out."

I tell her, "I think it's part of Tracie's master plan to impress the guests. It's supposed to come with a shower of confetti, a custom light show, and who knows what else."

"Sounds like Tracie," Carmen says. "Always the artist. Speaking of – she just walked in. I need to make sure she understands that if the murder makes the news, we're likely to get slammed with your ghoulish fans."

"I thought you embraced the fans," I tell her. "Good for business, look for opportunities, all of that."

"I do. But that doesn't mean they're not ghoulish. This is the second 'fan' who turned out to be a killer."

Which explains why she's not excited about them as she used to be.

Carmen and I hammer out a few more details, and then I hang up. I head for the kitchen to get the coffee started. Logan's mom is already there. Today, she's wearing a green satin top the same color as her eyes.

She smiles and offers me a cup, saying, "None of us got very much sleep last night."

I take the mug. "I'm sorry I got you all into this predicament. I should have known something bad would happen."

"Now don't go doing that," she says.

"Doing what?" I ask.

She says, "You and Logan are just alike. No wonder you two found each other. My son has made an art out of taking responsibility for things that are outside his control. It was tragic that that girl died when he was a bodyguard. But the only one to blame for that was the gunman that pulled the trigger. Same here. You put together a party, in good faith. The only person to blame for putting anyone in danger is the crazy person threatening to kill us if we leave."

"You're taking this very calmly," I point out.

She says, "Did Logan tell you that when I was young, I was a stunt pilot? I even did some work for a couple of movies. I've stared death in the face a lot closer than this."

"No," I admit. "He did tell me once that you're the reason he loves flying."

Ash wanders into the kitchen, yawning. He heads straight for the coffee pot. I've never seen him dressed this casually – in a black tee and lounge pants, instead of his usual button-up shirt and skinny tie. But his still doesn't lose a beat when he says, "That sounds amazing, Mrs. H. I'd love to interview you about it for the podcast. Logan plays a big part in it, and I'd love to hear some stories about where he comes from. And a few death-defying feats from an aviatrix would play well to the audience, too."

"Ash," I say in a warning tone. "We've discussed this. You don't get to interview my family."

"Technically," Ash says, "They're not legally your family until you and Logan tie the knot. Besides, we're all stuck in this hotel for literal days. What else are we going to do?"

"I don't suppose anyone wants to keep trying to solve the fictional mystery?" I ask.

Logan's mom says, "I doubt your friend Arlo would take kindly to anyone calling him McCowboybritches again."

I point out, "But if they're not playing the game, what are they going to do all day? We need to keep the guests occupied, so nobody tries to leave."

"I can try," Ash says halfheartedly. "I guess."

"After you interview me," Mrs. Hanlon says. "Now, there was this one time when I was doing a chandelle in an experimental aircraft – now, that's when you take it up to maximum climb, don't you know – and when I came out of the turn, I ran smack into a goose. Honestly, I should be dead, only-"

"Wait until I have the camera running," Ash says. "It's always hard to capture the same spontaneity on the second take."

"You betcha."

As they're leaving the kitchen, Arlo walks in, nodding at Ash as they cross in opposite directions. It's the first time Arlo and I have been alone since I made my choice between him and Logan. I think we've both been avoiding this. I'd have thought it would feel awkward. But it doesn't. Arlo is still my friend.

He just points at my coffee mug, and I move to fix him a cup. He looks very tired.

I ask, "Did the CSI guys find anything last night?"

Arlo holds up a finger and goes around the corner, to make sure there's no one in the dining room who could overhear what he has to say. Then he comes back, an excited smile coming over his extremely tired face. He says, "They didn't find any fingerprints on the door except for Logan's, your aunt's and your friend Tiff's – who isn't even here. And Ted must have been paranoid, because the reason it was so hard for Logan to kick the door in last night was because Ted had stuck one of those security wedges underneath it. Which means it really is a locked room, in the classic sense."

"Anything you can tell me about people's movements last night?" I ask.

After all, Arlo had questioned everybody, late into the night. It's the reason for the dark circles under his eyes so deep they almost look like bruises.

Arlo gives me a disapproving look. "You know I'm not supposed to discuss that kind of thing with civilians."

I shrug. "Worth a try. Besides, I thought this time might be different, since Logan and I were two of the detectives this killer has called out."

Arlo says, "Let's try not to bring attention to that. There was some talk at the station about evacuating this place by force, rather than have citizens in danger. That might still happen, if they can figure out a way to legally take everyone into custody."

That would actually solve a number of our problems – assuming the killer is one of us. There is always the chance that someone else could be in the hotel. It might not be huge as hotels go, but there are still a ton of vacant rooms and hiding places.

I say, "I still think Logan and I have to try to unmask this killer. There are clues here, somewhere, that are specifically meant for me to decipher. It's why the four of us have been granted the ability to leave, to follow threads of investigation."

Arlo says, "I still think it's odd that Dawn and I were included separately, by name, after saying that the police could come and go."

"You're a little insulted, aren't you?"

"Maybe," he admits, though he looks embarrassed to admit that this particular murderer has gotten to him.

I say, "Don't be. It means that you have been challenged. Logan's dad is a cop too, but he wasn't singled out. So he's not classed with the cops actively assigned to the case. The killer couldn't have known for sure that you'd be assigned as lead detective."

"That's a fair point," Arlo says, "But that's far from comforting."

Logan walks into the room, and instead of heading for the coffee pot, he heads straight for me and plants a kiss on my forehead. He says, "Good morning, Sunshine."

He looks put-together, wearing his signature pilot's jacket and jeans, which does little to obscure the memory of how built his abs had looked last night. He's shaved and smells fantastic.

I ask, "How is it you don't even have the decency to look tired?"

He says, "Experience with stakeouts and long nights doing personal protection. Trust me, I'll probably crash hard around two this afternoon. In the meantime, we need to make the most of our time." He casts a sour look at Arlo, which I assume is about him being here with me, but what he says is, "I had a little chat with my sister. She seems to think she's teaming up with you on this investigation. Cops versus amateurs. She's convinced that's what the killer intends. And she's so confident you two will figure out the killer's identity before we do that she talked me into a bet. If she figures out the clues first, I'll at least consider rejoining the force."

Arlo winces. "I don't think that would be good for your mental health. Or my ability to complain freely about my friends at the station."

Logan says, "Tell me about it."

Arlo looks at me. He says, "Fine. There weren't a whole lot of people last night with solid alibis for the time the shot was fired. The Wimbletons were in their room, and they alibi each other. You know where Hudson, Irene and Jordan were, since you ran into them yourselves. Your aunt and uncle also alibi each other. Elena claims she was at a restaurant last night, to get away from her brother, and someone there may or may not remember seeing her. He can't be sure. She has a receipt with a much later timestamp. Chloe also has a receipt from the bar she was at. Colin says he was asleep in his room, and heard nothing. Cynthia says the same thing."

I blink, taking in this sudden wealth of information. It is a bit frustrating that Aunt Naomi and Uncle Greg are so high up the suspect list. But I hadn't expected Arlo to be so forthcoming about all the work he'd put in last night – let alone summarize it for us.

Logan lets out a low whistle. "You must really not want to share an office with me."

Arlo says, "You're my friend. I don't want to see you lose to your sister."

Logan says, "We could get that same information ourselves, you know? All you did is talk to people who are already in this hotel."

Arlo scoffs. "See next time I do you a favor."

I say, "Logan may not appreciate it, but I do." I tell Logan, "I'd like to take another look at room 402, now that the police are done with it."

Logan says, "The way I busted the lock, I don't think that's going to be a problem."

I say, "I did always think you were better with lockpicks. Not nearly so destructive."

Logan says, "I'll remember that, next time we're in a life-or-death situation." He gestures with his chin towards my hands. "You're competent with a set of picks yourself now. I didn't see you offering to open the door. Not that it would have done any good with the door wedge in place."

Arlo says, "You two are impossible."

Still, he comes with us back up to the fourth floor.

"What about Dawn?" I ask. I look over at the door where her chair had been propped last night. It's not there. Presumably, someone else has taken charge of Hudson. "Isn't she expecting to team up with you?"

Arlo says, "Probably not before a couple more hours sleep and three cups of caffeinated beverage. If yesterday is anything to judge by."

Logan says, "Accurate."

I say, "Well, you guys are at least observant, to catch her habits. Let's see if we can find anything that everybody else missed."

We go into the room. Ted's body is gone, but the chair is still in the same place, though there's a tiny number underneath it. The laptop has been taken. On the surface of the desk where it was, there's a perfectly round sticky spot from some kind of clear adhesive. Had something been attached to the laptop, and later fallen off? Or had the desk been used to glue something, and the adhesive had gotten on the bottom of a cup, or the glue can itself?

I get down lower to examine the desk. It's a piece Aunt Naomi found at a yard sale, a writing desk with curved legs that end in dog's paws and a single wide front drawer with an iron handle. It's a beautiful piece, even if it does look a bit like it is preparing to run away.

I take a tissue out of the box on the nightstand to use to open the drawer, since the desk hasn't yet been cleaned. There's a weird tension. I pull out a second tissue, and it tears.

I dig into the box. There's a small leatherbound ledger shoved in with the tissues. Arlo was right. Ted really was paranoid. And I just found something the CSI guys obviously missed.

I flip the ledger open. The descriptions for most of the entries are vague. But the word Quiet is repeated on a number of the lines. And the name C. Lipscombe is in the book, dated last night. I show this to the guys. I say, "Do you think Quiet here could be some kind of code for hush money? I mean, Ted was involved in a number of shady things. Maybe he was blackmailing people." Of course, there's a darker possibility. After all, the last time I'd found a list like this, it had belonged to a killer for hire. *Quiet* could mean something much more ominous.

Logan, probably having the same memory, says, "Or he might have taken a job from Colin to quiet someone else."

Arlo says, "Sounds like I need to have another chat with old Cecil Flirty."

Logan says, "Don't you mean *we* should have a chat with him? Fee did find the evidence. We should at least get the possibility of a confession."

Arlo says, "I'll let Dawn know you were the one who cracked it if it turns out to be him."

I take a few more tissues from the box and use them to carefully open the desk drawer. There's a black circle glued to the inside of the drawer, of the same diameter as the goo spot on the desk. I say, "Now that's weird. I know that wasn't in the desk when Aunt Naomi brought it home."

The object is about half an inch thick.

Logan says, "It looks like a phone charger – only, there should be a cord coming off of it."

Arlo says, "Maybe it's solar." He gestures vaguely at the object. "Or maybe it's something else entirely." He gives me an odd look.

"What?" I ask.

Arlo says, "Like you said, your aunt bought this desk. Her fingerprints are on the door. She's the one who could have come into here hours or days in advance and set up the locked room. And she had a fight with the deceased the day of the murder. Who else had that kind of opportunity?"

"Anybody," I say, gesturing wildly. "We only have two security cameras in the hotel. One's at the front door, and one's at the kitchen. Some of the guests came early yesterday. Nobody would have been on this floor, and some of us weren't even in the hotel."

"Where were you?" Arlo asks, his head tilted in curiosity.

"Playing volleyball," Logan admits, looking chagrinned, as if he somehow should have known not to leave the premises unattended. Which is ridiculous. How would he have known there would actually be a murder.

Arlo looks at me. "You were playing volleyball?"

"He didn't say I was doing it well," I point out. "Besides, people have been in and out of the hotel throughout the remodel. Someone could have strolled in days ago, with the workers who were re-doing the wiring on the second floor."

Arlo knows this already. He requested Aunt Naomi give him copies of the recordings for the last two weeks so he can have someone review the footage.

"That's fair." Arlo takes a plastic bag out of his pocket and slips the ledger into it. "And honestly, I hope your aunt isn't involved. I like Naomi. She's good people. But even good people have been known to snap when presented with trauma."

I can't believe that Arlo honestly believes my aunt capable of murder – under any circumstance. He's known her for a long time. Since we were in high school, and she'd given us free Icees at the little tourist shop she and Greg used to own.

I look away, and I notice, in the corner, over by the air vent, there's a sparkly rhinestone bracelet, an inch wide in ombré shades of red and pink. I step over to it, saying, "This wasn't here last night."

"No," Logan agrees. "We would have noticed that, since it's on the same side of the room as the floor grate we were talking about."

The grate is still open. I peer into it. All I see is some silvery ductwork. No way the bracelet could have shot out of it, even if it had fallen into the system in a different room.

I say, "Maybe someone came in here this morning, and left it while searching the room."

Arlo says, "Isn't that the bracelet Mrs. Wimbleton was wearing last night?"

The evidence implicating the Wimbletons is adding up fast – almost too fast. What are the odds that Sasha would have come in here – in a state of panic over having left some evidence behind – and somehow managed to leave more evidence sitting neatly in the corner?

It feels more like someone might be trying to frame Sasha, since the person who invited Sasha here must know about her grief over her son. It's all very calculated. And quite twisted.

Logan says, "I'll get the door replaced ASAP. I'll take a door off one of the other rooms just so we can seal up this room."

I say, "I need to go down and oversee breakfast. Ash is going to try to revive the mystery party, and I have a feeling he's going to need all the help he can get."

Chapter Eight
Saturday

By the time I get back downstairs, Carmen and Enrique are setting up the breakfast buffet, and guests are trickling in. I am in need of sustenance, and not about to miss out on the spread that Carmen promised, so I wander over and grab a plate. Enrique is talking to Sasha, and he has a pleased yet embarrassed expression on his face. She must be saying good things about the food. I'm standing behind Sasha, so I give Enrique a double thumbs up. His only reaction is to widen the grin on his face.

He tells Sasha, "I'd be happy to get you copies of both. I self-published my cookbook, but Carmen has a publisher for hers."

As I move around them to fill my plate, I say, "Carmen's actually working on a second cookbook. One with light recipes, and gluten and dairy free options, to show ways that most people can enjoy chocolate."

"How interesting." Sasha doesn't seem impressed. She probably prefers smaller portions of more decadent food.

Watching her today, she doesn't seem nervous, the way you would expect someone who just committed a murder and is in a hotel full of cops and detectives. Cheeseburger, the ferret, is on her leash, this time on the floor. She rushes the length of the leash over to me, and taps my shoe with her front paw. She really is cute, once I get past my fear. I tell the ferret, "I'll pet you later, when I'm done with breakfast."

Cheeseburger makes a honking noise I don't know how to interpret. I decide to take it as agreement. I take a little bit of everything from the buffet and head for the table where Logan's dad is sitting with Fisher. They're quiet – another testament to how good the food is. I take a spoonful out of the little dish of atol de elote, which is something between a pudding and a beverage. It's like eating silk. There's huevos rancheros and beans and rice, which are seasoned on point. And the plantains are perfectly caramelized, with crema for dipping.

Chloe comes in and sits down next to me. She plucks a plantain off my plate and dips it in the crema. She says, "The food alone was worth coming back here for."

I tell her, "I still wish you'd gone to a hotel."

She says, "You think I'm just going to sit back and let people decide I had something to do with all of this?"

But her hand holding the plantain is trembling. She really is scared, trying to put on a brave front.

Logan's dad says, "It's better not to care what other people think. You know you did nothing wrong, then the investigation will prove that in the end. You'll be fine. Believe me, wanting to know people's opinions of you is a sure way to be disappointed."

Chloe pops the plantain into her mouth. After she chews, she says, "That's impossible for me. I live my life online. It's all about the slightly-edgy yet bubblegum pink life I live with my reformed jerk cat and my obsession for sushi. Tell you the truth?

Some days I hate sushi now. But I defined that as my thing, you know? Even the hint of suspicion that I was involved in orchestrating a murder – even if it's later proved false – and my sponsors disappear."

Logan's dad says, "That sounds like a wretched way to live."

Chloe taps her sparkly phone case. "I have tuition for college, and a tidy nest egg for when I move out of the house. I know more about marketing than some MBAs. It's a trade-off, and I'm coming out ahead." She gestures over at Hudson, who is sitting at a table with Irene and my aunt and uncle. He's telling a joke, showing off the tattoo at the back of his neck, partly obscured by his purple hair which seems to have lost some of its spikiness. "You know who he is? Hudson Nolan. He was a child actor in LA for years, but he never could get a breakout role. Wound up doing cereal commercials by the end of it. But then he turned 20, moved to Japan, and started his vlog. Now he has over a million subscribers watching him walk through the park with the sakura blossoms. He generally covers that tattoo when he's on the street in Tokyo – but how much of a price is that to pay for what he's found?"

Logan's dad gestures toward Ash, who has just walked into the room with Logan's mom. He must have changed before he interviewed her, because now he's wearing a button-up shirt and slacks. Logan's dad asks, "What about him and his podcast?"

"He's only got about thirty thousand listeners. But it's much more niche."

I have to keep my mouth from sliding open. I never really thought about how many people were actually listening to what Ash has been saying about me. Who would find my life that interesting, despite the high number of coincidences that had gotten me involved in solving so many murders? I'd pictured a couple hundred local people, maybe a few people who can't get enough of true crime in any form. But thirty thousand? It seems preposterous. I stammer, "That many?"

Chloe says, "It's nothing compared to Ash's blog. That's big enough to get him some real advertisers."

Logan's father makes a grumbling, considering noise. "A lot of people in this room are bigger deals than they would seem. Ash is a little goofy looking. That Hudson kid looks like he had a run-in with a truck. And Sasha looks like she's had one facelift too many."

"Dad!" Fisher exclaims, smacking his father-in-law's arm. "You can't say things like that."

Logan's father eats a few forkfuls of eggs, then belatedly says, "Why not, if it's true?"

"Because it's rude, Malcolm," Logan's mom says as she takes a seat next to him.

Ash goes to the front of the room, standing between everyone and the buffet table. He gives a half-hearted smile. "So. How's everyone doing this morning."

"I've been better," Jordan shouts in reply.

Everyone laughs, but there's a nervous edge to the vibe in the room.

Ash says, "I think we can all agree on that. But now that we're all here-"

"Not all," Cynthia points out. "Colin isn't here."

"I'm here. I'm here," Colin says, as he comes in from the hall.

That's a relief. Colin can't have any idea that we suspect him of – something. I'm not sure whether he's a blackmailee or a bad guy. Potentially both – being blackmailed about being a bad guy.

Ash starts again, "Now that we're all here, I think we should make a go of what we gathered here to do – solve the murder of Clementine Vanderclump."

"She can't have been murdered, she's right here." Jordan points at Chloe.

Chloe says, "Pretend I'm not here."

Jordan says, "It's a pointless exercise. There's a real murderer among us, and you want us to waste time looking for a fake one?"

Ash says, "I want us to try to maintain a sense of normalcy. We're going to do a virtual version of the chocolate tour in about an hour. So until then, if you could just play along, I would appreciate it."

Hudson stands up. He says, "Before we get started, I just wanted to apologize. I panicked last night. I was selfish, but I had some time to think about my actions. I wouldn't have been able to live with myself if I had left and someone had actually died. And now that I know Chloe came back because she was afraid we might not be safe without her – I'm deeply ashamed. *Mōshiwake arimasen.*" He nods his head in a way that feels close to a bow. Exactly how long has he been living in Japan?

Jordan says, "One less suspect, right?"

"I don't know," Cynthia says. "Chloe's name was on the email I got inviting me here. I don't care she's a kid, I don't trust her."

"But she came back," Dawn points out. "If she was the killer, don't you think she would want to get as far away from here as possible? Killers always make a mistake, and their best chance is to not be there when it gets uncovered. This place is crawling with cops."

Sebastian throws up his hands in frustration. "Of course Chloe came back! It actually makes her more suspicious. If she's the killer, she had to be here in order to enact the rest of her plans."

Jordon says, "Why don't we all leave? If the killer is threatening two of those left behind, and there's nobody left, who is he going to kill?"

Dawn says, "The text didn't say the killer was going to kill two more people in the house. Or even two of us. It just said two more people will die. It could even be people we care about. And we would be responsible."

Logan points out, "And even if the police relocated us, we would likely be taking the killer with us."

"What is the point of all this, anyway?" Irene asks. "All this staged drama? Keeping us here? The guy could have just shot Ted at home, and who would ever know he did it?"

Cynthia says, "The text says it's so that all our secrets can come out. But I don't have any secrets. I'm just a boring secretary from New Jersey with a chocolate addiction and a serious podcast habit."

"So you're saying you didn't know Ted?" Irene challenges.

"I did not," Cynthia says, drawing herself up on straighter posture. "And I doubt I'm the only one here who didn't. Some of us are just innocent bystanders."

Jordon says, "This feels like the work of a frustrated writer or a failed actor. Someone who wants to spin a narrative that Ted was such a bad human being that his murder was justified. This person has to be an absolute narcissist. Wanting to beat Felicity, and make sure everyone watches them do it. Making all these parallels with classic literature because they don't have an originally creative bone in their body."

"Careful," Hudson says. "It sounds like you're describing yourself."

"Says the failed child actor," Jordan quips back. "Get your Super Mac Snack Attack on, right Hudson? Your hair was purple back then, too."

Hudson snaps his jaw shut so loudly his teeth click.

I stand up and say, "This is getting out of hand. I'm sorry that you're all stuck here. But attacking each other isn't going to help anything."

Chloe says, "I'm still waiting for someone to uncover the reason for my untimely demise, so I can give them the prize."

"Prize?" Sebastian says, clearly intrigued. "People will do oh so many things when they think there's a prize involved. Pray tell what is it?"

Chloe says, "An all-expense paid trip to North Carolina to meet a certain YouTuber I happen to know. Plus ten thousand dollars cash."

Several people in the room gasp. Clearly, at least half of them know what Youtuber she's talking about. Of course, they're probably also excited by the thought of the money.

I give Chloe a questioning look. She whispers back, "I can afford it."

Logan asks, "Won't the fictional killer just turn themselves in?"

Ash says, "Unfortunately, that person still isn't eligible to play."

Imogen says, "We're not either. So it's fair."

Chloe says, "We were going to have everyone turn in their guesses on Sunday before leaving, but for a cash prize, there can be only one winner. So Ash will accept the first correct answer. You can only officially guess once, so don't turn in your answer until you're sure."

"But what about the real secrets we're supposed to share?" Irene asks. "I, for one, don't mind. It's not that much of a secret that I was married to Ted for four years. He was a jerk, so eventually I left. But I never hated Ted. Really, he was a scared little boy, trying to come across as self-confident when he could barely understand life. You just have to ignore his bluster and push back against it. Had. I mean you had to. Man. It's hard to think of him in the past tense."

Whelp. That's a big reveal for me. Obviously, Ted's sister Elena had known that Irene was Ted's ex, which explains a lot of what she said yesterday. Including the part about her still having a soft spot for Ted, which could include making excuses for him, justified or imagined. So while her connection with him and the failure of their marriage does give Irene a motive, her shock and pain last night had seemed very real – too real for a killer.

I look over at Elena, who is pointedly ignoring Irene, playing with her water bottle, twisting the filter. She seems so different from her brother. Ted had been arrogant and ambitious. Elena is somehow refined without seeming overbearing. She's a professor of literature, and all those words weigh in on her, broadening her view of the world. Yet, Irene had a serious problem with her. Is it possible that somewhere inside, Elena had the coldness necessary to kill her own brother? Maybe. She doesn't look like she's grieving. And she was unaccounted for at the time. But how could she have done it? The locked room angle has me stumped.

There's movement in the hallway. But who could it be? We're all here.

To my horror, it's Autumn. She waves and holds up a small gift bag.

I race over to her and grab her hand, pulling her back into the hallway and out into the lobby. My voice is unsteady when I ask, "What are you doing here?"

She opens her mouth and blinks at me. She tilts her head. "What do you mean what am I doing here? I thought I was invited – any time."

"Yes, but this is – oh, Autumn, there was a murder here last night."

Her face scrunches with confusion. "Then why are you still having a party this morning?"

"Because." I pause, trying to think how to break the news to her. "The killer made it clear that if anyone leaves, they are going to kill a couple more people. And now that you're here . . ."

I trail off, letting her make the connection. Her eyes go wide, and she brings a hand to her chest. "Well, that's not great."

Autumn is often the master of understatement.

"I'm sorry," I tell her. "You were supposed to be busy this weekend. And I already dragged you out here to take care of Knightley. If I had any idea you'd be coming back, I would have called you."

"You should have called me anyway. Your best friend should at least know when you're under the threat of death."

She's right. I've been working on being more connected to people, and being a better friend. But when there's a crisis, I tend to take ownership of the problem and lose focus of other things. I ask, "So why are you here? What's with the gift bag?"

She holds it out to me. I pull out the two pieces of tissue paper to reveal a mug. It says, *World's Greatest Aunt.*

For a second, I'm just stumped. Who is this mug for? But then I get it. Yesterday's spa day must have been more than an impulsive break from writing. It had been a private celebration. "Oh my gosh, Autumn. You and Drake?"

Her grin is infectious. "That's right. We're having a baby. You're the first person we've told. Aunt Fee."

"I like the sound of that," I say. I hook the handle of the mug through my thumb and grab both of her hands and we jump up and down and squee. But the weight of what I've let happen by not warning her to stay away from this tense situation tempers my joy.

I love kids, but found myself unable to have any of my own, so the thought of a little one to buy tiny clothes for and spoil almost brings tears to my eyes. I have to make sure Autumn stays safe. Which means catching this killer – right now.

I tell Autumn, "You know how I have problems with change? Well, this one is fantastic."

There are happy tears in Autumn's eyes. I explain to her a bit about what's going on, then we join the others in the dining room, where everyone is now standing in small groups. I guess they're questioning each other about their roles in the $10,000 mystery. Naomi and Greg are still sitting at a table, and Naomi has pulled over a second chair to rest her ankle. I tell Autumn, "Stay here and talk to Aunt Naomi. I'll be right back."

I trail after Logan and Arlo, wanting to be close enough to hear when they confront Colin about the ledger.

Colin is smiling as he takes in the three of us. He rubs at his oversized beard and says, "What can old Cecil Flirty do for you?"

"Nothing," Logan says. "But Colin Lipscombe can maybe help a lot. Why were you being blackmailed?"

"Blackmailed?" Colin tries to laugh it off, but there's a troubled look in his eyes. "What would make you say that?"

Arlo takes the ledger out of his pocket.

Colin says, "It's not what you think."

Hmmm. There were a lot of ledger entries with the word *Quiet*. Exactly how many of his patients was he blackmailing? And were they all even patients? I've never understood how someone would even get started blackmailing multiple people. How do you look at someone and go, yes, this person definitely has something to hide?

"So what is it, if not what we think?" Logan asks.

"Well, it was . . . why don't you ask her?" He points across the room, and all three of us instinctively follow his gaze – only to find out his's pointing at no one. Taking advantage of our moment of distraction, he pushes me into Arlo and takes off running.

Logan takes off after him, but Colin is spry for his age, and he manages to grab a food cart and throw it in Logan's way. Logan flips the cart out of his way. He loses time fumbling away from it, and Colin makes it into the hall. I can't sprint without risk of triggering my latent asthma, but I chase after them at a more reasonable pace anyway.

Colin grabs a gold bird sculpture off one of the lobby tables and chunks it at Logan's feet, further slowing him. Then he knocks another table over in Logan's path. And then Colin reaches the door.

I hear myself distantly shouting, "Noooooo!" as he opens it and slips through, out in the parking lot. Logan chases him down, catches him two blocks away. But the damage has been done.

Arlo pulls out his phone and calls the station, requesting all possible backup as we try to figure out a way to keep the murderer from making good his threat. Two people to die – but who knows who it will be. It could be me and Logan, now that the killer's experiment at beating us has been fouled. Or it could be any of the people I'd just had breakfast with. I feel hyperaware, find myself swinging my head like a cat with its back up, expecting threatening movement in my peripheral vision.

There's only one way I know of to feel safe. And that's if we've inadvertently caught the killer.

Arlo is marching Colin forward in handcuffs. I rush around in front of them, and I ask Colin, "Did you do all of this to get rid of Ted? Over whatever he's blackmailing you for?"

Colin looks stunned. "Me? Darlin' I may have done a lot of things, but I've never killed a man in me life. I lied. I didn't enter any contest. And I was shocked to show up here and see the man who's been blackmailing me. It didn't seem prudent to say anything. It felt like something out of one of the cheesier mystery movies."

Dang. Well, if he did it, he's certainly not going to be pressed into confessing.

"So what was he blackmailing you over?" Logan asks.

"Now that, I'm not telling you," Colin says. And given the determination on his craggy face, I doubt we are going to change his mind.

There's a veil of dread over the whole dining room – but nothing happens immediately to back it up. Maybe it was just a bluff. Maybe the killer is just trying to create a distraction around Ted's death.

Chapter Nine
Saturday

I rub at my temples. This is already shaping up to be quite a day. Colin is handcuffed to a chair in the dining room, and we're having trouble connecting to the giant monitor that we're using for the virtual tour. It's a Bluetooth thing, and it is absolutely refusing to accept my laptop as a device. Chloe and Ash are trying to fix it. If they can't, I doubt anyone else here can.

Normally, that wouldn't be a huge deal, but this crowd is already starting to be suspicious of each other, and they're basically trapped in this room, convinced they're sitting here with a killer. They're probably right. But there's nothing any of us can do about it. Which is why they need the distraction.

Logan and I are sitting at a table by ourselves, trying to come up with a plan B. We've already notified the historic homes tour folks that we aren't coming. I brought down a few board games, but so far no one has picked one up. Logan has an arm around my shoulders. He gives me a reassuring squeeze and says, "As long as we all stay here together, we stand a good chance of thwarting whatever Doc Frankenstein is trying to do."

"Doc Frankenstein?" I say absently. "Or the monster?"

Logan shrugs, moving against me in a somewhat distracting way. He says, "We have to start calling the killer something. And I refuse to keep saying Frankenstein's monster."

"You know," I say. "I keep thinking about the book. It just really doesn't seem to fit everything that's been going on. But the murderer must have meant something significant by it. Do you think it might be something so cheesy as that Ted was a doctor? Or that Elena – also a doctor – is signaling that she's the killer?"

Logan gives me a dismayed look. "I hope not. Elena's a literature professor."

"You sound like you'd be disappointed if the puzzle was that easy," I say.

"Not disappointed. Just unsure we'd actually solved it. Our Doc Frankenstein seems to like to be in control, manufacturing situations. Just like the Doc in the book, he craves power over life and death."

I say, "I thought you didn't much read fiction."

"I looked up the SparkNotes last night. But it sounded like a good book, so I started reading it. I'm a couple of chapters in. You know it was written in the form of letters? I suppose today it would be emails. Already, Victor Frankenstein is so arrogant."

I say, "That certainly sounds like Sasha and Sebastian. Arrogant. Possibly believing they're justified in taking a life for a life. Later in the book, Victor Frankenstein realizes his monster is responsible for the death of two innocents, one actually killed by the monster. Maybe Arlo was right, and Ted represents the monster."

"It's possible," Logan says. "But it could just as easily describe Elena. She almost seemed to be gloating over her brother's death last night."

"True," I admit. "And it's a little less on-the-nose than Sasha and Sebastian. We should talk to her." I look over at Elena, who is scrolling through something on her phone, detached from the anxious vibe in the room. Out of everyone here, she seems the most likely person to have challenged me.

Bea comes over to stand next to me. Satchmo flops down on my foot and sighs a satisfied doggie sigh. He looks hopefully up at me.

"Sorry," I tell the beagle. "I don't think there's anything that's good for dogs on the menu this morning."

Bea says, "Don't worry. He's got a Puppuccino coming."

I realize that Bea has on more makeup than she usually does, with winged eyeliner and soft glitter on her cheeks. I have an idea where this is going. I ask, "You have a good conversation with Fisk yesterday?"

"You caught that," Bea says, a little flush coming to her glittery cheeks. "We've been trying to keep things quiet until we're sure something is going to come of our conversations."

"So it wasn't just last night," Logan says. "How long has this been going on?"

"And how have we all missed it?" I ask. "I know I've been trying to pay more attention to my friends, but am I still being oblivious?"

Bea waves a dismissive hand. "It's been a couple of dates. He had a bad breakup a few months ago, and I don't want to jump into things if he's not ready. I will say, it's been a while for me, so I've been a bit nervous about looking overeager."

This is the first time I've seen her interested in anybody, since moving to the island, and she's always so reserved around people. I can't imagine she's coming on too strong. I admit, "Most of what I know about Fisk is from seeing him work crime scenes."

"Me too," Logan says. "What do you two talk about?"

Bea blushes again. "We have a lot in common, actually. Did you know he's a connoisseur of fine whiskey? Next week we're supposed to go to a Japanese whiskey tasting. And a couple of weeks after that, we're going to the opera."

"I had no idea you liked opera," I say. I always pictured Bea as more of a down-to-Earth type of person.

"I might," Bea says. "I've never been to one. But I love musicals, so it feels like kind of the same thing. Of course, I can't sing to save my life, while Fisk is in a band. I guess you can't expect to have everything in common."

Logan says, "A whiskey tasting sounds like fun. Mind if we show up? I'm sure Autumn and Drake would love it too. He's a real whiskey guy."

"I don't think that's a good idea," I say. After all, Autumn is in no condition to drink.

But Bea looks at me, hurt. "Oh, okay. If you don't want to double-date, I get it."

"It's not that," I say quickly. "I'd love spending time with y'all. It's just-" I look around. Autumn isn't in the dining room, so I can't ask her, but she didn't actually ask me to keep her news a secret. I lower my voice. "Okay, you can't tell her I told you, and you have to act surprised when she makes the announcement." They both nod, and Logan makes a hand rolling gesture telling me to get on with it. I do. "Autumn's pregnant."

Bea gasps, bringing a hand to her mouth. "That's wonderful."

I tell Logan, "She brought me a mug officially claiming me as the kid's aunt. Which makes you an uncle."

Logan looks pleased. He says, "Well, I don't have a shot at being the fun uncle, considering Autumn's brother and his karaoke nights. But I can be the protective uncle."

Bea laughs. "If it's a girl, you can scare off all the suitors in about sixteen years."

Logan says, "Drake has that covered. Have you ever seen his don't-mess-with-that look when people are poking around the rare books at the library?"

I say, "I should find Autumn. I know she was upset about being here, under the circumstances. I thought she understood why everyone was supposed to stay in this room."

Bea says, "I saw her heading towards the ladies' room in the lobby."

Really? Has no one been staying put? I guess we can't expect them to stay in this room all day without restroom breaks. Autumn should have at least taken someone with her. I tell myself she should be safe. Surely, Doc Frankenstein wouldn't pick on someone who wasn't even invited to this party – unless they're a killer of opportunity. I find myself rushing as I move out into the hallway and cross the lobby.

When I get to the restroom, Autumn's fine. Mostly. She's patting at her face with a wet towel, and her black skin looks ashen.

"Morning sickness," she says miserably. "Sweet plantains are my favorite, so I thought I could handle a couple off the buffet. Not so much."

I put a comforting hand on her back, rubbing between her shoulders. I say, "I hear it passes, after a couple of months."

"I hope so," she says. She gestures at her phone, on the counter nearby. "I talked to Drake. Explained the situation. He said he wants to meet me here, to be with me in case anything happens."

I say, "I hope you told him not to come. The last thing we need is more people showing up. It could put the killer on edge."

"Yeah," Autumn says. "I told him I didn't want him to put himself in danger."

"Besides," I say. "I'm totally selfish. I need somebody out there taking care of Knightley."

Autumn says, "Drake has been totally spoiling that bunny. He made a special trip last night to the grocery store just to get parsley. I think it's part of his reaction to finding out he's going to be a dad."

Parsley is Knightley's favorite food. All my friends know it. I say, "Bunnies are pretty cute and small."

Autumn comes back with me to join the group. When we get back, Logan's sister has joined her husband and Logan's father at their table. I guess she got a few hours of real sleep after her uncomfortable rest last night keeping tabs on Hudson.

Fisk comes into the dining room. He's wearing his CSI jacket, open over a sky-blue polo shirt. I guess he's not officially working today. Maybe he wants to remind the killer – Doc Frankenstein, as Logan has named that person – that Fisk is a cop, and therefore not part of the killer's game. Not that it matters, since one of the guests already left the premises. Bea heads over to meet him, Satchmo on his leash beside her. Fisk leans down and scratches Satchmo behind the ears, and he puts a cup of whipped cream down on the floor. Satchmo eagerly starts licking at it.

"Come on," Logan says. "While Fisk is here, we might as well put him to good use."

We walk over to join them. Bea is holding a single red rose, and she doesn't move to hide it. I guess she told Fisk she already broke the news that they're dating. He seems fine with it.

Logan asks, "You up to doing a little forensic investigating on somebody who's not dead?"

Fisk looks confused. "What's the problem?"

Logan gestures over to Colin, who is still cuffed to his chair. Logan says, "I need to ID this guy, but his face isn't in any databases I could find."

Fisk says, "What do you need me for? You could just scan his fingerprints using your phone."

"Ordinarily, yes," Logan says. "Only, this guy hasn't got any fingerprints."

"Really?" Fisk looks intrigued. "That means he probably should be in a database, somewhere."

Fisk goes over and sits down next to Colin, trying to strike up a conversation. Colin seems to rebuff him. Fisk takes Colin's plate and puts it on the cart where Carmen has been collecting dirty dishes.

"Well?" Logan asks. "You weren't over there very long."

Fisk says, "I think that guy had surgery to change his appearance. He probably grew the beard to try and hide the scars, but you can still tell, if you know what to look for."

I ask, "Then how are you going to find out who he is?"

Fisk pulls a fork half wrapped in a napkin out of his jacket pocket. "Didn't you say that Arlo is officially asking us to run a DNA test on this?" When neither of us say anything, Fisk whispers, "Bea told me about your bet with your sister. I'll make sure you get the results first."

"Oh, right," Logan says. He peers across the room, where Arlo and Dawn are in deep conversation, while Patsy stands nearby looking board. "Arlo definitely wants that."

"Good," Fisk says. "I promised Bea I'd take Satchmo out for a walk. I think I'll just take him with me and drop him back by when I have the test results."

"You can get the information that fast?" I ask.

He says, "You can when people owe you favors." Then he gets Satchmo and heads for the door.

As soon as the dog is gone, Sasha makes her way over to me. So does Jordan. Clearly, he's been drinking again. The only booze we have on offer is mimosas at the breakfast buffet. How many has he had? Or is this another part of his weird act?

"Hey, Koerber," Jordan says. "What are you doing about getting us out of here? You solve all these murders for everybody else, but we're your fans. And you can't solve this one for us?"

"We're working on it," I say.

Jordan says, "You even have all your suspects handy under one roof. That should make things easier, right?"

"Not necessarily," I stammer.

"Ignore him," Sasha says. "He's an idiot."

I tell her, "I still feel like I owe something to everyone here. If I hadn't solved those other murders, the killer wouldn't have called me out, or invited you all for the spectacle."

"Really?" Sasha says. "The killer called you out?"

The way she says it sends a shiver down my spine. I hadn't actually told any of the guests about receiving the copy of *Frankenstein*. Could Sasha be the killer? If so, she has nerves of ice, casually strolling over to talk about it. I don't mention the book. Instead, I say, "You got that text message. I was one of the four people the killer specified who could leave the building. Obviously, that was so we could try to catch said killer."

"True," Sasha says. "This is all so upsetting. But still, you wanted to pet my little baby."

She holds out Cheeseburger. So maybe she's not the one who sent the book. I take Cheeseburger. The ferret squirms in my arms. They are impossibly long creatures. But after a moment, she settles down and lets me hold her. She grabs at stands of my hair, which have fallen forward over my shoulder. It sounds like the ferret starts hyperventilating, making loud little pants. Alarmed, I try to hand her back to Sasha. "I don't know what to do here. Is she okay?"

Sasha presses Cheeseburger back over to me. "She's fine. That's the noise ferrets make when they're really happy. I think she likes you."

"Despite the fact that I was just petting a dog?"

Sasha shrugs. "Ferrets and dogs have been known to get along. Not always, but it has happened."

I say, "I wasn't trying to push you on Carmen's new cookbook earlier. I know you have a lot of influence, and people must do that all the time. I'm just used to talking up my business, and she's an integral part of it."

Sasha says, "I try not to judge things until I've tasted them – or read them. No offense to you or your pastry chef. What I've tasted so far is divine. But can she write? That's a totally different skill."

My phone buzzes in my pocket. When I check my texts, there's a notification from the drone delivery company Tracie hired. I say, "If you'll excuse me, the drone's almost here. I will need to open the front door to let it inside." I look over, and Ash and Chloe must have gotten the screen to connect, because there's a live feed to Tracie and Miles waving at us from the shop.

Sasha says, "One thing before you go. I already told you I don't believe in ghosts."

"That you did," I say as I scratch Cheeseburger's chin. The ferret still seems happy but has calmed down from the panting. She reaches up to sniff my chin.

"Which means there has to be some other explanation for things going missing from my room. I want to know what you plan to do about it."

My heart sinks. One more thing going wrong. I'm not sure I can deal with that, in the face of a potential second and third murder. I stammer, "We're actually not a functional hotel. So there's no security. But tell me what's gone, and I can do my best to look into it."

She starts counting on her fingers. "First, there was the Austrian crystal bracelet I had on yesterday. It wasn't expensive, but it was a gift from Brad – one of the last things he ever gave me – so there is a ton of sentimental value attached to it. Then there was Sebastian's shaving brush. And later, I noticed my lip balm was missing, which was annoying, and then this morning, my reading glasses were gone. I don't know. It's possible they were all stolen at once and they were such little things, I didn't realize they were gone until we needed them."

I look down at the ferret in my arms, the most probable culprit for small-object theft. Except – she specifically mentioned the bracelet we'd found in Ted's room. It seems unlikely that there's a ferret going around planting evidence. Still, I ask, "Are you sure Cheeseburger didn't just misplace a few things for you?"

Sasha looks surprised, but seems to think about it. She says, "The bracelet, maybe, but not the other things. She's taken shiny objects before, but she hates the smell of Sebastian's shaving soap, so she wouldn't touch the brush."

Hmm. I'm not sure how to put this together. Maybe Sasha realizes she left the bracelet in Ted's room, and now she's concocting an elaborate lie. Or maybe she even planted it there herself, to make it look like someone is framing her.

I get another text. The drone is here. I hand Cheeseburger back to Sasha and go to open the door.

The drone is the strangest thing I've ever greeted at a doorstep. It's basically a box with four spinning helicopter blades, one at each corner. This drone is pink, and suspended under it, there's a disco ball. Under that, there's a shipping box from Greetings and Felicitations.

There must be a camera on it somewhere, because Tracie told me there's a pilot on the other end of this thing. I wave it inside and gesture for it to follow me down the corridor. I know this is unusual, even for drone delivery services, but I guess somebody had to design a party delivery drone. Chloe dims the lights. The disco ball starts spinning and lights up. The drone releases its package on the floor, then it flies up to the ceiling at the center of the room. It starts playing lyricless, upbeat music, and little cannons, shoot out confetti and glitter. Inwardly, I groan. Tracie had mentioned the confetti – but does she not know how hard glitter is to clean up?

Someone dims the lights. Despite the tension in the room, with the death threat and all, several people start clapping, and Chloe stands up to dance, bathed in colored lights from the light show. Ash and Imogen join in, and then Arlo and Patsy. Nobody else seems inclined to join them, though. And Jordan is openly scowling.

Chloe calls, "Who's ready for some chocolate?"

Jordan says, "Not me, if you're serving it. I still believe you killed Ted."

Hudson says, "Well, I think you did it."

Jordan says, "Don't worry – you're my second most likely suspect. I just can't figure out your connection to him."

Hudson doesn't say anything. After several beats, he says, "I, for one, look forward to enjoying the chocolate."

Interesting. He didn't say he doesn't have a connection to Ted. Which doesn't necessarily mean he does – but I need to at least look into it. Later. Right now, I have to diffuse this situation.

I say, "Look. This box has arrived sealed, directly from Greetings and Felicitations. Nobody here has touched it. Why don't we get Detective Romero to hand around the samples."

Jordan says, "I'll still pass." But he says it with much less conviction.

"Fine," I say.

Arlo asks the group, "Is it okay if I ask Patsy to help me? She's only here as my girlfriend."

There are a number of nods, and Logan says, "I'm sure that's fine."

The song ends, and the drone descends from the ceiling, and I see all those little cannons, and I think – what if something like this could be used to commit a murder? Maybe that thing in the drawer in Ted's desk hadn't been a charger. Maybe it had been some kind of signal booster to make sure a drone could be controlled remotely, and the killer had left it, and a small drone inside Ted's room – potentially while Logan and I were down at the beach and no one was paying attention. Could the drone then have flown away on its own – through that open floor grate? Only – doesn't metal impede the kind of signal you would need to navigate a drone through the duct system? Which means it's probably not a workable solution – unless the drone is still in the duct.

Arlo comes over and takes out a pocketknife, which he uses to slit the seal on the box. Inside, there are stacked trays filled with paper cups, and on the side of each tray there's a number.

Over the audio coming from the monitor Tracie says, "Arlo, the numbers correspond with the processes we're going to be showing here at our micro factory. The first thing everyone should get is a cup of cacao nibs." Arlo and Patsy move around the room, Arlo holding the tray and Patsy handing out cups, while Tracie explains, "Nibs are basically broken up cacao beans."

Miles moves forward and takes the camera, which he uses to follow Tracie behind the counter at the shop, on through the kitchen and into the bean room, panning over the large sacks of cacao beans that are sitting behind the equipment.

Tracie says from off camera, "Cacao grows in pods, similar in size and shape to a Nerf football. The beans are inside, roughly forty to a pod. They must be hand harvested by cutting the pods off of the tree because the pods grow on pads on the trunk of the tree and pulling them off would damage the pads. By the time we get them, the beans have to be fermented in the pod pulp, and then dried. Once here they are sorted, roasted and winnowed, before being broken into nibs and processed. Let's watch Miles, as he takes us through an abbreviated version of the steps."

She takes the camera and points it at Miles. He hefts a bucket of beans and pours them into the sorter. He says, "Meanwhile, taste the nibs. They may give you a hint of what the chocolate made from them might be, but they're mostly nutty in flavor."

Sasha says, "I like to keep a bag of cacao nibs in my desk, for snacking. You get just that vague shadow of chocolate, and you can munch on them without worrying there's too many calories."

"That's a good point," Miles tells her. I hadn't realized there was a microphone here, but it is good that the presentation goes both ways. He goes through the rest of the processes, answering questions and getting the guests to taste samples along the way.

The response is positive, with calling our Madagascar chocolate, "Sweet like cherries," and, "Bright and fruity."

Hudson says, "I've never had anything like this. I thought dark chocolate was dull and bitter."

Miles says, "Saying you don't like dark chocolate is like saying you don't like wine. There are so many different types and flavor profiles in wine, you can easily like one and not another. The next chocolate sample we're going to share is more lemony, from the tannins, which are a compound that chocolate shares with wine and tea. You know how oversteeped tea can become astringent? That's tannins at work. But you can use them in a good way."

I'm impressed at how much Miles has learned from working at the shop, especially since he only took the job to help me out.

There are three different single origin bars being discussed, highlighting different flavor profiles. I have fond memories attached to each of those bars. I'd taken sourcing trips for two of them, met the farmers, seen the trees. It's part of what makes my job so precious to me. We've been trying to plan a sourcing trip for a group of our friends, to a plantation we've been invited to in Brazil, and we were waiting for Drake to have more vacation time, after his and Autumn's splashy honeymoon. But I guess that's going to have to wait a while – at least for going anywhere by plane. Maybe Logan and I can arrange for the trip after the baby arrives and is old enough to be left with a sitter. It's wild to think that Logan and I will be married ourselves by then.

"Turn up the lights!" Arlo says urgently, breaking my train of thought.

"But the presentation's not finished," Chloe protests.

"I don't care. Elena's in trouble."

The lights come up. Logan, Bea, Dawn and I rush over to where Elena has fallen from her chair to the floor. Arlo rolls her over. There's not a mark on her. But she's not breathing, and there's slobber on her mouth. Arlo grimaces and then leans closer to her face. He looks back at us and says, "I smell bitter almonds. Which can mean only one thing."

Half the people in the room say, "Cyanide," or "Poison," at the same time. Trust the true crime fans to know.

He puts his fingers to her neck, trying to find a pulse. Still looking at her elegant face, he says, "She's dead."

There's upset mumbling around the room, and someone screams.

Jordan says, "I knew better than to eat the chocolate."

I say, "There's no evidence saying the poison was even in the chocolate."

From the kitchen, Enrique calls, "Don't you dare say it was in the breakfast! My food is perfection."

Arlo has everyone move to the lobby, where Dawn and Logan's dad are keeping an eye on the guests, while he does his best to preserve the scene. Considering the poisoning, nobody seems much in the mood for being fed, or to hold onto warm beverages, so my usual response to a tense situation is off the table. It makes me feel antsy.

I'm standing with Logan off to one side, by the check-in desk, just watching the others interact.

Jordan is pacing back and forth, saying, "Don't eat or drink anything. Stay safe. Stay in control," over and over to himself. I'm interested to see how long that lasts – and if it includes staying away from the booze.

I ask Logan, "Any chance you can get him to stop doing that?"

"Afraid not," Logan says. "I tried to calm him down, and he started hyperventilating."

"Poor guy." I try to ignore Jordan's panic attack, since bringing attention to it will make things worse. Instead, I try to focus on what some of the others are doing. Hudson is standing near the palm tree, talking to Logan's dad.

Logan's dad, blunt as always, asks the vlogger, "Son, what happened to your face?"

"Motorcycle accident," Hudson says.

Wait – that's not what he told Sasha yesterday. I pull out my phone and Google Hudson. Not surprisingly, he has an extensive Wikipedia entry. But when I look at his biography, it just says that there was a mysterious accident that ended his acting career, leaving his face and body scarred, and that he disappeared from public view for a year, before returning to the spotlight as a Youtuber. Apparently, he chose Japan in search of a fresh start, where few people would recognize him. I look up the citations for the entry – which usually give more reliable and in-depth information – but it's all speculation.

I spend a little time Googling "Hudson Nolan Face Accident" and I get a ton of wild speculation, including one hit that claims Hudson wasn't in an accident at all, and that his face was the only part of him to receive scarring. The article's speculation is that he was injured by his then girlfriend, Savannah Blythe, after he broke up with her – despite the popular opinion that it was Savannah who broke up with him. There's even a photo of Hudson with his shirt off showing off his unmarked torso as proof.

Logan's dad tells Hudson, "It must have taken guts to go on camera again, given how much your looks had changed. I can appreciate that, and respect you for it."

Malcolm can be blunt – but he's also not shy with praise. Suddenly, I want him to be proud of me, too, to make me feel like a real part of his family. Maybe if we can solve this murder, he will be.

Logan whispers, "If my dad says he respects someone, that's high praise." Then he catches sight of what's on my phone and tilts it so he can get a better look. He looks from the shirtless image on the phone, to Hudson standing there in real life, looking just as fit as in the photo, to me, then he says in a teasing tone, "Should I be worried?"

"Nah," I whisper back. "I'm just interested in his medical records."

Logan says, "I can probably help you out with that. Where did you say he's from?"

I say, "He would have still been living in Los Angeles when whatever happened to his face."

Logan takes out his own phone and says, "Let me see what I can do."

While he's busy typing, Cynthia comes up to me and whispers, "You should keep an eye on that guy." Her gaze follows Hudson, who is walking off to talk to Patsy. Patsy is standing with Uncle Greg, by a settee Aunt Naomi is using to elevate her ankle. Patsy notices me looking at them and waves.

I wave back.

But Hudson thinks she is waving at him and waves back too. It doesn't look flirtatious. Or menacing. In fact, he seems completely innocuous.

I ask Cynthia, "What's so suspicious about Hudson?"

Cynthia says, "I saw him talking to Elena this morning, only a few hours before she died, and he looked none too happy. I think that last night, Hudson killed Ted, and Elena figured something out, so today, she had to die, too, so Hudson could cover his tracks." Cynthia gives me a bland half-grin. "If I'm right, and that helps the case, I'll get a mention on the podcast, won't I?"

I give her a careful smile in return. I still find the whole true-crime aficionado thing a bit unsettling. I say, "That's Ash's department. But if you really did break the case, I'm sure you'd get coverage on the local news."

Cynthia says, "Oh, I'm not ready for a news interview. My sister tried to get me to go on a makeover show, but I turned them down flat."

"That sounds like it could have been fun," I tell her, trying to be diplomatic. But her sister had probably been coming from a place of genuine concern, and it is a bit sad she didn't give it a shot. I know I'm the last one to embrace change, so it's unfair of me to think others should.

"Oh no," Cynthia says. "I would have been petrified the whole time I was on camera."

I realize I don't know much about Cynthia – other than that she didn't know Ted. I ask, "What do you do for fun? When you're not being a secretary?"

She says, "I do a lot of macramé. And I practice knife throwing. You know, like at the circus. I used to do this act with my sister – only she wanted us to do it in front of people, since I was so good, but I said absolutely not. Because one of my biggest fears is getting embarrassed in front of other people."

I say, "And still you came here. It must have taken a lot of courage to participate in an event like this."

She gets a frozen look on her face, as though this hasn't occurred to her and now she wants to hold up a piece of macramé to shield herself. Maybe she had planned to just listen in on the event and not speak up. She says, "I think I'd like to go lie down in my room now."

"I don't think you can," Logan says. "Everybody needs to stay here until the police get a chance to question you."

She looks frustrated, but she makes her way over to a chair and sits down. She pulls a half-completed piece of macramé out of her tote bag.

Logan whispers, "Could it be she's the mastermind behind all of this? It's always the quiet ones, you know."

I say, "Knife throwing is an unusual hobby. But she doesn't have a connection to Ted."

"Or so she says," Logan points out. "But I have never met anybody who's been working so hard at being nondescript.

Irene approaches us. She has a clue sheet from the boardgame Clue, and she's marked out the suspect names that correspond to the game pieces and written in the characters names Ash assigned yesterday. Given her strong block handwriting, Mitch McCowboybritches takes up the entire width of his line.

She comes over to us and asks, "Do either of you know where Walt Wishman or Rhonda Vanderclump were at the time of Clementine Vanderclump's murder?"

Logan gives her a reproachful look. He says, "You do realize the people playing both of those characters are dead."

Irene blushes prettily. She says, "I guess it's in poor taste, since Elena's body isn't even cold. But Ash and Chloe wanted us to continue the game. And I could really use ten thousand dollars. Travel agencies got hit hard during the pandemic, you know?"

I ask Logan, "Would you mind playing along? I encouraged Ash to keep the game going, to give the guests something to do other than dwell on the unpleasantness."

Logan doesn't look happy. But he takes the folded-up character sheet out of his jacket pocket and consults it. "It says here that I saw Mitch McCowboybritches talking to Rhonda

Vanderclump right before the lights went out. I don't have any notes about Ted – I mean Walt Wishman."

Irene looks at me, her pencil still poised after drawing an x beside Rhonda's name.

I say, "I didn't actually get a character sheet. I was too busy coordinating things as host."

"Oh," she says. "Well, at least I got one piece of useful information."

My curiosity gets the better of me, and I ask her, "Why did you stay in the travel business, if times were so hard?"

Irene says, "I've listened to the podcast. You have the travel bug yourself. Travel agents get invited to try out new cruise ships and hotels, for cheap or sometimes even free. Airlines encourage us to try out their services, too. And when I'm not traveling myself, I get to plan perfect itineraries for other people. I do a lot of work as a travel advisor, which means I get to spend a lot of time researching destinations and getting feedback. And I love making connections with new people. Now that I know about Logan's services, I can put his puddle jump and destination flights on my list to recommend."

"That's kind of you," Logan says.

Irene shrugs and adds, "Besides. I knew things would bounce back. Cooped up people couldn't wait to travel again. It was just a matter of waiting, and taking a couple of work-from-home gigs in the meantime. I'm a very patient person."

"I get that," I say.

Patsy wanders over to us. She gives me a brief hug and says, "Congratulations again on your engagement. Logan is quite a catch."

"He can hear you, you know," I quip. "The praise is going to go to his head."

"Nah," Logan says. "I already know I'm a catch. Even with the emotional baggage."

I tell Patsy, "See what I have to deal with?"

She says, "It looked like you were trying to get my attention. What's up?"

I say, "I was just saying hi. We haven't gotten to talk much lately."

Patsy says, "I would invite you to go to the concert at my favorite jazz club with me next week, but every time you have an outing, someone seems to wind up dead."

"Not every time," I say. It is kind of her to be sort-of inviting me somewhere – despite the complicated past between me and Arlo. A lot of girls would be more jealous over her current boyfriend's ex still being a part of the couple's current life – but I'm glad Patsy isn't the kind of girl that would want Arlo to separate from his friend group, just because his ex was there. I tell her, "I love jazz, so if you decide you're willing to take the risk, I'd love to have a girl's night."

Irene asks Patsy, "Since you're here, do you have any clues about Rhonda Vanderclump? I'm still trying to place her whereabouts at the time of the fictional murder."

Patsy says, "She wasn't on my clue sheet either."

The two of them start comparing notes, so Logan and I excuse ourselves.

I walk over to Aunt Naomi and sit down in the chair closest to the settee. "How are you holding up?" I ask.

She says, "I'm pretty sure the police think I killed Ted. I thought Arlo knew me better that that. Apparently, my fingerprints are all over that room. And I was like, yeah, I just decorated it."

I ask her, "You didn't remove the floor vent in there, did you? When you redid the floors?"

Her brow wrinkles as she tries to remember. "I think I replaced it, once we finished with the wood. But that was a long time ago. I can't be a hundred percent sure."

"Thanks," I say. "That's helpful."

Aunt Naomi reaches out and takes my hand. "You're going to keep me out of jail, aren't you?"

"I'm certainly going to try." I squeeze her hand, then let go. I stand up and make my way over to Chloe to ask if she has a selfie stick I can borrow. Of course she does, but it's in her bag. She pops back into the dining room to get it.

I tell Logan, "I want to check out Ted's room again. I had an idea during the chocolate demo."

Logan scans the room and I follow his gaze. Jordan is still looking agitated, but at least he has stopped pacing. Logan's mom is talking to him, and she seems to be calming him down.

Sasha and Cheeseburger are on opposite sides of the room from Bea and Satchmo. Ash is standing by the fireplace, recording Sebastian, who is sitting in a chair, talking about how much therapy helped him after he had been abducted as a child, and why he had decided to become a therapist in order to help others at their weakest hour. Which gives me even more empathy for him, and makes me hope that he and Sasha have nothing to do with the murders – despite the fact that they are the most obvious suspects. Logan's sister is standing with her husband, and Autumn is sitting by them, chatting. Fisher is digging in Dawn's purse, and he comes out with a mint, which he hands to Autumn.

Chloe returns with the selfie stick and hands it to me without question.

Logan says, "It looks like everything is under control here. I don't think anyone's going to notice if we sneak off."

But Logan's mom notices as we head for the stairs, trying to avoid the obvious noise of the elevator. She gives me a big wink, and I can almost hear her say, *time for a little cuddling*. I try to telepathically convey, *actually no, time for a big investigating*. But the way Logan takes my hand and pulls me closer to him as we start up the stairs doesn't help the impression any. I don't know why I care. After all, Logan and I are engaged. But I want his mom to have an honest impression of me.

Chapter Eleven
Saturday

At the top of the stairs, we move over to the elevator and take it the rest of the way up.

When we turn the corner into the hall, Dawn is already there, leaning against the wall next to the door to 402, her arms crossed, a skeptical look on her face. She pushes herself away from the wall and says, "What gives? You really think I wasn't going to notice you're investigating without me?"

Logan grunts. "The whole premise of a bet implies that we'd be investigating without you."

Dawn gestures at me. "But this one figured something out."

Logan tells me, "One thing you should know about my sister. She never did play fair."

I say, "The important thing is solving the murder." I move to the replacement door and unlock it. Logan follows me in and lets it close in Dawn's face.

"Hey!" she says, knocking loudly on it from the other side.

Logan says, "Hurry. We only have a few minutes before she picks the lock and lets herself in."

"Right," I say. I cross the room and kneel down next to the open grate. I tell Logan, "If I'm right, whatever was used to kill Ted should still be in the ductwork. It's the only way out of the room, right?"

"Right," Logan says skeptically. "But only for something very small."

I attach my phone to the selfie stick and set it to video. Then I push the selfie stick into the ductwork, doing my best to take a complete image of the inside.

The stick seems to snag on something, and I wiggle it free very carefully, holding my breath in the fear that each jostle is risking knocking my phone off the stick and losing it in the ductwork. Finally, it comes free, and I pull the stick back, not sure what I'm going to do if my phone isn't still attached.

But it is, and I let out that breath in relief.

By the time I get my phone off of the selfie stick, Dawn has let herself into the room.

She asks, "What's in there?"

I look to Logan, but he just shrugs like, *might as well show her*. Not that he knows what I'm hoping to have captured anyway.

I say, "What I'm hoping is that in that duct, there's the wreckage of a drone. I figure that whatever killed Ted has to have gone somewhere, and a drone could have been configured to fire a projectile and then fly into the open floor register. But inside all that metal, it would be hard to fly accurately – if it could get a signal at all."

Logan peers over one shoulder and Dawn over the other as I play the video. At first the duct seems empty, apart from some accumulated dust. But then there's an object resting on the bottom. As I get closer, it becomes clear that it is not a drone.

"What is that?" Dawn asks, trying to peer closer.

"I don't know," I say. It's a long, skinny object, dark against the surrounding metal.

Logan says, "That's poop."

Gross. But he's right. "Ewe! Does the hotel have rats?"

"No," Dawn says. "That's way too big for rat droppings. Something closer to the size of a cat."

"Like a ferret?" I ask.

The three of us just stand there, staring at the paused video of ferret poop like it is going to solve the murder for us. And I guess it might, at that. After all, there's only one ferret in the building, and we know exactly who that belongs to.

Logan says, "So what you're saying is that you think a drone killed Ted, and that Sasha's ferret then made off with it."

I shrug. "It makes as much sense as anything else. The big question in my mind is whether the ferret took it accidentally – or if someone trained it to retrieve something out of air ducts."

"Someone meaning Sasha," Logan says.

I say, "Her room is almost directly under this one. So it's plausible. But she seems like such an empathetic person – it's hard to imagine her killing someone in cold blood."

Dawn says, "Sometimes the nicest people do the most horrible things." She smacks Logan on the shoulder. "This is exactly what I mean abut untrained investigators. *Too much* empathy."

Logan says, "I don't know about that. Fee has an excellent track record of using that empathy to solve cases."

Ignoring the fact that they're talking about me like I'm not in the room, I point out, "Sasha did say something about her ferret going missing for a while yesterday. It's possible that Cheeseburger got up here on her own, well before the murder happened. Maybe she didn't carry off the murder weapon after all. But we can't exactly question her."

"But we can talk to Sasha," Dawn says.

So we go downstairs and ask Sasha to follow us into the office. She does, looking leery. She asks, "What is this about? Usually Sebastian handles any official unpleasantness."

Which makes me wonder – exactly how much unpleasantness has there been?

There's a knock in the door, and Sebastian asks, "Can I come in?"

Logan says that's fine, but there isn't a chair, so Sebastian stands behind his wife, one hand on her shoulder.

At the same time, both Logan and Dawn say, "We'd just like to ask you a few questions."

They both pull up short, similar looks of frustration on their faces highlighting the family resemblance. Logan makes an *after you* gesture with his hand.

Dawn says, "As we said, just a few questions. Felicity told us your ferret went missing yesterday. What time was that?"

"I don't know. Well before dinner, I guess."

Dawn lets out a frustrated breath. That's well before the timeline we're interested in.

Logan asks, "Was Cheeseburger with you when Ted was shot?"

"Of course. All three of us were in this room. Remember, I had her in my arms when you knocked and said we all needed to go downstairs to give statements?"

Logan says, "I remember. What about after that, though? Could she have escaped again later in the night while you were asleep?"

"No," Sasha says. "I crate her at night. Otherwise, she thinks my hair is a toy, and I wake up to her pulling on it, and the whole next day is a mess."

"Huh," Dawn says.

Sasha pulls out her phone and shows us a picture of a sleeping ferret in a relatively large wire cage. There's a litter box in the corner. Sasha says, "She looked so cute last night that I couldn't help take a picture."

Dawn asks Sasha if she can see the phone and checks the time stamp. She says, "This is shortly before Ted was shot."

"Yes," Sasha says. "We were getting ready for bed." She looks at each of us in turn. "Will one of you please tell me what this is about?"

"Just a theory I had," I tell her. I had been so sure the ferret had had something to do with Ted's murder. How else can I explain the poop in the air duct? It was definitely a fresh poo, too. So it couldn't have been from some random animal living in the hotel before Aunt Naomi had started her renovation. "And you're sure Cheeseburger was in her cage all night?"

Of course, Sasha could just lie to me, if she's guilty. So I don't know how useful the question is.

Sasha asks, "She didn't eat something she shouldn't have or anything, did she?"

Sebastian asks, "Why not just check the cage cam?"

"Cage cam?" I repeat.

Sebastian says, "There's a webcam on Cheeseburger's crate. It records her when she eats or plays or sleeps, and she has followers who actually pay to watch her." Sebastian looks sympathetically at Sasha. Then he tells us, "After we lost Brad, Sasha had a really hard time. She took an absence from work, and then needed something to fill the hole in her days. She spent so much time researching how to take care of the darn things, she started following ferret accounts all over social media."

Sebastian gives me the link information and I pull up the site. There's archived feed. And sure enough, last night, Cheeseburger was in her crate exactly when the Wimbletons said she was. I spot-check through the hours after Ted's death. And in the later footage, there's a reflected image of Sebastian's foot poking out from under the covers showing in the sliver of mirror behind the crate that the cam captured, meaning he was exactly where he said he was, too. I know some of this could be faked or altered, but somehow I doubt it.

And yet. It feels like the ferret has to be involved in all of this somehow. Or – I don't know. Maybe I'm just trying too hard, and committing to a theory because I want to be right in front of Logan's sister.

I must be missing something. But what?

I tell Logan I'm going back up to my suite. He says, "You of all people should know better than to go alone when there's a killer threatening another murder."

"I don't think I'm the target," I say. "Why call me out to solve the case and then kill me before I've given it a good solid try?"

Still, I wait for Logan to join me. This time we skip the pretense of the stairs and just take the elevator.

Logan takes a seat on my living room sofa, while I go into my bedroom and take the copy of *Frankenstein* from the locked drawer in my nightstand, where I keep valuables. I take it with me and go sit next to Logan on the sofa. He puts an arm around me and pulls me in close, and it feels so easy being here with him. I just fit. It feels like the kind of moment we'll have together once we're married, and I can see our future. And for a second that scares me. After all, I've been happy before – and then lost everything because of a stupid accident. I can have a great deal of happiness with Logan. But the more you have, the more that can be taken away.

I have to remind myself that it's worth the risk.

Logan takes the book from me with his other hand. "What exactly are we looking for?"

I tell him, "It's the book the killer left in my bed. Everything was such a jumble last night, I didn't examine it closely. We're looking for a hidden code marking one of the pages, or something tucked into the book, or . . . I don't know, a confession note from the killer would be nice. Just saying."

Logan flips through the pages one by one, while still cradling me with his other arm. And I let myself feel safe inside his embrace.

He gets to a part where two pages are stuck together. He has to move his arm so he can use both hands to gently pull the pages apart. He says, "This was done using a glue that's meant to peel off. So no damage to the book."

In between the pages, there's a $10,000 bill. And there's a small typed slip of paper that says, *Unmask me and you can keep it*.

"This is a joke, right?" I ask Logan as I peer down at the money. "They don't even make bills that large."

"They used to," Logan says. "And at a glance, this looks legit. That serious looking guy in the pic is Salmon P. Chase, President Lincoln's Secretary of the Treasury."

"Why do you even know that?" I ask.

Logan says, "When I worked private security, one time I escorted a courier who got paid with one of these, and it was a long flight back from Washington DC to Paris. We talked a lot. $10,000 bills are actually worth about five times face value at auction or to the right collector. Though they are legal currency, so technically you could just take this down to the store and buy a countertop chocolate depositor for cash."

I say, "I thought we decided to hold out for the conveyer belt model." I take a deep breath. "But that's not the point. Obviously. Because I can't accept this. It's blood money. Ted and Elena both died just so our Frankenstein could play some twisted game with me."

Logan says, "Personally, I wouldn't have any problem spending money a killer paid me to put him in jail."

I tell him, "Then you hold onto it."

He arches an eyebrow. "You don't mind that we have different opinions on this?"

I say, "We have different opinions on a lot of things. Guns, Taco Tuesdays, music. But the only reason what we have works is that we respect each other's preferences and beliefs."

Logan says, "Even if I still say Taco Tuesday is a marketing ploy."

I shrug. "I'm still not saying it isn't. But if I'm being encouraged to eat tacos at a restaurant, I'm going to do it."

"Okay." Logan takes the money and the note and puts them carefully on the side table.

I say, "The question is – what kind of person gives somebody an antique bank note? This could just as easily have been a stack of hundreds, which would be a lot less traceable."

Logan points out, "The single bill is far more dramatic. And much easier to slip unnoticed into the pages of a book."

"True. Jordan is all about drama. He's a theater teacher and an acting coach – even if he is a terrible actor. And we still have no idea what he carried in here in that duffle bag."

Logan says, "Fair point. But Sasha and Sebastian seem loaded. They're the ones who could have most easily afforded to burn money on a gesture like this."

"I still don't think they did it," I say. "I know that's where the evidence is pointing, but it seems like they would have covered their tracks better. And there's something about it being $10,000. Do you think it is coincidence that it's the same amount of money being offered to solve the fictional murder that happened in Ash's game?"

Logan's eyes widen in surprise. "Are you saying you think Chloe did this, after all?"

"No, not really," I admit. "Though it wouldn't hurt to find out more about her."

Logan says, "We need to find out more about all of them. Hudson and Cynthia both claim to have no connection to Ted. If that's true, then why are they here? The killer seems to have orchestrated all of this down to the smallest detail, so why put wild cards into the guest list?"

"And don't forget Colin," I say. "He's not talking about his connection to anything. We need to figure out who he is and why he's here."

Logan says, "We need to do it quick, before Doc Frankenstein makes good on the promise to kill somebody else."

Chapter Twelve
Saturday

Good thing for us, Fisk was already heading back when he got the notice about Elena's death. Unfortunately, now he is here in his official capacity.

We're back in the dining room, now that the scene has been contained and people were complaining about being crowded in the lobby. They were hoping to be allowed to go back to their rooms instead of back into a larger space together, so there's an air of frustration – especially because there's a yellow band of police tape around the area of the dining room where Elena's draped form still lies. Logan and I are standing just beyond the tape, while most everyone else is sitting at the tables again.

"Here," Fisk reaches in his jacket and hands Logan a yellow envelope. "The DNA results. Arlo will get the official copy in his email in an hour."

"Thanks." Logan opens the envelope, and I read over his shoulder. Colin Lipscombe is in fact one Lyle Crandall, on the run after escaping prison, where he had been incarcerated for antiquities theft and armed robbery. The picture we're looking at shows a guy with a distinctive Roman nose and a narrow face. Pretty much the opposite of the gregarious Englishman with the generous beard. But if you look really closely, the eyes are Colin's.

I say, "He must have gone to Ted for the cosmetic surgery. So Ted would have been the only one who knew who he was."

Logan says, "That's what I figure too."

I say, "I can't imagine living life like that, on the run. Away from everyone you've ever known, pretending to be somebody else. It must be so lonely. I wonder why he did it?"

"Let's go ask him," Logan says.

Arlo and another cop are busy interviewing everyone again, so why not? We walk over to Colin and sit down at the table.

I say, "Lyle, I figured out why your accent sounds so over the top. You're not really British, are you?"

He gives me a glassy deer-in-headlights look. Then he seems to collapse, his shoulder slumping forward, his gaze turning to the table in front of him. "No," he says, dropping the accent. "I'm actually from Queens."

Logan asks, "Why skip out on prison? You'd served over half your sentence."

Colin/Lyle says, "It was complicated. I got on the wrong side of some of the guys in prison, who thought I could tell them where I stashed the loot from the armed robbery. They didn't believe me when I told them I'd lost it in the car chase with the cops. That it – and my car – are somewhere at the bottom of the Atlantic Ocean, and cash don't hold up too good down there, you know?" He makes eye contact. "It was in my best interest to skedaddle. They'd started to threaten my mother, on the outside. So I got my face fixed and then went to her place to get her out of there. I was in pain, and in bandages, and my mamma took care of me in one seedy hotel after another. But Doc Ted hired a private investigator to follow us."

I say, "So he found out your new identity and blackmailed you."

Colin grunts assent. "I guess I can't blame him too much. I did show up at his office after hours and demand a rush job. I tried to do it at gunpoint – I was so jacked up on the adrenaline, I wasn't thinking straight. How am I going to keep a gun on the guy when he has to use anesthesia on me? But he thought it was funny. He did good work. I made the mistake of giving him most of the cash I had salvaged after the car crash. Once he found me in Des Moines, he demanded more money. And in New Orleans, even more. I thought I had finally escaped him – but then he showed up here."

"And last night, he demanded another payment, didn't he?" Logan says. "We saw the ledger."

Colin looks down at the table again.

I add, "Or what? He was going to turn you in to the cops?"

Colin looks amused. "That I could handle. He was going to turn me in to the guys from prison. I couldn't take a risk that they'd hurt my poor mamma before I could get home from Texas, so I paid him."

"And then you felt trapped, so you decided to kill him," Logan prompts.

"What? Lord, no." Colin's lips go into a hard line. "If I had killed him, I'd have just done it. No locked room puzzles, or fancy traps. Who needs all the attention?"

"Then why come here in the first place?" I ask. "Wasn't it a risk?"

He says, "I lied when I told you I'd entered your contest. I got an email offering me a job. I'm a safe cracker, ya know? I may have a different face, but I still gotta eat. I was told to meet my contact here, and join the party, and to wait until I heard the right response to my code phrase."

Well, that explains why Colin had gone around saying, *Top of the morning to ya*, to everyone – even when it wasn't morning anymore.

I tell Logan, "I don't think this guy killed Ted."

Colin says, "That's right, Logan, listen to the lass. She knows, ya know?"

"Lass," Logan says, stifling a chuckle.

"Sorry," Colin says. "Force of habit. But if you let me go, I promise you wouldn't be aiding Ted's murderer."

Logan looks at me. "Notice he didn't say a murderer. Meaning he's only denying the one specific murder."

I say, "Well, he couldn't have murdered Elena. He's been cuffed to that chair this whole time."

Logan says, "If he tampered with the chocolates, he could have done it in advance."

"I don't think so," I say. "He was eating the chocolates along with everyone else. The only one who didn't is Jordan."

We both cast a look over at Jordan, who has started packing again, now that he's back in the room with the body. But he looks genuinely agitated this time, unlike last night's drunk act. Irene is by his side now, trying to calm him down. Hudson doesn't seem to mind that she's left the table. He's on his phone, doing something that doesn't involve streaming. Thank goodness.

Fisk clears his throat and waves us over. "I think Felicity is right. There's no trace of poison in the chocolates, or on Elena's plate. It was on the filter of her water bottle."

Logan says, "I saw Elena take a drink out of that bottle maybe half an hour before the presentation started. She took some kind of pills. Cyanide is fast acting. So the bottle had to be tampered with within that time span."

I say, "Maybe she left the bottle unattended at her spot on the table, to go to the bathroom or back up to the buffet. Someone could have applied cyanide to the filter, or even switched out the bottle for a poisoned one."

"Agreed," Logan says. "And it could have been practically anyone in this room – except Colin."

I say, "It doesn't feel like this was a random choice of victim. If the water bottle was changed out, it would have to have been arranged by someone who knew Elena carried it, and then brought it along to this event."

Logan says, "It could be that Doc Frankenstein followed her on social media and saw the bottle. But yeah, that implies planning."

I scan the room. Which one of the people out there is that cold and meticulous? To be honest, none of them seem all that organized.

Fisk packs away his equipment and samples, then goes and washes up. Someone else on his team will arrive to take away Elena's body. I can't help but worry about her mother, who has been living in Elena's spare room. With both twins dead, who will be left to take care of her?

Fisk comes back in, dolloping sanitizer on his hands. He walks over to where Enrique is packing up the leftover from the breakfast buffet. He tells Enrique, "I hope you have some of that left for me."

Enrique says, "Always, for a foodie like yourself."

Fisk's reputation as a gourmand is as much news to me as was learning he's an opera fan.

Jordan says, "Don't eat that. Don't you know somebody was poisoned in this room?"

Fisk straightens the edges of his CSI jacket. "I am aware. But if something on the buffet was poisoned, most of you should be dead already."

"I can't watch this," Jordan says, stalking out of the room, into the lobby.

Bea turns to follow him, either to protect him since he's alone, or to make sure he doesn't try to leave the building. She forgets to grab Satchmo's leash. Satchmo, momentarily ignored and without a command to heel or stay, takes the opportunity to check out the ferret. Before Satchmo can even get close, Cheeseburger flees the room.

Sasha shouts, "Somebody catch my baby."

There's noise out in the lobby, and the sound of Bea calling the ferret. Satchmo cocks his head, and then follows his owner's voice. There's more noise, and the sound of something heavy falling over. Jordan comes back into the room carrying Cheeseburger, trailing the rhinestone lead behind him. Cheeseburger seems to be trying to burrow into his armpit for safety.

Jordan announces, "There were two ferrets, but I only caught the leash for this one. I figure it has to be yours."

Seriously? Does Jordan expect us to believe that he's so drunk, he's seeing double? It feels even more like a calculated act.

Sasha doesn't seem to care. She tells the ferret, "I'm so glad you're safe, Sweetheart." Then she turns to Jordan. "Thank you. I don't know what I would do if I lost Cheeseburger. She went missing for a little while yesterday, and I was frantic."

Bea walks back in, and now that we're all together again, phones start dinging all over the room. There's another text from the same burner phone number belonging to Doc Frankenstein. This time it says, *I promised to kill two. Elena was to show I'm serious. But you can buy the other one back if you all share your secrets and uncomfortable truths.*

"That's it," Jordan shouts. "I'm tired of being controlled by my phone." He throws his on the floor and walks away from it. Irene picks it up and follows him, to give it back.

Carmen walks out from the kitchen, pushing a trolley laden with chips and various dips. There will be sandwiches too, and more pastries, for lunch and snacks throughout the afternoon. We were supposed to have lunch while touring historic homes, so this is a last-minute substitution.

Right now seems like an appropriate time to break for chips and queso before we get into the discussion that has been proposed to us by a killer.

Once we have everyone organized and sitting down again, Cynthia says, "I already told you all, I'm not part of this. I never even met Ted before the night he died."

"We understand that," I reassure her. Honestly, I'm not sure what the killer's motive is in pushing us all to share. To muddy the water, by showing how many people have a motive for killing Ted? To move things along, because I haven't been uncovering the clues fast enough? Or just to show off how good they are at games like Two Truths and a Lie? Still. Whatever Doc Frankenstein's reasoning, why not take advantage of it to get a few answers of my own? I say, "Obviously, not all of us have secrets about Doctor Durango. But everybody has secrets about something. And I think the killer invited each of you here for a reason. That person probably knows whether what you are sharing is true or not. So how about this. If you have a connection to the murder victim, share that. If not, share something that will help us get to know you."

"What about you?" Jordan asks.

"Okay," I say reluctantly. "I guess I should go first. I never met any of you before you arrived at the hotel. My secret is that I once cheated on a big exam in college. I've always been big on following the rules, but I fell asleep the night before while studying. I was racked with guilt afterwards and didn't sleep for a week." I've never told anyone this, and admitting it somehow makes me feel lighter.

Sasha laughs. "You must be one poor sheltered thing if that's the worst thing that's happened to you."

It's not – but most of the tragedies in my life aren't secrets.

Next to her, Sebastian says, "That kind of need for structure can be the result of trauma, you know. Maybe you should schedule a session with someone."

Sasha waves her hand at him dismissively. "Obviously, Felicity has been working through her problems by solving murders." She turns and waves at the group. "My uncomfortable truth is that I feel guilty for letting my son play sports. If I hadn't, then he never would have gotten injured and needed an operation in the first place. I know, it's not logical." She turns to Sebastian and he squeezes her hand supportively.

Sebastian clears his throat and, still looking at his wife, says, "My secret is that I sent Ted a number of death threats. I obviously wouldn't have acted on them, and I've discussed this need to lash out in great depth with my own therapist." Someone laughs, and Sebastian adds, "Yes, even therapists see therapists."

See? Even though so much evidence points towards them, I can't see the Wimbletons as capable of murder. Plus, it seems unlikely that Sebastian would have realized that the cage cam had recorded his foot while he slept. So while it is possible Sasha left the room, Sebastian hadn't so much as stirred.

Colin says, "Logan already has the police report that lays out all my secrets."

"Oh?" Arlo asks.

"He didn't tell you?" Colin asks, sounding amused. "The short of it is, Ted was blackmailing me to keep my identity a secret. Did I think about killing him? Yes. Did I do it? No."

Hudson says, "My secret is that I'm afraid of heights. I didn't used to be. I took a tumble down one of the trails on Mt. Fuji while I was filming a video. I busted my camera and sprained a wrist."

Irene asks, "Is that how you scarred your face?"

Hudson says, "No. Logging accident. I was in a movie, on set in Alaska."

Logan's dad asks, "Is that the real truth?"

Hudson shrugs. "It could be."

Sasha stands up and says, "If you're lying, you could be putting yourself in the killer's sights. Given the stakes of this game, you had better tell the truth."

Hudson says, "I did. I honestly am afraid of heights."

Sasha looks like she wants to protest, but she thinks better of it and sits back down.

Irene says, "My secret is that I was married once before I met Ted. It was an impulsive weekend-in-Vegas thing, and he wanted to get it annulled. But I don't give up on things easily, so I didn't sign the papers until I decided to marry Ted."

Jordan says, "That's harsh." He looks dismayed. I'd inferred from the conversation I'd overheard last night that he and Irene are in some stage of romantic involvement. I wonder if he's realizing right now that he doesn't know her as well as he thought he did.

I mean, Logan and I are still figuring out things about each other, but it's little things – preferences, anecdotes, small bits of personal history. Irene not telling Jordan that she'd been married before feels like a major oversight.

Logan says, "My secret is that I intentionally left my sister behind on a family vacation when we were teenagers. I locked her in the cabin bathroom and headed out after Mom and Dad, and she wound up hitchhiking through the Appalachians."

"I knew it!" Dawn shouts. "I've always said you knew perfectly well I didn't go with Mom and Dad. I could have died, you know?"

Logan says, "You should have thought about that before you started a prank war. Or escalated it."

I am a bit surprised that Logan would do something like that. He's always seemed so serious, so responsible. So maybe I do still have a bit to learn about him.

Dawn says, "My secret is that I am the one who sabotaged Logan's science fair project when he was in ninth grade and I was in eleventh." She flashes Logan a wicked grin. "Oh no! Where are all the purple bubbles coming from?"

Logan's dad says, "My secret is that sometimes, I used to go to the station and do paperwork just to get away from you two."

"That's no secret, dear," Logan's mom says. "I was just glad we knew where you were. A cop's wife is always bound to worry. My secret is that I would sometimes schedule a flight just for me, even if there was no cargo, just so I could get some alone time when the kids were little."

I whisper to Logan, "Your mom's a cargo pilot? I thought you said she worked retail occasionally, just get out of the house."

He whispers back, "That's accurate. But she was a cargo pilot, for a couple of years. Can you imagine her flying to Canada just to get away from us?"

Bea says, "My secret is that I sing show tunes in the shower. Satchmo usually howls along from the other side of the door. I know I can't sing, but that's okay."

No one seems to know what to do with that information.

Autumn says, "My uncomfortable truth is that I may never be able to eat guacamole again. If you'll excuse me, I think I need to go back to the bathroom."

She gets up and exits the room.

Poor thing! Under any other circumstance I'd have jumped up immediately to go with her to be supportive. I'm conflicted. I shouldn't let her go alone, when we're all staying together to keep anyone from getting hurt, and she's the one who seems the most vulnerable.

Imogen stands up. She looks at me and says, "I'll go with her. It will be fine."

I nod, gratefully. Imogen sees Autumn as a writing mentor, so it makes sense she'd want to help Autumn in return.

I look back at Jordan and say, "You didn't actually tell us your secret."

Jordan says, "My uncomfortable truth is that I am a coward. I have never seen a dead body before last night, never been to a funeral – not even when my aunt died, or my grandmother. I just skipped out on both of their services. And seeing Ted, all broken and cold – it just brings home the reality of our mortality."

Ash asks, "Why come to a murder mystery weekend if you're that touchy about death."

Jordan straightens his posture and juts out his chin. "I am an actor at heart. It sounded like a fun way to play a role. I didn't expect for anybody to actually die. As I said before, I am not actually a listener of your podcast. I merely filled out a form that someone forwarded into my inbox."

"Forwarded," I repeat. "Who sent it to you?"

Jordan winces as he realizes his slip-up. "I – uh-" He looks over at Irene.

"For Christ's sake," Irene says. She looks at me. "I forwarded him the ad. I told him that if we both entered, we'd be twice as likely to win. Only – we both won. Which in retrospect seems kind of suspicious, since obviously I was selected-" She makes air quotes around the word. "-to come because I'm Ted's ex."

Logan asks Jordan, "Then why pretend not to know each other? There wasn't any rule that says you can't both win."

Jordan says, "We were going to try to team up to win the mystery game without anybody knowing we were working together."

It's a somewhat plausible explanation. Though it seems quite cold of Irene to have been showing attention to Hudson the whole time her boyfriend has been in the building.

Hudson looks a little hurt, too. He asks Irene, "So when you said you wanted to team up and share clues with me – you were already sharing everything with Jordan?"

Irene says, "It's not like I knew there was going to turn out to be a cash prize. I just get competitive."

Jordan and Hudson make wary eye contact across the tables – and I wonder if Irene is going to wind up losing her friendship with both of them before the weekend is over.

Aunt Naomi says, "My uncomfortable truth is that you never forget your past. You just learn to live with it. And for the record – I held no remaining anger towards Ted, and I am saddened by his passing and the senseless death of his sister."

Uncle Greg says, "My uncomfortable truth is that sometimes I hate working offshore. I miss my wife, and I feel powerless to help her when she needs me. But to be clear – I didn't kill Ted either."

"Right," Jordan says skeptically. "Who better to set up two murders than the guy who lives here?"

"That's a bit of a stretch," Hudson says.

Jordan scoffs. "Now you're just saying the opposite of whatever I say."

Chloe stands up and says, "My secret is that I tried the skin care line Ted was touting. It wasn't just my friends who got cheated by him. I invested money, too. I even met him once. I'm sorry I lied about that."

"It's okay," I tell her. "We understand."

"You keep cutting her slack because she's your friend," Cynthia says. "But there's a lot of circumstantial evidence that says she could have committed both murders."

Chloe puts a hand on her hip. "You're quick to cast judgement, but you've been awful quiet yourself."

Cynthia says, "That's because I don't want to play this game. It's undignified. Besides, as I told you, I don't have any secrets."

Chloe says, "That's exactly what someone hiding something would say."

Chloe's not wrong. But since I don't know what Cynthia is hiding, I don't know if she's dangerous.

The killer has to be here, at one of these tables. It's only fair, as part of the game. Doc Frankenstein is playing with me. Yes, it is possible a drone could have been hidden in the hotel by one of the workers days before and operated from a distance, but Elena's filter couldn't have been tampered with the same way. The person had to be in the room during the presentation. Besides, a killer who killed by remote and watched the suspects and sleuths from a hidden camera could not be knowable, and could not be discovered. I've been offered money to catch this person. They would have wanted to be here, watching me work, gloating at passing off their own innocuous lies as a way to hide their real connections in this case.

It's chilling to think that someone in this room has coldly killed two people – and I have no idea who it is.

Chapter Thirteen
Saturday

It's been hours since Doc Frankenstein's little impromptu game of Truth of Dare, and nothing's happened. The fact that no one else has died has most of the group off their guard, either feeling the anticlimactic nature of something promised and not delivered, or convinced that, even though not everyone shared real secrets, it was enough to fulfill Doc Frankenstein's conditions. People have gotten restless, and some of them have decided to go back to their own rooms, despite our urging for them to stay in one place. Others have scattered throughout the lobby and the dining room, a few even retreating to tables in the room behind the office that will be the business center, to work at the long built-in tables, or charge their devices. Logan and I have joined that group, so he can charge his phone.

Arlo enters the room and walks over to us. He says, "I finally got the email with Colin's file. Seems a little odd that my own guys would be favoring you with early information. But they're making up for that by coming to pick him up and take him to jail."

Logan says, "What can I say? They must think I'd be a pain to have around the office. Everybody knows about the bet we have going on."

Arlo sighs. "You have a bet. With your sister. All I want to do is stop anyone else from getting murdered."

I ask, "You don't think we're safe, even though we played along with the killer's game, do you?"

Arlo says, "I think whoever is doing this is off on a power trip and is enjoying the sense of being in control of all of us. And the threat of continued violence is a big part of that."

"What about moving Colin?" I ask. "Won't that interfere with the killer's sense of control."

Arlo says, "I sent a text back to the number the threats have been coming from, notifying them that Colin will be taken into custody. There wasn't a reply."

Reacting to the need for urgency, Logan says, "I don't mind sharing information. And I've called in a few favors to learn more about some of the people here. Do you want the somewhat predictable information or the really surprising information first?"

Arlo says, "The surprising information."

"Chloe has a record."

"What?" I lean towards him, shocked, part of my brain waiting for the punch line.

Several people at the other tables turn towards me at the sound of my outburst.

"I know," Logan says softly. "I was surprised, too. She was arrested for assault, two years ago after some awards show. She was fifteen, and they somehow managed to keep it out of the news."

"We need to talk to her," I say. "Last I saw, she was chatting with Aunt Naomi in the kitchen."

Logan unplugs his phone from the charger. "Let's go." But before we leave the table, he puts a hand on my arm, stopping me. "Fee, I know you don't want Chloe to turn out to be a killer, but she is smart and capable, and she's almost an adult. You need to make sure you treat her like any other suspect."

I tell Logan, "Now you're starting to sound like your sister."

For a brief moment, there's a flicker of hurt in his eyes. But then he laughs. "And now you're starting to sound like part of the family."

I give him a careful smile. Maybe we're starting to find ourselves in a more secure place.

"Come on, you two," Arlo says. "Have you forgotten how recently I was part of this love triangle? I'm happy for you, but you don't have to flaunt how lovey-dovey you are right in front of me."

"Sorry," I say. "Let's go find Chloe." But Logan winks at me, and I feel all warm and melty inside, so I'm sure there's a ridiculous grin on my face as I head for the kitchen.

We find Chloe standing with a giant bowl, snapping the ends off green beans. Patsy is helping her. Rosemary and Bea are pulling empty glass jars out of an even bigger pot of boiling water, while Aunt Noami is sitting in a chair, mixing vinegar and sugar in a large saucepan.

"What's going on in here?" I ask, though I can take a guess.

Bea says, "Naomi was talking about how she's hoping for vegetables this summer from the garden she's putting in on the side of the hotel."

Naomi says, "It would be perfect for someone wanting to do a farm-to-table restaurant in here once they buy the place. But in the meantime, I'm going to take advantage of having a small bit of land."

I gesture towards Chloe. "Where'd you get all the green beans?"

Bea says, "Fisk brought them, along with all the canning supplies. I told him we've been going stir-crazy, cooped up in here with nothing to do, so I made a list, and voilà – all these ladies get to try their hand at canning for the first time. I even shared my favorite recipe – dilled green beans."

Logan asks, "What's Enrique going to say when he gets back and finds you in his kitchen?"

Chloe says, "He already asked for a couple of jars of beans. And we promised we'd wrap this up before dinner."

Chloe seems like such a responsible kid. And she's so upbeat and sweet. How could she really have a record?

Arlo tells Chloe, "I thought you and Ash were trying to keep people occupied playing the game. You did offer quite the incentive."

Chloe snaps another green bean. "I've had two people come up to me and ask me to flat out tell them who did it. And I was honest – I have no idea."

Bea says, "I've been listening to people ask each other questions. And I have a good idea who might have killed poor Clementine. I just need to verify a few more things, but it all comes down to the palm tree."

"Really?" Logan's mom asks. "How would that play in? I thought we were trying to figure out who switched the jewelry boxes and took the ring. Whoever has the ring has to be the culprit, right?"

"Probably," Bea says. "But that person would have been the same one who moved the palm tree to obstruct the line of sight, so we wouldn't see them fire the gun."

I say, "I haven't had much time to look into the game myself, but it sounds like a complex puzzle."

Chloe says, "Oh, it is. The problem is that Ted and Elena both had lists of clues, what their characters had seen and what they knew. So it's impossible to question everyone and make sure of the solution."

Logan's mom volunteers, "My character, Ethel Waggsbottom, was the one who saw Clementine put the ring into the box and say, 'No, I won't marry him.' So I think her boyfriend Walt must have overheard, and then later switched the boxes."

"You're not supposed to say that out loud," Bea chides. "If you're sure Walt killed Chloe, you should write it down and go find Ash to claim the prize."

Chloe helpfully adds, "Ash is in the sauna."

I look at Aunt Naomi, "You got the sauna up and working?"

As far as I knew, the space was still in need of a little TLC. Okay, honestly, a lot of TLC.

Aunt Naomi says, "Ash volunteered to try and get it working. I told him the whole space needs to be cleaned, but he said he'd deal with that if he could get the system fixed."

The look on Logan's face says he would like nothing more than to go help Ash tinker with the sauna. Logan likes doing maintenance on his planes, and working with the machines at the chocolate shop. But we have more important things to focus on right now. His jaw tenses as he forces himself to stay on track.

Rosemary says, "Oh, I never win anything. Besides, even if Walt felt jilted and did take his ring back, that doesn't mean he murdered Clementine."

"Fair enough," Chloe says. "I doubt the mystery would be that simple."

Patsy says, "My character talked to Walt last night – shortly before Ted went up to his room." She hesitates, looking unsettled that she was one of the last people to see Ted alive. She says, "He said he was secretly in love with somebody else. Maybe he was glad he took back the ring, so he could give it to her."

I don't think Patsy means to insinuate anything about art imitating life. But the looks she gives me says she's afraid she's offended me. We're all trying to be so careful around each other, given the complex past of our relationships. She'd dated Arlo, then broken up with him after he'd arrested her brother. Then, Arlo had gotten interested in me again – since we'd been each other's first loves in high school. But by then, I had already started a tentative relationship with Logan. Honestly, though, Arlo had still been pining for Patsy.

I say, "Then Walt would have had no reason to hurt Clementine, since clearly he's moved on."

Patsy looks relieved we're keeping this in the context of the game. She says, "Maybe they'd even become friends."

Arlo says, "Probably so. I'd like to think all four of them become close friends. But I think we've lost focus of why we came in here. Chloe, do you mind coming with us to the office for a short chat?"

"Me?" Chloe asks as she drops another green bean into the bowl. She giggles nervously. "Why do I feel like I'm being pulled into the principal's office?"

"You're not in trouble," Logan assures her. "We just want to clarify a few things."

"Sure," Chloe says. She looks over at Bea. "Don't let them pull all the jars out without me."

Patsy asks, "Would you like me to go with you? For moral support?"

I'm surprised. Patsy has been very stand-offish about Arlo's job, or anything to do with solving cases – especially given the whole Arlo-arrested-her-brother thing, and the recent death of her dad in the last case I'd gotten involved in. But maybe she's taking the whole Arlo-clearly-asking-for-us-all-to-be-couple-friends thing to heart. Or maybe she can just see that Chloe is scared.

Chloe says, "I'd like that, Miss Nash."

So the four of us make our way to the office. There's still only four chairs. Arlo and Patsy wind up behind the desk, with me and Chloe facing him, while Logan stands.

I'm not sure where to start. I ask Chloe, "Have you ever read *Frankenstein*?"

Chloe giggles. She says, "I've seen the Abbot and Costello version. My mom and I love watching old movies together."

"That's not the same thing," Patsy tells her sympathetically. "I think Felicity is talking about the book." Patsy gives me a questioning look, and I nod. She nods back, though she still looks confused why I'm bringing this up, and says, "It's about the abuse of power, the absolute hubris of playing God over another creature. And about the pain of feeling like an outsider. The doctor creates a monster, and the monster asks the doctor to create a female counterpart, and at first the doctor is going to do it, but then he gets scared and throws the half-completed second monster in the lake. So the monster kills someone the doctor cares about in revenge."

"That sounds awful," Chloe says.

"Wait a minute," Arlo protests. "I saw the original *Frankenstein* movie, with Boris Karloff, and that's not what happens at all. The monster is tragic, yet innocent. It kills that little girl, but it had no idea that it was doing it. They were throwing flower petals in a lake, and when they ran out of flower petals, it threw her in instead."

Patsy says, "The movie was an adaption of a play which was an adaptation of the book. It was a very different take, but it's the one that a lot of subsequent adaptations were based on. There's not a lot of media that stays true to the book."

"But why is this important?" Chloe asks. Then her eyes go wide. "Wait a minute. Did you find a copy of *Frankenstein*? Is this another one of your book-murder connections?"

"Maybe," I say, trying to sound noncommittal. But it's obvious she's guessed right.

Chloe giggles nervously. She says, "I knew I might be a suspect in all of this, but I promise you, I'm not a violent person."

Logan asks, "If that's true, then why were you arrested for assault?"

Chloe's face sinks instantly into a somber expression. She says, "The judge told me that was going to be sealed."

Arlo says, "Well, Logan has a way of getting information that has restricted access. You should know that if you're going to hang out with Felicity. Given the situations she tends to find herself in, there could also be an element of risk."

Chloe nods. "I understood that. I've listened to all of Ash's podcast, since first meeting you guys. And he's still only starting on the second case y'all were involved in."

Arlo says, "Tell us what prompted the assault."

Chloe leans back in her chair and closes her eyes. "It was a weird day. I'd been nominated for an award at a pet media event. I lost, but afterwards, one of the other nominees kept touching Mr. Tunaface. I told her to stop, but she kept insinuating that I didn't deserve such a beautiful cat. She never came out and said it, but the implication was that she wanted to take my cat home with her. It was creepy. Stalkerish. I lost it. I'd never been in a fight before, but I knocked that girl out. Since I couldn't prove that she'd been threatening me, I was the one who got in trouble."

Logan asks, "Has there been any trouble since then?"

I can't tell if he's worried about Chloe's violent streak – or if he's more concerned for her safety with a potentially unhinged cat fancier out there.

"No," Chloe says. "I've never seen that girl again. It's not like we were neighbors, or anything. Her parents filed a restraining order, but I haven't been back in California anyway, so what does it matter?"

Arlo asks, "And you haven't been in trouble again? Even for something minor?"

Chloe raises both her hands in the air, clearly exasperated. "Okay, so you know. I only snuck into that club just one time. I saw Lindsay M. – she's this hot fashion designer – go in there, and I wanted to talk to her about this idea I had for a collab. Please don't tell my mom."

"We didn't know about that incident, actually," I tell her. "But if that's the worst thing you've got, I'm sure you have nothing to worry about."

Patsy says, "We know you're a good kid."

"So I can go now?" she asks.

I look to Arlo. He says, "Unless you remember anything else about where any of the others were around the time of either murder."

Chloe says, "When Ted was shot, I wasn't even at the hotel. And when Elena fell over, I was busy trying to keep the connection stable on the computer. So how could I have noticed anything?"

Arlo shrugs. "These murders both seem to have had elements set up in advance. You could easily have seen something. Just try to remember details you might have missed."

Chloe says, "I'll think on it." Then she slips out of her chair and heads back to the kitchen.

Logan sits down in the unoccupied spot. He says, "If she did do it, she's got moxie, lying straight to our faces."

"I don't think she's lying," I protest.

I sound defensive, even to myself. Because thin of a motive as it is, she does have a reason for disliking Dr. Ted Durango. And there's a lot more to Chloe than I had realized – including a willingness to use her fists. But surely, she's not a killer.

Arlo leans forward, steepling his hands on the desk. "And the somewhat predictable information?"

I had all but forgotten that Logan had said he's come up with more than one revelation from those favors he had called in.

"Jordan is on suspension from his last teaching job, pending an investigation into accusations he brought alcohol on campus."

"Why does that not surprise me?" I ask.

Arlo says, "It does me a bit. I thought the alcohol thing was just an act."

Logan's phone buzzes. He looks down at his screen, then chuckles. "How about this one? I just got the info on Hudson's medical records, and he wasn't in an accident after all. The scars on his face? They're the result of botched plastic surgery."

"Let me guess," Arlo says. "Ted was his doctor?"

Logan says, "You got it in one."

"Anybody know where Hudson is?" I ask.

"Last I saw, he was playing checkers with Dawn," Logan says.

"That's a bit odd," I say. "You would think she'd be busy investigating, considering she's trying to beat us to the punch in unraveling all of this."

"She probably *is* investigating," Logan says. "She can be disarming, even charming if she wants. If she has any of the same information about Hudson that we do, she may well be trying to get him comfortable enough to share information she can use to force a confession."

"Well, dang," I say. "I don't think we should disrupt that. If he is the killer, we might spook him."

"And if he's not," Logan adds, "then we've just invited Dawn right back into our business."

"Okay," I say. "Then let's go find Ash and see how his progress is going on the sauna. Maybe someone said something to him about the game that might give away intentions in the real world."

"I wanted to get a look at that thing anyway," Logan says. "I wasn't even aware this hotel had a sauna."

"Neither were we, until a little while ago. There was a room at the far end of the hall being used as a storage room. When Aunt Naomi cleaned it out, she realized that it must have once been a small gym. She pulled down some drywall and found a whole locker room area that had been walled over, with two sets of showers, and a sauna and hot tub. The hot tub looked pretty gross, like the water had dried in it."

Arlo says, "That sounds like a black mold situation waiting to happen."

I say, "That's why Aunt Naomi had the hot tub removed. There's still a lot of cleaning that needs to happen in there – maybe even some remediation."

Logan asks, "Are you sure you should go in there?"

I'd undergone experimental treatments to deal with my asthma issues, which has mostly gone away. I still carry an inhaler – just in case – but I haven't needed it in ages. I tap my pocket. "I'll be fine. Nothing really irritated me the last time I looked at the space."

Chapter Fourteen
Saturday

So the four of us make our way to the far end of the building. At first, it doesn't look like Ash is even still in there. But then I hear banging, and Ash talking to the machinery as though to another person.

We enter the sauna and hot tub area and I realize he *is* talking to another person – Sasha, who is sitting inside the sauna itself, on the wooden seat as though her pants suit is gym-ready attire. Ash has the door propped open.

Cheeseburger is playing at her feet, jumping and then rolling over. Sasha has one high heel off to pet the ferret's belly with her foot. When Cheeseburger spots me, she starts making a panting noise and races out of the sauna and across the room towards me. Half way there, she gets distracted by the pieces of machinery Ash has laid out in the middle of the room. She starts to climb into it, but Patsy moves over to stop her, lifting the ferret by the midsection to pull Cheeseburger out of a pipe.

"Hold on, little girl," Patsy says. "You don't know where that goes."

She flips Cheeseburger onto her belly and scratches the ferret's chin. Cheeseburger squeaks happily and waves her paws in the air.

Sasha leans forward and asks, "Are you fond of ferrets?"

Patsy says, "We used to have three of them, when I was growing up. They were the sweetest things ever."

"You don't have one now?" Sasha asks.

Patsy shakes her head, making a cute-baby face down at the ferret. "Not at the moment. I have a big orange cat named Juice. He's enough of a handful."

Arlo laughs. "Remember the time he jumped in the hamper, and it closed on him?"

Patsy giggles, while trying to look serious. She says, "You know he chewed a hole in it. I had to buy a new hamper after that."

Arlo says, "How is it that cats can be total jerks, but completely endearing at the same time?

Sasha says, "I feel the same way about ferrets."

I say, "Knightley used to jump into the tall kitchen trash can Kevin and I had. It was funny, but we finally bought one of the ones with the lid, that you operate with your foot."

I meant to join in the light-hearted conversation, but the looks my friends are giving me are sympathetic. "It's okay," I tell them. "Being with Kevin was a big part of my life. If I can't remember him, and share the good times, that diminishes his memory."

Patsy says, "You've come a long way, since I first met you. Arlo didn't dare mention Kevin's name. I hope I can get to that point someday, about my dad."

Sasha says, "Me too, about Brad."

I say, "I still miss him sometimes. But like everyone kept telling me when I was at my lowest – he wouldn't have wanted me to be miserable forever."

Logan says, "If you're ready, maybe we can talk about him a bit. I've felt like that is a whole part of your life that's been closed off from me. And I want to be able to share anything with the woman I'm going to marry, happy or sad."

Heat suddenly builds behind my eyes. I reach out and hug him, holding on tight.

Ash says, "I have a cat. Does anybody want to hug me?"

I snort a laugh against Logan's chest and let him go. I turn to Ash and ask, "How's the mystery game coming?"

Logan starts looking at the pieces of the sauna, finally unable to resist.

Ash says, "So far, I've had two wrong guesses. Hudson and Jordan came in separately and accused each other." Ash gestures over at Sasha. "She came in here asking for a clue, and that's the information I gave her."

I'm surprised that Sasha is that into the game. She looks like the one person here who doesn't need the ten thousand dollars.

Sasha says, "If I win, the cash goes to a charity I set up for a scholarship fund." She waves a hand. "Besides, Sebastian said it's impossible to figure out all the clues without Ted and Elena still playing. He's given up. So I thought I'd ask Ash to fill in the gaps in the narrative. It's not really cheating."

Patsy leans towards me, and the ferret jumps out of her arms into mine, begging to be petted. She's right – ferrets can be super sweet. Patsy says, "I think Arlo and I have an advantage, since he's a cop."

I don't mention that there are a number of people here who either are or used to be cops. We're getting along so well, I don't want to say anything negative.

"Who do you think the game killer is?" I ask.

She leans even closer and whispers into my ear, "Logan's mom. She acted like she doesn't plan to turn in a guess. Who else would have done that, except someone who can't play?"

"Smart logic," I whisper back. It's not a bad guess – though I can see why Arlo would want more to go on, given his police training.

But it gets me back thinking about the two people who had refused to play the real killer's game: Hudson and Cynthia. Part of me thinks one of them is guilty of a very real murder. And we still know very little about them – especially Cynthia.

Cradling the ferret in one arm, I pull out my phone and do a quick search for *Cynthia Reed secretary*. There's not much useful in the way of results, but on the second page, Cynthia has a LinkedIn entry, with a photo, connecting her to a company called Ratherson, Inc. It says her hobbies include snowboarding, knife throwing and doing crossword puzzles. Which could point to skills needed by a killer intent on setting up the crimes as a game. I look up Ratherson, and I nearly drop the ferret in excitement. It's a company that sells drones.

Cheeseburger makes a honking noise and tries to grab the phone with her mouth. I hold it out away from her, still trying to read what's on the screen. The company sells drones for a variety of uses – including police and military applications. I still don't know what Cynthia's motive for killing Ted might have been, but she certainly had the means.

I draft a text to Logan and Arlo. After a second, I add Patsy to the list. I screenshot Cynthia's Linked-In and the company's "About" page.

A few seconds later, Logan puts down the pipe he's been examining and says, "I guess we really should get out of your way."

"Right," Arlo says. "We have to go check on something."

Ash looks at me, his eyes troubled. He says, "Before you go, I really ought to give you something." Ash hands me an envelope. He says, "This was under my door this morning."

The envelope has my name on it. I ask, "Why would they deliver this to you instead of me?" I flip the envelope over, but the seal's already ripped.

Ash says, "Come on. Did you expect me not to open it?"

I take out a typed note that says, *Meet me in the sauna at 4 PM. I have information that could help the case.*

Ash says, "That's why I came in here. I wanted to see if there was anything in here that might be a trap."

I gesture to the machinery splayed across the room. "Then what is all this about?"

Ash shrugs. "I thought I might be able to fix it. You know how I get when I think I might be onto something."

"That I do." I had first met Ash when he had been convinced I'd murdered one of my employees. Convincing him otherwise had been an undertaking.

Logan gestures at the machinery on the floor. "Let me know how it goes with the heating unit."

He looks back once, then we go looking for Cynthia. She's not in the lobby or the dining room. We check the kitchen, where the pickle-making process is nearly complete, with jars of dilled green beans lined up neatly on the counter. Cynthia's not there, but Bea asks, "Can you walk Satchmo? Fisk couldn't stay, and I presume the killer still doesn't want us leaving the building."

"Sure," I say. "I'll come get him as soon as we track down Cynthia. She's got to be here somewhere."

After all, Logan's dad is still watching the front door. He would have told us if anybody left.

I call the number Cynthia provided when she'd accepted the trip out here. There's no answer.

Patsy says, "Maybe she decided to take a nap in her room."

I say, "Well, this time we should bring the master key."

I get it from Aunt Naomi, and we go up to Cynthia's room. Logan gestures Arlo, Patsy, and me to take a few steps back while he knocks on the door. There is no answer. Logan gives it a few minutes, then he opens the door and steps inside. After a moment, he looks back into the says, "She's not here."

We all head into the room. There's a window in here, but we're on the second floor. Still – I suppose Cynthia could have gone out that way if she had just jumped from the small balcony. The window is closed, but the lock isn't engaged.

I move over to the closet, which is ajar.

I ask Logan, "Did you open this?"

"No," Logan says. "It was like that when I cleared the space."

I nudge the closet door farther open with my elbow. The clothes inside have been hung up haphazardly. It looks like the space has been rifled through, but that could just as easily have been Cynthia's unpacking method.

Her suitcase is on the floor, partly open, and between the case and the wall, there's something wrapped in a towel.

I say, "Hey, y'all. What is that?"

"Let me see." Arlo takes out a pair of gloves and puts them on before leaning down and carefully removing the towel. He unwraps it, and there in his hands is a small broken drone – presumably the weapon used to kill Ted.

Part of me feels validated that my wild speculation about murder by drone had been right.

Patsy gasps. Then she says, "I cannot believe Cynthia's the murderer. I had a long talk with her last night, and it sounds like the most interesting thing that happened to her in her whole life is when she went with her sister on vacation to Niagara Falls.

I say, "Let's not jump to conclusions. Somebody had to get that weapon into Ted's room. It's possible that the same person planted it here, to frame Cynthia."

Arlo says, "Though we all know it's more likely that the person hiding evidence in her room is the killer."

"Well either way," Logan says, "she's gone. But she didn't take her clothes."

"And she didn't take her phone," Patsy adds.

Arlo says, "I'm starting to hate locked room murders. Nothing that has happened on this case has made any sense." He takes out his phone and starts calling in an APB for Cynthia.

A voice from the hallway asks, "What are you all doing in here?"

I turn, and there's Dawn. How does she keep doing that? It's like she can smell when we've uncovered a clue. She gives Arlo a disappointed look. She had hoped to recruit him into her bet against Logan – and here he's investigating with Logan, again.

Arlo finishes his call and says, "I thought you were playing checkers with Hudson."

"I was," Dawn says. "Long enough to decide that he probably didn't kill anybody. Do you know he volunteers at an old folk's home in Japan? I think he feels lonely about not having his own family close by." She gestures sharply with her chin at Patsy. "And what's she doing here? One civilian impeding a police investigation is enough."

Arlo's face flushes. "Patsy actually talked to Cynthia last night. Her insight here might be useful."

Dawn doesn't look convinced. "Right. That's going to help with a suspect that's obviously fled the scene."

"I'll go," Patsy says. "I didn't mean to cause any trouble."

"I'll go too," I say. I turn to Logan. "Let me know if you find the cyanide bottle. And be sure not to touch anything in here without gloves."

"He already knows that," Dawn says, clearly irritated at being left out of the loop.

Logan says, "She's just trying to say she cares what happens to me because she doesn't want me accidentally poisoned. Give it a rest, would ya?"

Chapter Fifteen
Saturday

Patsy and I take the elevator back downstairs together. The minute the doors close, Patsy turns to me and asks, "Are you sure you want to marry into that family?"

I say, "Logan's mom is an absolute doll. And I think his dad likes me. Besides, I'm marrying Logan. He's the one who's going to have to set boundaries with his family."

Patsy says, "Is that how it was in your first marriage?"

I sigh. "Kevin's brothers were a handful, but they were good guys' you know? And his mom wanted everyone over for family meals. But we all got along, and they weren't nosy or controlling. And they tried to make me feel like part of the family, even after the accident. Only – I pulled away from everyone. And then I moved home. They've tried to keep in touch, but most of the time, I just don't know what to say."

Patsy says, "I don't think Arlo's mom likes me. After I broke up with her son, I'm not sure there's any way back into her good graces."

I say, "I can't really help you there. I'm pretty sure she feels the same way about me. But she's not unreasonable. I'm sure you can win her over."

"Wow," she says. "Did you ever think we'd be having this conversation?"

"No," I say. "I did not."

After all, we'd been rivals for Arlo's affection at one point. But now, I think we're really becoming friends. I ask her, "How come you know so much about Frankenstein?"

Patsy says, "I read a lot of classic authors, and I remember having the same disconnect that Arlo did about the movie version. Only my rule has always been to read the book before I see any related movie, so it seems like the 'real' version in my head."

"You've mentioned that before," I tell her. "A long time ago. I have the same rule. I like to imagine what characters look like before a movie sticks a certain vision of them in my head."

Exactly!" Patsy says. "I started looking up why the film was so different than the book, and I found myself going down a rabbit hole of Frankenstein film history. I never guessed it would be useful for anything."

Patsy heads back to the kitchen to claim her jars of dilled green beans, and I head the other direction, to check on Ash.

Logan's dad stops me in the lobby, waving me over to where he's been sitting, in a comfy chair with a clear line of sight to the door.

I sit down across from him and ask, "You feeling okay?"

After all, Logan's dad had had to take early retirement from the police force due to illness.

"I'm fine," he says. "There's good days and bad. I think the salt air here is doing me a world of good."

"I'm glad to hear it. Logan told me you're thinking about buying a house out here."

"Buying you a house," he corrects. "But Logan said he's not sure you're interested. Want to keep your space separate from the in-laws. I can respect that. It was different for Rosemary and me. We had two kids by the time we'd been married for three years. My parents offered to help with child care, so we couldn't really say no."

I don't bring up the fact that Logan and I aren't likely to have kids of our own. Which still hurts to think about. I swallow back a lump in my throat and force a smile. "It's not that I want distance. I'm just having a hard time giving up the hotel."

Logan's dad studies the lobby, with the elegant reception desk and the retro fireplace. "It is a beautiful place. I can see all the work you and your aunt have put into it."

"Mostly Naomi. I just invested in it, and helped out a few weekends when she needed extra hands." I point at the elaborate molding at the top of the wall behind us. "I painted that. But I'm busy with the chocolate micro factory. Thanks to Logan, we're expanding operations."

He says, "I had been looking forward to seeing your café. Especially the construction work Logan did in the expansion. You know, when he was a kid, he built a tree house? It wasn't the most well-constructed thing, and one of his friends fell through the floor. After that, he was determined to learn how to do things right, build a better tree house. Same thing with his planes. I have never seen anyone be so careful about maintenance."

"Logan never told me about that," I say. Which seems a little oversight-ish, given that I'd told him about the car accident I'd had back in high school that had led to me becoming very much about following the rules. The one where Arlo had gotten hurt.

"Well," Logan's dad says, "He probably didn't think much about it. The kid who fell was fine. There was two feet of snow on the ground."

"Oh," I say. "Well, I'm sure you'll appreciate his work at Greetings and Felicitations. Plus, you'll get to see our chocolate work." I wince, preparing for him to be just as dismissive as Dawn had been about chocolate making. Though he's been polite about it in the past.

He says, "I rather enjoyed the virtual presentation – up until the unfortunate incident with the poisoning. I've never thought much about how chocolate is made before. I'll certainly appreciate it more in the future."

"I'm glad." I feel quiet joy that he appreciates my work.

"Only – I'm still confused how you took a left turn from chocolate making into detective work." He scratches at his head. "It seems dangerous. It's even led to the whole situation we find ourselves in here."

"That's not fair," I protest. "I never set out to get involved in solving murders. It just kept happening."

"Logan said he almost died, the last time a killer called you out."

That's really not fair. Frustrated, I say, "Did Logan happen to mention that he got singled out because of somebody he arrested? If I hadn't been there, that killer would have gotten revenge another way."

"Maybe," Logan's dad says. "But if you're going to keep getting involved in these kinds of things, you need to be careful. Start carrying a weapon."

I tap my pocket. "I carry pepper spray. It's what I'm comfortable with."

He looks doubtful. "If you were at my precinct, that kind of answer would have been enough to see you out the door."

"Well, it's a good thing I'm not," I say. "And like I said, I don't get involved in solving crimes on purpose."

Logan's dad's face is hard and craggy. He says, "I guess I'll see you at dinner, then."

Is that his way of saying I've been dismissed? Geesh. It's no wonder that Logan has had a difficult relationship with his father.

"I guess I will," I say. I turn and head for the long hallway, leading to the little room where Ash is presumably still working. But before I can get there, the ferret comes loping around the corner from the elevator. She has a piece of paper in her mouth.

How did she get away from Sasha? I notice she has her collar on, but not her harness. Maybe she slipped out of it somehow. Sasha is probably frantic, looking for her.

"Come here, Cheeseburger," I coax, but the ferret runs away, honking. I guess she assumes that this is a game, as I chase after her. I get her cornered and make a grab for her, managing to pick her up. I wrinkle my nose. The ferret smell coming off of her is a lot stronger and more musky. I don't know. Maybe something scared her, or she needs a bath.

Suddenly, Cheeseburger lets go of the piece of paper and bites at my arm. Instinctively, I drop her, and she scurries around the corner, out of sight. I pick up the paper and run after her, in time to see her making for the stairs. By the time I get there, and up to the second floor, she's gone.

I text Sasha that I've seen her ferret somewhere on the second floor, but there's no immediate reply. I look around a bit, but Cheeseburger is gone, and there's nothing else I can do.

I don't get it. The ferret had been so sweet when Sasha had been nearby. Every time I've interacted with Cheeseburger, she's basically tried to jump into my arms. So why would she try to run away now? It's almost like she's a different ferret.

I look down at the sheet of paper in my hand. Cheeseburger has clearly taken it from someone. Despite what Sasha said, could this be the explanation for how the bracelet wound up in Ted's room? Maybe she had managed to get away for a few moments some time when the cage cam wasn't on. Though I still don't think the timing would work out for that.

I unfold the sheet of paper and get a whiff of perfume. It's Cynthia's character sheet for the murder mystery game, and she must have been carrying it in her pocket. I peruse the details. Miss Shirley Doright had had a number of clues, including proof that Paisley Vain couldn't have been the killer, because he had instinctively protected Shirley from the gunshot – which may well have been meant for her, instead of Clementine.

Which puts me back in mind of *A Murder is Announced*, since it reads similar to what happened in the main murder in the book. And it makes me think of something with the real murders. In the book, there had been two lamps, and one was traded out because the cord had been frayed to cause the lights to go out. Two lamps, to hide the method of the crime.

Jordan had said he's seen two ferrets. What if he wasn't play acting the drunk – but there had actually been two ferrets in the lobby? It had seemed ridiculous at the time, but I could easily be convinced that the ferret I'd just picked up was not Cheeseburger.

And if that is the case, the idea that this other muskier ferret could have been trained to retrieve the drone we'd found means that my theory had made sense after all.

So what does it mean that this ferret has brought me Cynthia's character sheet? If Cynthia is indeed the murderer, did the ferret escape from her room at the same time she left? Or has it been running around the hotel, holding onto the last thing it picked up, hoping to find Cynthia and give it back to her?

Of course Cynthia might not be the killer, in which case maybe the ferret was in Cynthia's room when its owner was planting the evidence. Which means that either way, Cynthia is clearly in trouble.

I go back down to talk to Ash, maybe get some more details on how this mystery note got delivered this morning. It's possible that it is from Cynthia, that she's hiding out somewhere until the set meeting time.

But Ash says, "I was asleep when that note came in under the door. I have no idea why they gave it to me. I'm not even on the same floor as you."

I say, "Maybe something happened, and whoever had it needed to get rid of it. Whoever it is might not realize that you passed on the message."

He points out, "But they probably hope I would. Honestly, I almost didn't because it feels like a trap. And I know you won't be able to resist going."

I tell him, "I just wish I could figure out who it is from. It had to have been printed in the business center. There's no way to tell who was on any of the computers connected to the printers, is there?"

"Not really," Ash says. "When this opens officially as a hotel, there will probably be logins and software for recording information on laptops hooked up to the machines, but right now, there are just a couple of computers anyone could have gotten on. Maybe you could dust for prints?"

I scoff. "Half the people here probably hopped onto one of those computers to check email. We've all been feeling cooped up."

"Says one of the few people allowed to leave."

Which reminds me that I promised to walk Bea's dog. I gesture at the progress Ash has made with the sauna. I say, "That heating unit looks promising."

Ash says, "It's pretty close to being back together. But that still doesn't mean it's going to work when I turn it on."

I say, "I should let you get back to it. Satchmo probably really has to pee by now."

I text the Logan-Arlo-Patsy thread to let them know I'm taking Satchmo outside so they don't think I've gone MIA too. Logan texts back that he prefers I not go anywhere alone, but I promise I won't go far.

So I go back to the kitchen and get the dog from Bea. When Satchmo realizes we are going outside, he starts a little excited prancing dance. He must really have to go potty.

We go around to the side of the hotel, where he will have plenty of green spots to choose from. He relieves himself for an embarrassingly long time, during which I pointedly look in the other direction. At least I don't need the poop bag Bea had given me.

I pull out my phone, to tell everyone I'm heading back inside, but the paper falls out of my pocket and lands right in front of Satchmo's nose. He sniffs at it and then at the ground nearby and starts barking. Satchmo used to be a cadaver dog, so it makes sense for him to scent off of a person's perfume. Does that mean Cynthia had come this way?

The reasonable thing would be to get someone out here with me before I go off and follow a possible killer. But Satchmo is pulling at his lead, barking his head off. And I really don't think the killer is planning to randomly shoot me, after going through all this trouble to challenge me. So I text Logan and the others to meet me ASAP, and I take out the pepper spray, holding it at the ready.

Satchmo leads me into the space that's meant to become a garden. There's already a big water feature. On the other side of it, where weeds and saplings still need to be cleared away, Cynthia is lying face-up on the ground. She's been stabbed with the very knife that Logan had locked away after it had mysteriously showed up during the murder mystery game.

I stop short, trying to take in the reality of this, find myself looking away from the damage that's been done to her. I'm ready to believe that she didn't have anything to do with any of this – now, that it's too late to comfort her or save her. Maybe Logan's dad was right – everything I've done solving cases in the past has led to this moment where someone clearly innocent is lying dead.

I take out my phone and call Arlo.

He says, "Sorry about Dawn. She's kind of a force of nature, isn't she?"

I say, "She's fine. But you know how you were convinced Cynthia was behind all the murders?"

"Yeah," Arlo says warily.

"I have a pretty good idea that she didn't do it. You need to come out to the garden."

"That doesn't sound good," Arlo says. "She's dead, isn't she."

"Unfortunately."

Satchmo is sitting not far from the body, looking up at me like he's expecting a treat. Which he deserves, having done the job he'd been trained for. Unfortunately, I didn't bring any treats, so he has to settle for a pat on the head, and me repeatedly telling him he's a, "Good boy."

I must smell of the ferret I had held earlier, because Satchmo starts snuffling my arm, like he's ID'ing the ferret I still believe isn't Cheeseburger. It can't be a coincidence, someone bringing a pet ferret to the same place where a criminal is using a ferret to help enact a nefarious plan. But who of the guests would have known that Sasha even has a ferret, let alone that she travels with it?

But that logic is backwards. Given the cage cam is connected to Sasha's name, anyone researching Sasha would know about Cheeseburger. And clearly, the killer researched everyone who was invited this weekend. So the knowledge of the ferret's existence doesn't narrow down the suspects.

Nothing here feels random. I doubt Elena as the killer's second victim was a random choice either. Cynthia had refused to play the game, so it is possible that she was killed for that reason. Or there could have been another motive. Maybe Cynthia and the killer had been working together, and it had been Cynthia's drone. If she had cracked, threatened to go to the police, who know what might have happened?

Cynthia had gone outside, without her phone or other belongings. Which means she probably didn't leave the hotel on her own. Had she been lured out here? Or had she been chased?

When the others arrive, Arlo and Dawn move to secure the scene, while Logan gathers me up in a hug.

"You okay?" he asks, finally letting me go.

"I'm fine," I say. "Just trying to figure this out, before anybody else gets hurt. Did you talk to Hudson?"

Logan says, "I got my dad to challenge him to a couple of games of checkers to keep him visible and protected. This whole setup is a tactical nightmare. If everyone would have just agreed to stay together in the dining room, it would be so much simpler."

I don't bother telling him that a lot of the guests didn't feel particularly safe with that strategy after Elena got poisoned right in front of everyone else.

Instead, I ask, "What happened with that knife? I thought you locked it up?"

He says, "I did. In the old hotel safe. So you can add safecracker to Doc Frankenstein's skill set."

Dawn stands up from examining something at the scene and turns to tell us, "Cynthia didn't go down easy. From the look of this, I think she may have injured her attacker."

Logan says, "That makes perfect sense for someone whose hobby is throwing knives."

"That's it then," I say. "We just bring in a doctor to examine everyone for knife wounds. Case solved."

"It's not that simple," Arlo says. "That kind of warrant will take time."

I say, "Well, at least this should eliminate my aunt. Naomi can barely walk – let alone engage in a knife fight."

"True," Arlo admits. "But it doesn't clear your uncle. Greg does a bit of fishing. He knows how to handle a knife."

I say, "You only know that because you've gone fishing with him. Come on, you really think he would kill three people because one of them was Aunt Naomi's ex? He's not the theatrical kind of person. He's more the beer on the back porch and let's talk it out kind."

"I agree," Arlo says. "They made more sense as suspects when this was just about Ted. Despite having been in on the planning for this weekend."

My phone buzzes. Sasha has texted me a selfie of her and Cheeseburger, with the caption, *You must be mistaken. We're fine.*

So either she hasn't lost her ferret and the one I'd seen is a different one – or she's lying. Either way, things keep getting more and more complicated.

Chapter Sixteen
Saturday

I've retreated to the business center, trying to think all of this through. I have my tablet out to do some more research on our remaining guests. So far I've found out that the travel agency that Irene works for has won a number of awards, and that she is sought out by clients wanting concierge services for high-end vacations. According to the reviews, she is very detail oriented, and able to make impossible-to-get reservations happen and to pull together once-in-a-lifetime proposals and excursions. There are also images coming up in the Google results, showing Irene in costume at a number of galas and events. Apparently, showing up here in the singing telegram girl costume is just her style when she wants to make an entrance. She's been a female version of Mr. Monopoly, one of the aliens from Star Trek, a princess who may well be Rapunzel, and Charlotte from Charlotte's Web. That one was for the opening of a children's library one of her clients had funded somewhere in South America.

She was even in a couple of commercials — including one for the same shampoo company Hudson had had a spot with when he was a teen. Could there be a connection there? Probably not, since Hudson hadn't seemed to recognize Irene when she had arrived. Or had he? Irene claimed she had only been flirting with Hudson to make Jordan jealous, and that the only reason he had been in her room was because he was helping her with her website. But could that have been a convenient lie? Could Hudson have been using Irene to get easy access to Ted's room, the better to retrieve the ferret?

Hudson certainly seems suspicious, especially since Logan found out his connection to Ted. All of the Frankenstein references seem to point pretty heavily to him. After all, it was Ted who scarred Hudson's face, probably ending his acting career. I checked the dates when Hudson had his surgery, and it was only a few weeks after his last acting job. Had Ted talked him into it? And what had gone wrong, exactly? You'd think for botched surgery, he would have come out with an asymmetrical smile, or a lumpy nose or something. Not looking like something attacked the side of his face. Interestingly, although Hudson seems to have made videos of everything else he's done in Japan, I can't find anything about him visiting the elderly, or doing any other sort of community service. So either he'd been lying to Patsy, or he considers that side of his life private. Which is interesting, because a lot of social media personalities would have been all over posting anything that might make them seem empathetic to others.

I looked up Jordan, too, but I didn't find as much as you would think for an acting coach. He's a theater teacher, like he said, for a magnet high school in New York, and he is also a freelance acting coach. His page for the school seems fairly standard, listing his hobbies as travel, ballroom dancing, and star gazing. There's no mention of his suspension – but part of me wonders if that could have been manufactured to get him into trouble and make him want a weekend away. His photo, taken in front of a stage, with him in a school polo and khakis, looks responsible and easy-going. Nothing like the bumbling, drunken persona he'd tried to present before the murders had started happening. Especially considering the ballroom dancing part, which takes a great deal of coordination. I find a clip of him in the finals for some minor celebrity charity competition, and he's good. I mean really good. Tango that leaves me a little breathless watching it good. His acting credits are listed, and he has had one-episode appearances on an impressive number of television shows, but the dates are all at least a decade ago. I wonder why he got out of acting, right when a lot of people are looking for their breakout role? I try looking up Jordan's name combined with Ted's, but there doesn't seem to be a connection between them.

I know a bit about Chloe, but I looked her up anyway. There doesn't seem to be a connection between her and Ted either, past what she already told us about her investing in his skin care line. Chloe is a huge cat person – or at least cats are a big part of her online persona. She's done a number of videos where she's gone on cycling tours across Texas to raise money for cat welfare. She'd gotten a number of Youtubers involved in one series of videos where they tag-teamed to take a cat toy from California to North Carolina. It was a massive undertaking, requiring a good deal of organization. Ted wasn't a great human being. If we find out he hated cats, then who knows, Chloe might actually have killed him.

I bring my fingers to the bridge of my nose. I'm getting nowhere. My most probable suspect is dead. The others don't seem the type to kill people. And I have an impending meeting with a mystery person who could be dangerous.

Autumn is sitting in a chair in the corner, typing on her phone, which is plugged in to charge. She's been typing for a really long time.

"Updating Drake?" I ask.

"Nope," she says. "I'm still on deadline. And if I wanted inspiration to crank out the last few chapters of a mystery, this is certainly the perfect setting."

I shudder. I know she's not trying to be mean, but I never wanted this hotel, which I love, to feel ominous. Trying not to let my frustration show over my inability to keep crimes from touching places and people I care about, I ask, "Any bits of reality trickling into the book?"

"A bit," Autumn says. "A couple vaguely reminiscent of Sasha and Sebastian may have shown up at the party where my detective is about to do her big reveal. I know the gather-the-suspects-together bit is a tad old-fashioned, but sometimes classic tropes are classic for a reason."

"Speaking of parties." I put my tablet down, because this is the one bit no research is going to help. "You were the one who came up with the idea for the mystery weekend, right? Exactly where did that idea come from?"

Autumn laughs, "I thought you knew better than to ask a writer where she gets her ideas."

"I'm serious, Autumn. This is important. Ash and Chloe pitched it to me as a marketing tool, but you had the original idea, and Imogen said you helped plan out the story."

Autumn stops typing. "I know we were at your shop. It was after my writer's group meeting, remember? You had just told us that Logan was going to do a line of chocolate bars, and Chloe got all excited about the marketing opportunities for mystery flavors. I think she and Ash were there working on some marketing ideas for Carmen's new book."

"Okay," I say. "I vaguely remember that."

Autumn says, "I had been thinking about mystery weekends as a plot line for a book. It's weird. I've been seeing an online therapist, and we've talked a lot about my writing, and how I've been using it to work out the trauma in my past. It was a conversation we had maybe six months ago, she suggested I should host a mystery weekend. It came back up a couple of times. I assumed it was just something she wanted to do. I told her you took the suggestion and decided to hold a contest to choose guests, and she seemed pleased."

Could Autumn have been talking to the killer, and been influenced to help set the setting for these murders? But if that was the case, she surely would have recognized that person immediately upon showing up at the event. Unless I've been wrong this whole time, and the killer is enacting their plan remotely. I ask Autumn, "What was this therapist's name?"

Autumn says, "I went with a service that used pseudonyms for both the therapist and the client. And I really didn't want to look at someone and tell them a bunch of uncomfortable stuff about myself, so I chose the voice-only option."

Well, that leaves everything wide open. I say, "So given today's technology, the therapist could have changed her voice to sound different, right?"

Autumn looks at me sharply as she realizes where I'm going with this. She smacks herself in the forehead with the palm of her hand. "Lis, if I hadn't been on deadline and puking my guts up all weekend, I probably would have put it together myself. I probably gave the killer all the information they needed to know, about all of us, about the hotel, everything. And, given the voice changing tech you're talking about, I couldn't even guarantee I was talking to a woman. So I can't even help you narrow down the suspect pool. I feel like such a moron."

I move over to her and give her a hug. I tell her, "It is such an obscure connection, I doubt I would have made it myself."

Autumn sniffles. Normally, she's not an overly emotional person. But I guess with hormone shifts and lack of rest, she's allowed. She leans her head against my shoulder and says, "How am I going to be a good mom if I'm that gullible?"

I tell her, "You're going to be a fantastic mom. And you will have all of your friends here to help you."

Autumn says, "You'd better not get hurt solving this case. You know I'm going to need you."

"I'll do my best to stay safe," I promise her. She picks up her phone again and I assume it's going to be to start typing, but instead she turns the camera on and takes a selfie of the two of us.

She says, "I'll send this to Drake, to remind him I'm in good hands."

She formats the text, and almost immediately Drake responds with a picture of Knightley flopped comfortably on top of one of Drake's wingtips, looking sleepily up at the camera. Bunnies only flop when they feel super-secure. I tell Autumn, "Look. Knightley has claimed Drake as his person."

"Aww," she says. "That's so sweet." She looks like she might cry again.

I tell her, "Maybe we should get you some protein. If you think you can keep something down."

We go back into the kitchen, where Carmen and Enrique are unpacking everything they've prepared for dinner.

I ask Enrique if he can come up with something easy for Autumn to eat. He takes out a pan and starts scrambling lightly salted eggs.

Autumn says, "That actually smells fantastic."

Ash comes around the corner and starts looking into the bags and trays laid out on the counters, everything prepped for dinner. He says, "This is promising to be quite a feast."

Enrique says, "Dinner isn't going to be for a while. Want me to whip you up some eggs too, while I'm at it? I could do them over easy with bacon and toast?"

Ash grimaces. "No thanks. I'm not a huge fan of eggs. Especially runny ones."

"What?" I say. "I've never seen you turn down food."

Ash looks at Autumn and says, "Cover your ears." Then he whispers to me, "Eggs remind me of snot. And runny ones always feel raw. But if Autumn wants to eat them, I don't want to gross her out."

"How gentlemanly of you," Enrique says. "So just the toast, then?"

"You know it," Ash says. He turns back to me and adds, "The reason you've never seen me turn down food at your shop is that everything there is always outstanding. I do have a picky side, you know."

"I did not know that," I tell him.

Autumn says, "I'm putting my hands down now. But I guarantee you whatever egg-based scary story you just told, I imagined something worse. Hazards of being a writer."

"Sorry," Ash says.

Autumn shrugs. "It's not going to turn me off eggs. I'm not that picky. Usually."

I ask Ash, "Did you give up on the sauna?"

"No," Ash says. "I got it working." He rubs his knuckles against his shirt, clearly pleased with himself. He peeks back around the corner to make sure no one is in the dining room, listening. I follow suit. Jordan is at a table in the corner, just staring off into space. Irene is sitting across from him, her back towards us, knitting a table runner. At least that's what I think it's supposed to be. She has headphones in, and occasionally she says a single word in Italian. Not one to waste time, she must be learning Italian for an upcoming trip.

We move back, more completely into the kitchen.

Ash says, "Everything should be set up for your mystery meeting. I put in a web cam pointed into the sauna, and one pointing out at the empty room. Say the word spaghetti, and the calvary will come running." After a moment, he clarifies, "The calvary meaning Logan and his sister. Not me, obviously."

I tell Ash, "Whatever video you come up with, don't expect to put it up on the internet."

"I wouldn't be that presumptuous," Ash says. "Oh, and I pulled the lock mechanism off the sauna door. Nobody can stick anything through it and trap you inside. And if anyone tries to lean anything against it, Logan should be able to move it before you get broiled."

Carmen says, "Sometimes I guess it pays to have a true crime obsessed friend."

"Exactly," Ash says. "I know all of the tropes, so I can help keep you from falling for them."

Enrique asks, "Are you planning to confront the killer?"

"No," I say. "At least I don't think so. Someone wants to give me information about the murder. I doubt the killer would be that audacious."

I show them all the message that Ash had passed on to me.

Autumn says, "If this was a book, that message would be from Cynthia. You never want to be the character who promises to offer information at a later time. That character always winds up dead."

"That's possible," I say. "But that's the problem with an anonymous note. You never know."

Enrique asks, "Do you still think Sasha Wimbleton is the killer? Please say no, because she told me she might be able to get me a spot on a cooking competition show. She knows absolutely everyone in the business."

Ash asks, "You are still in college, right?"

Enrique says, "I can take a semester off if it means a big cash prize, and the kind of publicity that will open doors later. But if you arrest her, Sasha is going to lose a lot of credibility."

Carmen says, "The important thing here is the truth. I was arrested once for a murder I didn't commit. Nothing would have been worth letting the real killer go free."

Enrique says, "Still. There are other suspects, no?"

Thinking about what Autumn had disclosed, I say, "It's possible that this case may have something to do with a therapist using inappropriate influence. Which means Sasha's husband is even more suspicious than she is."

Enrique looks relieved. He spreads jam onto toast with an extra flourish. Though I'm not sure how having Mr. Wimbleton be guilty instead of Mrs. makes anything better.

I consider what I had seen on the cage cam. It is true that Sebastian's foot had been in the frame the whole time. But we're talking about a crime that had been set up in advance, presumably by someone who had gotten a peek at the rooming list on the way into the hotel or somehow snuck a look at the file, which was created two days in advance. But a foot does not a complete picture make. If the crime was committed by drone, with the evidence hidden by the second ferret, Sebastian could, in theory, have orchestrated the whole thing from his bed. He's the one person here who is the most likely to have had credibly conversed with Autumn for months as a real therapist – albeit not under his own name.

But he's not the only other viable suspect. Chloe is also good with electronics, and has a skilled way of talking to people where I could see her faking being a therapist, despite her youth. I still don't see her as the type to murder three people. While I really hope it's not her, it's hard to ignore the fact that she had a copy of the advance file of the rooming list. It's all circumstantial, but she had access to all the information needed to set up these very elaborate crimes. Whereas, most of the other suspects don't seem computer savvy enough to have stolen the data.

There is Hudson, who showed up so early in the morning, wanting to look around and take video of everything. He could have gotten an image of Ted's room number and gone up there while we were all finishing brunch. It would have been possible for him to have a ferret hidden in his hoodie, and the drone and cyanide in his suitcase. He's probably the most computer-proficient of the remaining suspects, too.

I still never figured out what Jordan had in his duffle bag. He could have had the knife on him, along with a ton of electronics. And we just helped him bring them all upstairs. He's still the biggest mystery out of all my suspects, with all his obvious over-acting and him lying about knowing Irene. He's clearly up to something, but is it murder?

Irene's a suspect too. She knew the most about Ted and his habits and what would actually get him here. And she's certainly organized enough to have orchestrated everything that has happened here. But she didn't seem to have a grudge against him, so where's the motive? And if she needed Hudson's help to build a website, presumably she's not the one who hacked into our RaffleSchnaz account and rigged the contest, to collect together the ragtag group of guests with all their hidden connections.

The others with potential motives are my aunt and uncle, and I know they didn't do it. They may be on the police's list of suspects, but they're not on mine. Looking at all the other suspects together, they would make one perfect culprit, with the access to information about the party and the know-how to plan the elaborate setup and get the guests here, easy ability to have brought in the drone and the second ferret, along with the cyanide bottle and the knife. It's a tall order for any one of the suspects to pull off. So maybe this is mimicking classic Agatha Christie, and they all did it.

Only – these people don't seem to be working together. And the killer hadn't phrased anything so ambiguously as to suggest that, "*They all did it*," is the solution. I suspect I'm just looking for an easy answer.

Chapter Seventeen
Saturday

Logan is still with his sister and Arlo, trying to find all of the guests to gauge their locations at the time of Cynthia's murder. It's taking a long time to get statements, but Logan keeps texting me that he's going to be back before I meet whoever sent me the note to meet in the sauna.

I still have a bit of time before that happens. And there's so much I still don't know. I keep thinking about Jordan's duffle bag.

Patsy comes into the kitchen and heads straight for the coffee pot. I grab her arm and tell her, "I need a favor."

She looks hesitant. "What do you want me to do?"

I gesture back towards the dining room. I say, "Ask Jordan for an acting lesson."

"Hey," Ash says, crossing his arms over his chest. "That's the kind of thing I usually do."

"Sure," I say, "But you already do reenactments and stuff. It's less believable if you ask for an acting lesson."

Patsy says, "I have no reason to want an acting lesson. Isn't that even less believable?"

Ash says, "Tell him you're thinking about doing community theater. There's actually a production of *Kiss Me Kate* coming up at one of the playhouses in the Strand District. Tell him you want to play Lois, who plays Bianca."

"Bianca," Patsy repeats.

"Trust me," Ash says. "It's the secondary romance, so it's not like you're asking for the lead. Lois has a gambler boyfriend, so she gets some of the best songs."

I tell Ash, "You and Imogen should double date to see it with Bea and Fisk. Bea is huge into showtunes."

Ash says, "I can ask. Imogen tends to-"

"Can we focus on me?" Patsy says. "Why do you want me to do this?"

I say, "I want to take a look around his room, and I need to know he's not going to come in while I'm doing it."

"Okay," she says. "I think we should have gone through everyone's belongings already to try and solve this thing." She turns back to Ash. "Lois who plays Bianca."

"Break a leg," Ash tells her.

Patsy rolls her eyes, and walks out into the dining room. I listen at the corner as she approaches Jordan and makes her request.

He says, "Sure. Anything to take my mind off the fact that any of us could die at any moment."

"Morbid," Patsy says. She asks, "You still aren't eating or drinking anything?"

"Absolutely not," he says. "Am I thirsty? Yeah. But is it worth it, to feel safer? Absolutely."

The two of them start speaking more quietly. I move out into the dining room, acting like I don't care about what is going on over at that table. Out of the corner of my eye, I register that Jordan has pulled up the script, and Patsy is hesitantly reading from it. Irene, still knitting, is watching. I have no idea what she's making, but it keeps getting longer. Does she just know the one stitch?

I keep myself from hurrying, trying to look casual as I cross the room and enter the hallway. Logan's dad nods at me as I head for the elevator. I swear he can tell what I'm up to, from across the room. If so, he doesn't seem to disapprove.

I take the elevator up. I glance at the elevator flooring and notice more ferret poop in the corner. If that ferret is Cynthia's and it did get loose during the altercation that led to her death, it could be anywhere in the hotel by now. I feel like I made a good decision sending Knightley elsewhere. But what if the second ferret wasn't Cynthia's? Shouldn't someone be looking for it? The elevator stops on the second floor. Hudson gets on.

He sees the poop in the corner, and an expression crosses his face that I can't read. Could he be the one who's missing a ferret? And hence the murderer?

"Going up?" I ask, trying to sound casual.

He says, "I think I left something in Irene's room. I was going to ask her to let me look for it."

I find myself shrinking towards the elevator wall. I hadn't expected to be alone in an enclosed space with a possible killer.

"Oh," I say. "I don't think she's upstairs. I saw her just a few minutes ago knitting in the dining room."

Hudson says, "That's inconvenient. You haven't seen a black hoodie lying around, have you?"

I say, "I'll keep an eye out."

Hudson says, "Thanks. And thanks for trying to find whoever killed Doctor Ted and the others."

The elevator dings for the third floor and the doors open. I get out, half expecting Hudson to follow me. But he doesn't. He just stands there as the doors close and the elevator heads up. If he is searching floor by floor for the ferret, that makes sense. Of course, he could have just decided to stay on because the button had already been pressed for four, and it would have to go up before he could punch a button to go back down.

I take a quick glance up and down the hallway. It seems empty. I still have the master key Aunt Naomi gave me, so I just walk up to Jordan's room and let myself in.

The room is neat, to the point where it hardly seems like anyone is staying here. We're not doing housekeeping tasks until the weekend is over, but the bed is neatly made and the towel folded over the towel bar. Looking at his toothbrush angled in a small glass on the bathroom counter, I suddenly feel embarrassed at how invasive what I'm doing really is.

I slip on a pair of plastic gloves I brought up from the kitchen and go to open his closet door. There are a few things hung up in the closet, but the duffle on the floor seems mostly full. I kneel down and open the duffle. Inside, there's a box, and inside the box there are dozens of gold coins.

Jordan hadn't been lying when he'd said his bag was full of gold. But what is he doing with this, here? Had he stolen it? Or bought it? Neither seem likely.

I pull out my phone and take pictures of the box and the coins. It all seems rather elaborate. Kind of like this weekend. Could Jordan have brought these coins to sell to Ted? But unless he's the killer, how would he even know Ted would be here? If he'd arranged to meet Ted, how would he have managed to get an invite? It all goes around in circles.

I send the pics to Logan along with info on my current location.

My phone gets a text, just as I hit send. It's from Patsy, and it just says, *Get out now*.

I scramble to get the box closed and back in the duffle. I stand up and close the closet door.

The room door rattles, then opens. Jordan is looking back in the hall, laughing.

I hear Patsy say, "Really, it isn't necessary. I don't need a DVD."

Jordan says, "Nonsense. Enunciation is everything. The drills will help. Besides, we're all stuck in this hotel. What else are you going to-" He stops short as he notices me standing in the middle of his room. "Oh, hello."

"Hi," I say back, not sure whether I ought to be embarrassed. I am a little scared, because Patsy and I are in the room with another person who's potential killer, and I've clearly uncovered evidence.

"What are you doing here?" he asks.

There's no point in trying to lie. I hold up the pic on my phone. With a lot more confidence than I feel, I say, "Exactly what I'm supposed to be. I was called on to investigate everyone here, and one of the most suspicious things I've seen so far is your duffle bag."

Jordan steps into the room, and gestures Patsy to follow him inside. "I didn't lie. I said there was gold, and there's gold."

Patsy shakes her head and says, "I think I'd prefer to stay here." She gestures meaningfully at her phone. "I'm one button away from calling Arlo."

Jordan coughs. "You two think I'm dangerous? I'm in terror for my life, and you think I'm the killer?"

"I think you're a better actor than you let on. Which makes that bumbling act last night even more confusing."

Jordan says, "That was Irene's idea. She told me to show up and act like a fool, so no one would guess why I was here."

I say, "You didn't come across so much like a fool as like someone badly trying to hide something."

Jordan sighs and waves a dramatic hand, "Sometimes, the truth will out."

Patsy asks, "If you're not the killer, then what are you hiding?"

I add, "It has something to do with the gold, doesn't it?"

Jordan says, "Irene wasn't the one that forwarded me the information on the contest to come here. It was from Ted. Ted told me that he had a way to guarantee he would be here this weekend, and if I wanted to buy back some embarrassing information he'd uncovered on me, I should try to be here too. And he told me what I needed to buy it back – an artifact in the private collection of one of the school's alumni."

"So you're a thief," Patsy says.

"More of a borrower. I'm hoping to replace the chest before it's missed. I brought it, hoping to use it to get him to show me where he'd stashed the evidence. Irene and I don't have secrets from each other. When I told her that Ted was trying to blackmail me, she said not to pay, that if I did, I'd never be free of him. Instead, she said we needed to find the document Ted was going to use as blackmail and destroy it. She said we should both enter the contest separately, because that meant we would have double the chance of winning. It was such a surprise when we both won. We decided it would be better if people didn't know we were a couple, so they wouldn't figure out we had an ulterior motive for being here."

I ask, "What was the information he was blackmailing you over?"

Jordan draws back, his body posture folding in from embarrassment. "I'd rather not say."

I think how to slot this in with everything I know so far about how the killer had set up the weekend. All of the other guests – with the possible exception of Cynthia – had had some kind of connection to or grudge against Ted. But for Jordan, the connection was to Irene, assuming Jordan is telling the truth about the blackmail threat he received. It does sound on brand for Ted, who was blackmailing at least one other person who'd been invited for the weekend, to want to also blackmail his ex-wife's new love interest. Part of me wonders if Ted somehow set all of this up himself to toy with people he didn't like – only to have things go horribly wrong, when one of them decided to murder him. Only, Ted didn't strike me as a stupid man. He would have foreseen that taunting people he'd wronged or blackmailed is a dangerous proposition. And he'd seemed sincerely upset when he'd accused me of setting the guest list just to make him uncomfortable.

Given that, it seems implausible that Ted would have invited Jordan here, before we'd chosen the winners of the contest. I mean, it is possible the killer had sent Ted information in advance, assuring him of a spot at the mystery weekend. And he might have contacted Jordan and asked him to enter, in order to have an easy way to get the blackmail process started. But it is equally possible that Jordan had been contacted by the killer pretending to be Ted, and that either the blackmail threat was a bluff – or that the killer had dug up the unsavory information on him. Whatever that information was.

Of course, Jordan wouldn't be in the blackmailer's headlights – whether Ted or Doc Frankenstein – if he hadn't been dating someone with a real connection to Ted.

I ask, "Sow how did you meet Irene?"

Jordan says, "She was the travel agent for a trip I took last year. It was a destination wedding in the Maldives, and my cousin was paying, so I impulsively asked Irene to be my plus one. Separate accommodations, of course."

"How did your cousin take that?" Patsy asks.

"He thought it was romantic as heck." Jordan laughs to himself, at a memory. "Plus, it was perfect that she was onsite to handle it when the bakery misplaced the cake."

Patsy says, "Talk about concierge service."

Jordan says, "Irene has been through a lot. She has this thing about not making mistakes or missing communications that probably isn't healthy – but it does make her excellent at her job. The fact that someone so smart, caring and driven is actually in love with me makes me feel fortunate every day."

Given the smitten look on his face, I know I'm going to have to ask my next question carefully. I say, "The police haven't been able to locate Ted's will. Did Irene talk to you about what happens if it doesn't show up?"

"I asked her," Jordan admits. "She said that when she left, Ted told her he was changing his will to leave everything to his dogs. He has three whippets – Larry, Moe, and Curly. And then anything past that would go to the whippet rescue. Honestly, I don't think he really cared that much about dogs. He just wanted her to know how little he still cared for her."

I wince. "Poor Irene."

Patsy says, "If the will never shows up, Irene inherits by default, at least in most states. I believe that's the case for California."

I remember Arlo once saying that Patsy does crosswords in pen, because she remembers the details. Which makes sense, since she's a CPA. She also often remembers random trivia. I point out, "That does give Irene motive – at least as much as everyone else."

"Right," Patsy says. "Because how could she possibly know the will wouldn't turn up? And it still might. If Ted lived alone and used a different lawyer, he might have stashed the document somewhere nobody's looked yet."

Jordan says, "Right. Think about it. She's in just as much danger as anyone else, and yet she's still determined to win the game. She didn't care before they added a cash prize. Does that sound like someone who's expecting a windfall inheritance? She was taking pictures out the window this morning, so she can class this as a work trip."

Patsy says, "She came here to stop you from being blackmailed, and that's a work trip?"

Jordan says, "She's a travel agent. If she blogs about everything she's seen in a cruise port town, that's a work trip." He moves and sits down at the desk.

I slip my hand into my pocket, gripping the pepper spray, in case he makes any sudden moves towards the desk drawer.

"Relax," Jordan says. "I'm just getting the DVD I promised Patsy. Don't you know all of us with a side hustle are ready to turn anything into a work trip? I'm surprised you don't have a chocolate making instructional video or anything."

He slides open the drawer and takes out a case with his face on it, with the title *Acting Up: Volume 3: Diction, Enunciation and Vocal Projecting.*

I gesture at the picture and ask him, "Why did you quit acting to become a teacher? From your IMDB listing, it looks like you were gaining momentum, and then you just quit."

Jordan says, "It was too much. I realized I was missing out on life."

Patsy says, "That sounds thin. What really happened?"

Jordan starts to protest, then he sighs and says, "I had a stalker. A woman who was obsessed with me. She even showed up at my house, claimed we were engaged and threatened to kill me for not returning her phone calls. I know, a lot of people wouldn't have given up on living a public life, but the experience shook me."

"Right," I say, trying to sound like I accept his explanation at face value. But I wonder – did his abrupt exit from acting actually have something to do with whatever Ted was planning to blackmail him over?

I ask, "Did you talk to Ted about the blackmail, or make any arrangements to pay him?" After all, Ted had already managed to settle his accounts with one blackmail victim here before he died. But I hadn't seen Jordon's name on Ted's ledger.

Jordan says, "I tried to bring it up, but Ted said he was busy. He brushed me off, so he could have a conversation with Hudson. I figured he wanted to let me stew a bit, which was irritating." He blinks at the skeptical look Patsy gives him. "I said irritated. Not angry enough to kill him." When Patsy splutters incredulously, he says, "Just look, if you find a yellow envelope with Ted's stuff, don't open it okay?"

Patsy and I meet up with Dawn and Arlo back in the lobby. Logan apparently went directly to get in position to try and see whoever it is heading into the sauna – although he's agreed not to disrupt this person until I've gotten whatever message they are waiting to give. Assuming anyone even shows up.

Logan's dad is still hanging out, but he has a book in his hand and looks half asleep. He probably figures that if anyone was going to try to flee the scene, they'd have done it by now. He probably expected for the police to evacuate us, but that hasn't happened either, and I don't really want to disrupt things by asking about it – not when I'm about to have my meetup. I feel like I'm close to figuring all of this out – in part because my strongest suspects are both dead.

I don't want anyone else to get hurt – but I also don't want Doc Frankenstein to get away with the three murders already committed.

I ask Arlo, "Did you happen to find a yellow envelope in with Ted's things?"

Dawn gives Arlo a sharp look, but he ignores her. I guess he's still miffed about her sending Patsy away from the investigation earlier. He says, "No. Should we have?"

I explain what Jordan had said about the blackmail evidence.

Dawn says, "If your ferret theory is right, then maybe Cheeseburger took off with it. Ferrets are known to hide things."

I haven't mentioned my two-ferret theory to her yet. I'm holding onto that information until I'm more sure what to do with it. Given the bet, I don't think that's impeding the police. After all, Dawn is trying to control Logan's future with the bet they've made. And I resent that. I never asked him to invest in the chocolate business. He'd decided to help me out when my equipment had been damaged by a killer, and he'd chosen to become an active part of the business instead of just a financial partner because he'd become interested in chocolate making. If he decided to chuck his puddle jump business and step back from Greetings and Felicitations because he wanted to get back into his old job – that would be one thing. I wouldn't pressure him not to, even though I'd be disappointed not to have him around the shop brightening up my day with his easy wit and creativity. But honestly, I don't think that's what he wants.

Dawn says, "I have a bulletproof vest up in my room, if you want."

"Really?" I can't help but feel a bit relieved at that thought. "Like the one the guy gets to wear on *Castle*? Except instead of *Writer*, it should say *Chocolate Maker*."

Logan would have laughed at that, and told me I'm being excessive. Dawn just frowns at me and sighs. She says, "This isn't like a television show. Do you know how many inaccuracies they have?"

Arlo comes to my rescue, asking Dawn, "Why exactly would you pack a bulletproof vest to go on vacation?"

Dawn looks at him like he's clueless. She asks, "You don't?"

Arlo and Patsy look at each other, nonplussed at first, but then they both crack up laughing.

Dawn ignores them, gesturing for me to follow her to the elevator. She says, "I still wish you'd let me show up to this meeting in your place. If I was in charge of this investigation, I'd absolutely forbid you putting yourself in danger."

I tell her, "That message was for me."

She says, "Then I wish I had a riot helmet."

When the elevator doors open, Sasha is getting off. Sasha has Cheeseburger draped around her neck like a stole. The ferret honks on seeing me and scrambles around to where she's sitting in Sasha's arms. I'm more convinced than ever that the unattended ferret I'd encountered earlier wasn't this sweet one.

Sasha says, "See, Felicity? I told you Cheeseburger hadn't escaped again. I'm not sure what you saw earlier, but it wasn't her."

"Really?" I say, acting surprised. "I hope we don't have rodents running wild in the hotel."

Sasha says, "It's fairly hard to mistake a rat for a ferret."

I make a puzzled face, then shrug like I don't have a better answer.

Dawn gives me a sharp look. I guess it's obvious I'm hiding something, but she doesn't ask what, not in front of Sasha. Which makes sense, since she's all about keeping the civilians out of the investigation.

I ask Sasha, "Does Hudson strike you as a ferret person?"

She says, "He seems to like Cheeseburger well enough. Why do you ask?"

I say, "I just got the idea he was looking for something earlier. I was wondering if it might have been a ferret."

Sasha blinks. "Why?"

I shrug. "It's just a theory. He seems to be hiding something."

Sasha looks at me sharply. "Hudson is a very kind young man. I know you don't trust him, but I don't want to see you accuse him of murdering people."

"Whoa," I say. "That's a big leap from hiding something to murder. After all, I'm pretty sure almost everyone here is hiding something."

She blushes. "Maybe what we hide is just how broken we are."

I ask Sasha, "Do you know Hudson from somewhere, before this weekend?"

"It's not that," Dawn says, answering for her. She makes eye contact with Sasha and asks, "it's because Hudson reminds you of someone, doesn't he? Take away the purple hair and the tattoo, and he looks a lot like Brad."

I haven't looked for a photo of Brad, but Dawn obviously has the whole file on the negligence case. She opens up a pic of Brad on her phone and shows it to me. He was a good-looking young man, with kind eyes and floppy brown hair, wearing a polo shirt. It's the opposite of Hudson's spiked purple hair and black hoodie, but there is something similar in the face shape, and the directness of his gaze. They don't look related, but they do look – I don't know if kindred is the right word.

Sasha looks down at Cheeseburger, like the ferret can protect her from this conversation. She says, "It's not just superficial. He's a kind soul."

"Come on," I tell Dawn. The elevator is long gone, so I punch the button to call it back. As we wait, I turn and tell Sasha, "I'll do my best to prove him innocent."

She looks so relieved I feed bad not telling her that that means I might well prove him — or someone else she cares about— guilty in the process.

I'm less convinced of Sasha herself as a viable suspect. Of course, she could be protesting Hudson's innocence so strongly because she knows exactly who did it and she doesn't want someone she feels a connection to taking the blame. Which just leaves me stepping into the elevator feeling confused. Even if I can almost see Sasha killing Ted in revenge, she doesn't sound like someone who would kill two other people just to keep things interesting.

When the doors close, Dawn tells me, "The first thing you learn in the academy is not to make promises you're not sure you can keep. Often, they wind up hurting the person you're trying to help more than if you'd been blunt with them. You know as well as I do that Hudson's probably guilty. He blamed Ted for what happened to his face. I've seen his deposition before the negligence trial. He said Ted went from one patient to another, in his presence, without washing his hands. The testimony was deemed inadmissible, since he was still coming out of the anesthesia, and had wandered out of the recovery room."

I have had about enough of Dawn for one day. If we weren't in an elevator, I probably would just tell her to forget the bulletproof vest and just walk away. Since we're stuck together, I can't help myself. I say, "All I promised is that I'm going to do my best. And, honestly, I think you're a bit *too* blunt. And pushy."

"Oh, really?" Dawn says. The elevator dings and the doors open for the fourth floor.

I snake around her and out onto the landing, intent on heading to my own suite, rather than her room. She follows me, and when I pass her door, she grabs my shoulder and says, "Where do you think you're going?"

I shrug out of her grasp. I say, "I've been being nice for Logan's sake. I really don't want to put a rift between him and his family. But you completely dismissed me yesterday, and when you realized I'd heard you, you didn't do anything to make it right. I'm marrying Logan whether you like it or not, and the decisions we make right now are together. Trying to go around that, and convince him to give up what we've built together – that's just dishonest."

At first, Dawn looks like I've slapped her. But then she laughs, and says, "Exactly what I wanted in a sister."

"Don't call me that," I say. "You haven't earned it."

The just-slapped look returns to her eyes, and I realize that this time I've hit a nerve. I'm not sure why. She sighs and says, "Come on, let's get you ready for your rendezvous. Have you ever worn a bulletproof vest before?"

"No," I say. "Though there's a couple of times when I would have been glad to have one."

In her room, her suitcase is on the desk, taking up most of the space, zipped open to reveal a colorful assortment of clothes. There's a smaller gym bag sitting on the chair – presumably Fisher's things. It's also zipped open and spilling out clothes – mainly a pair of boxers with characters from Super Mario Brothers printed on them. It's a perfect metaphor for their relationship – Fisher seems smaller and quieter compared to Dawn's over-the-top confidence – but somehow they fit together.

Dawn lifts up most of the clothes in the suitcase and pulls out the vest. She hands it to me, saying, "Kevlar is relatively thin, but this is still going to show under your clothes."

I say, "I could just wear it on top, like on *Ca* – like on certain TV shows. Unless you think that's to inauthentic, too?"

"It would probably be easier, actually," Dawn says. She gets me zipped into the vest, which is bulky and hard to move in – and hot. Immediately, I feel myself sweating. Being on an island means it is humid enough, without any help from such solid fabric. Dawn explains, "This is effective against projectiles – but less so against knives. And of course, it means absolutely nothing if someone decides to shoot you in the face."

I say, "You did hear what I said about being too blunt?"

She says, "If you can't face that thought, then you shouldn't be doing this."

"Agree to disagree," I say. I head for the door. It's time to go back downstairs. And I think I'm going to do better at this if I'm not too nervous, or too concerned about dying. I could be walking into danger, sure. But I have to be optimistic. Still, in a way it is nice that Dawn wants to look out for me. I look back and say, "And thank you. I'll try not to do anything too stupid."

"Too late," she says, but she's smiling, and her tone says she's joking.

The elevator ride back down feels ten times as long as the one up did. And the walk through the lobby even longer than that. Logan's dad arches an eyebrow at me and gives me a look I can't quite read. I assume he thinks I'm being stupid, but maybe he's wondering if I'm going to get anything out of this.

I nod at him, and then I head down the hall to the sauna, wondering how this mystery person plans to join me without everyone seeing them marching down the hall.

When I reach the room that used to be a gym, I scan the space. There's no sign of anyone waiting for me – though if they are in the locker area or the sauna, I wouldn't be able to see them from here. There's a small closet in this part of the room. Pepper spray in hand, I make my way over to it. Just as I put my hand on the knob, there's a soft sneeze from inside. It sounds familiar.

I put my face close to the door and ask, "Logan?"

It sounds muffled when he says, "Yeah. Pretend you don't hear me. It's dusty in here. This weight bench has to be fifty years old."

"I think it's too late to pretend you're not in there. But I don't see anybody out here."

"Neither do I," Logan says. "I'm watching on the webcams Ash set up. He can be quite useful sometimes. I've actually got a whole setup with a laptop and a surge protector in here. And a fan, because it's terribly stuffy."

I cross the room over to the sauna area and turn the corner. The space with the hole where the hot tub was taken out is cast in shadow, but it's not deep enough for anyone to be hiding in it. The machinery that had been littering the floor is all gone, presumably put back into place by Ash. The door beyond it leading to the split locker rooms is open – and it's too intimidating to even think about going inside. I turn towards the sauna itself. As promised, Ash has removed the locking mechanism, leaving a fist-sized hole. I try to use it as a peep hole, but I can only see a small portion of the sauna room, with its benches. It's impossible to see the rest of what's on the other side without opening the door.

Right. I can do this. Logan's right here for backup. He can even see me, on the webcam.

I pull the door open, and an arm snakes out, dragging me into the space. I let out a startled squeak. What the heck? I thought nobody was in here.

"Quiet, Mrs. Koerber, please." It's Hudson's voice. "I fed a static loop into the camera pointing at us. No one can see we're here."

I turn and look him in the eyes. I say, "You should be dead. Don't you know you never promise to share the information you know later? That's just asking for trouble." I gulp. "Unless you're the killer."

Hudson says, "Let's just take a breath. Enjoy the sauna for a second." He moves towards the switch.

"No thanks," I say quickly. "This vest is warm enough. Why don't you start by telling me how you got in here without anyone noticing."

"It wasn't hard," Hudson says. He touches the switch, and the sauna comes on for a moment, but then the circuit breaker blows, quieting the machinery and bathing us in darkness. Did it kill Ash's cameras too? Am I truly alone? And did he rig it to do that on purpose?

I hear something metal rasping in the dark. Dawn had warned me that the vest I'm wearing is only partly effective against blades, and I can't help but picture the knife that had killed Cynthia. "Don't touch me!" I screech as I try to fumble for the door. I'm holding up my pepper spray, but I can't tell where Hudson is in the darkness.

"Quiet, please," Hudson says, but the last thing I want to be is quiet.

I find the door and push it open with a wordless cry. There isn't a window in this space. I rush forward, and Hudson grabs for me. Belatedly, I hear the word, "Careful." I'm already spraying the pepper spray while falling backwards through open space. My brain registers that I've fallen into the open hole left by the missing hot tub, about the same time I realize the whimpering noise above me is Hudson, dealing with having been sprayed in the face.

The lights come back on, and Logan has Hudson by the collar. Hudson's arm is bleeding – possibly from the pipe sticking out of the side of the hot tub hole. My body aches, and when I look down, I realize I have a gash on my leg.

"Wait," Hudson wails. "Please. I won't tell her, I promise. Just don't kill me."

Logan says, "Who exactly do you think I am?"

Hudson rubs at his eyes, trying to see, but it looks like that only makes things worse. He says, "Mr. Logan?" Tears are streaming from his eyes, and it's hard to tell how much is the pepper spray, and how much is clear relief.

"Come on," Logan says. "Let's get you under the showers. Then you can tell us what's going on."

"Sorry!" I call after them. "I only pepper sprayed you because I thought you were the killer."

"Me?" Hudson squeaks.

I focus on getting myself out of the hole, and rinsing off my cut, which isn't as deep as it looked. I am going to need a tetanus shot, if I survive the weekend.

The three of us meet in front of the sauna, which sounds like it is working just fine now.

Hudson looks a bit better, but his eyes are still red, and there's snot running down his nose. He asks, "What's with the vest?"

I say, "I got a mysterious note to meet someone alone in a place where there's been three murders. If you wanted to tell me something, couldn't you just text?"

Hudson says, "I wanted to show you something I found this morning."

He goes back into the sauna and picks up a backpack which has a sword sticking out of it. I hadn't been imagining things when it had sounded like someone sharpening a knife – it had probably been Hudson scraping the blade on something as he turned. He starts to pull the sword out of the bag.

"Careful," Logan warns, and I realize his hand is not far from his gun.

I don't think Hudson registers this – or Logan's tone. He says, "Right. I've already messed up the fingerprint evidence. I probably shouldn't make it any worse." He gestures for Logan to take the bag.

Logan does, carefully. Hudson says, "This bag was not in my room last night, but it was this morning. Look at what's in it."

Logan carefully opens the bag. "A cage?"

"Not just a cage," Hudson says. "There was a ferret in there. The poor thing was in it, inside the bag. The bag was open, but when I took the ferret out of the cage, it squirmed out of my arms and ran off. My room door was cracked open, and the ferret made it into the hallway. At first, I thought it was Cheeseburger, with the same collar and everything, but I'm not so sure now." He gestures at the sword. "I mean, who randomly leaves a person a sword? With what happened to Cynthia, I'm sure that this is a sign I'm next. Because I didn't tell the whole truth."

"Wait a minute," I say. "I thought you said all of this happened this morning. That's when Ash said he got the note – before we all played Doc Frankenstein's little game of Two Truths and a Lie."

"Doc Frankenstein?" Hudson says, sounding puzzled.

"Our nickname for the killer," Logan clarifies. "Focus on Fee's question."

Hudson says, "I found the ferret cage and the backpack this morning, before breakfast. And it was weird, right? I thought it might somehow be connected to Ted's murder, so I wrote the note. There were some people coming up the hall when I was heading for the elevator, and I freaked and pushed the note under Ash's door. I figured if anyone was going to get it to you, it would be him. Either that, or he'd show up to talk to me himself."

I splutter. "Ash is not one for putting himself in danger, or showing up in the middle of confrontations."

Logan says, "And the sword?"

"That's the part that scared me," Hudson says. "I went back up to my room after everyone left the truth sharing session. Detective Romero had been questioning me like he thought I had something to do with all of this, since I was sitting closest to Elena, and I just wanted to be by myself and calm down. I was walking down the hallway to my room, and Cynthia came out of hers, running like someone was chasing her, swatting at the air. She hit the stairs, still at a flat out run."

"Who was chasing her?" Logan asks.

"That's just it. Nobody. She'd left her room door open, and there was nobody inside. I hurried to my own room – and that sword was on my bed."

I ask, "Did you tell Detective Romero any of this, when he questioned you about where you were when Cynthia died?"

Hudson says, "No. The sword was a clear message not to. Instead, I came downstairs and started challenging all the cops to play checkers, just so I'd be around someone safe. But I had to tell someone. I'm scared, Mrs. Koerber. Since I had already left the note to meet you, I snuck out of my window and around the building. I came back in at that boarded up gap in the wall that leads into the locker room."

I say, "Assuming I believe all that – which I'm not sure yet if I do – then tell me, what were you and Ted talking about for so long last night."

Hudson sighs and rolls his neck, like he's trying to get comfortable with what he's going to say. Finally, he says, "Dr. Ted said he wanted to make amends. He had a near death experience himself and wanted to find peace over his regrets. He asked me about my life. And he told me about his."

Logan says, "We know Ted was your plastic surgeon, and that you sued him. But the reports only have the clinical aspects of it. What really happened?"

Hudson says, "It's a stupid story. I was desperate to hold onto my acting career. I had been a cute little kid, but even as a teenager, it was obvious I wasn't going to turn into an A list heartthrob. My agent was about to drop me, so I volunteered to get surgery on my face. Higher cheekbones, a more prominent jawline. But I was also broke. So I went to a guy my mom knew who owed her a favor."

"How did your mom know Ted?" I ask.

"My mom knew his wife, who was also on the commercial audition circuit. I guess it must have been Irene, before her divorce. She recommended my mom get a nose job, and even though mom has a beautiful face, she kept the card. Those kinds of comments can really get to you, you know? Especially when beauty becomes competitive."

Logan asks, "Then why didn't you recognize Irene here at the hotel?"

Hudson sighs. "I don't think I ever met her, or I would have remembered. She's quite a striking woman. Older than me, but not too much older, you know? I know she has a boyfriend, and she probably doesn't see me in a romantic way. But she has the kind of face I won't forget."

So yes, we all know he's smitten. I don't see that Irene is all that striking, myself. But she does have a strong air of self-confidence – though it is possible that's all bluster. Considering that she was married to Ted, I wonder if she had any work done on her face? It could have been a way to mask her own lack of self-confidence at the time leading her to talk to Hudson's mom that way. But whatever happened between Ted and Hudson's mom – however Ted came to owe her a favor – Hudson wound up under the knife.

I say, "So it's years later, and your mom hands over the card when your agent says changing your face will save your career. Then what went wrong?" He had complained about unsanitary conditions, so I think I know where this might be heading.

Hudson says, "There was an infection. It spread, and I lost part of the bone in my jaw. Mom tried to sue for carelessness at the clinic, but the lawyer she talked to said it would be hard to prove. I gave a deposition, and it just made me look stupid and angry. When the clinic offered us some money as a no-fault settlement, I didn't push it. In a way, it was *my* fault. I had been willing to chase fame at any cost. And I paid with months of pain."

"That's why you broke up with your girlfriend," I say, suddenly realizing the frame of mind Hudson must have been in. "It wasn't the other way around, was it? You were ashamed of what you had done, and you were the one acting out, pushing her away."

"I was ashamed of my face," Hudson says. "I didn't want her to feel obligated to stay, when I wasn't the person she had signed on to be with. It took me a long time to realize that all she wanted was to stay by me and support me, and I demeaned her by not letting her. My face may be disfigured, but once you get used to looking at it in the mirror – honestly, it's not that bad. Not enough to drive people away. And Savannah knew I was still the same person inside. Breaking things off with her was the worst decision I ever made. Even worse than having the plastic surgery in the first place."

"Given that," I say, "It must have taken a great deal of courage to pick up a camera and become a Youtuber."

Hudson says, "You have no idea. For a long time, I couldn't even look at myself in the mirror. My vanity had gotten the better of me, and my desperation to hold onto a career that wasn't happening. I felt like Beast from *Beauty and the Beast*. I used to watch that animated film all the time when I was a kid. I never understood why his appearance was such a curse, because he actually looked kind of cool."

I say, "So you decided you were like Beast, and people just needed to appreciate your differences?"

"I wish," Hudson says. "That would imply that I had self-esteem. My sense of self-worth had been battered, first by my inability to get a big role, and then the reactions I kept getting to my scars. Even though in retrospect, a lot of it was probably concern, there was a time when I wouldn't go out in public. My parents finally kicked me out of the house – not because they weren't sympathetic, but because they were afraid I was becoming agoraphobic. I was living for the past I could no longer have, not sure what to do with myself in the present. Except eat Cheetos and binge watch reality TV."

My heart squeezes with empathy. "I've been there," I tell him. "Except for the Cheetos part. After my husband died, I went through life living for his memory, choosing things I thought he would have wanted. I even opened my chocolate shop because traveling to source beans for craft chocolate had been a dream of ours together – one he didn't live to see. But it wasn't until I faced off against that first killer that I realized I wanted the chocolate business because it was more my passion, my way to move forward. And more importantly, that I wanted to live every day in the present."

Hudson is nodding along. "I remember listening to those moments in Ash's podcast. He weaves it as a good story – but to think about you actually living it is inspiring. For me, it wasn't throwing a fistful of cacao nibs into some crazy guy's face. Instead, it was a video contest. At first, I wanted to prove that people couldn't look past my scars, that I was doomed to loneliness. But I placed second in the contest, and when I started reading the comments – sure there were some jerky ones, but there were also people talking about how brave I was for defying conventional beauty. And a couple of people even said the scars made me look hot. I took it as a challenge. Confront what I really look like – on camera. And show myself living an ordinary life. I hopped a plane to Japan and never looked back."

Logan says, "So you weren't angry with Ted for scarring you, turning you into a monster?"

"You think I'm a monster?" Hudson asks, sounding hurt. Considering that's the part he clued in on, I guess that's a no on the fomenting anger front.

"Of course not," Logan says. His ears have turned pink, a clear sign that he's embarrassed. "It's just somebody left Felicity a copy of *Frankenstein*, and I'm trying to make the clues fit."

Hudson gasps. "A murder book? Of course! We should have been looking for one sooner. I knew the killer here must have challenged you, the way you dove into investigating, despite there being half a dozen cops on the scene."

I give Logan a reproving look. Then I tell Hudson, "You can't tell anybody about the book. Not anybody online, or here in the hotel. Promise?"

"Promise," Hudson says, but after a beat he asks, "Can I see it?"

"No!" Logan and I both say at the same time.

Chapter Nineteen
Saturday

We bring Hudson over to Logan's dad, who promises to keep him safe.

"How are you going to do that?" Hudson asks.

Logan's dad says, "My wife and I are going to escort you to a random unoccupied room upstairs, and we'll play checkers or whatever you want until all of this is over. It would take a determined killer to search this entire hotel. And if anyone tries to sneak in a drone or a camera, I've got an EMP gun. I had Fisk bring it to me after there was first chatter about drones. I've searched this lobby, and Rosemary has been sweeping for bugs and looking for cameras all over, ever since lunch. She smashed a couple of cameras in the elevator and in the hallways, so the route should be safe."

Logan says, "I had wondered where Mom had gotten off to."

Logan's dad says, "We may not have the stamina we used to – especially me. But this won't be the first time she's helped me with a protection detail." He looks at me. "You've been surprisingly resourceful."

I whisper to Logan, "Was that a compliment?"

He whispers back, "Yes. I think."

The elevator dings, and Logan's mom steps out of it. She's carrying a hammer and a picnic hamper.

"What's in the basket?" I ask.

She replies, "Sustenance. I sweet-talked Enrique out of some beautiful paella, garlic bread, and a bottle of wine."

I whisper to Logan, "Your mom is about the coolest mother-in-law anyone could hope to have."

Logan's mom puts the hammer on top of the picnic basket and holds out her hand for the master key. She stage whispers, "I heard that." Then she winks. "Nice vest."

And I would follow her anywhere, if she promised to keep me safe.

Hudson, on the other hand, looks like he is having second thoughts as they usher him towards the elevator. I hear Logan's dad ask him, "What's the deal with the snake tattoo?"

Hudson says, "It was supposed to be about reinvention. Shedding my old life like a snake sheds its skin, when I moved to Japan. Turns out, it was a bad idea. You know tattoos in Japan are associated with organized crime?"

Logan's dad says, "Bad ideas build character."

Then the elevator dings and they get on.

Logan smiles after them. He says, "I told you my mom loves you. And I think my dad might be warming up."

I huff. "If you call a backhanded compliment warming up. You should have heard what he said to me earlier."

"I can only imagine," Logan says, and the look on his face says he's remembering the difficult time he's had in his relationship with his father. I'm starting to see why. Logan's dad is excessively blunt, and very judgmental – but there's an air of the hero about him that's impossible to deny, and hard not to want to emulate. It's not difficult to believe that Logan could believe that, once he had failed on the force, and again in private security, his father would never respect him again. He had chosen Galveston as a form of self-imposed exile to get away from everyone he used to know, in an attempt not to be reminded of that failure.

But I can see how much Logan's self-confidence and self-respect have returned, since he has realized his dad didn't see just his mistakes.

Now that we're back in the lobby, I unzip the vest, the better to breathe, but I leave it on because apparently it makes me look cool.

"Let's just say the kid is telling the truth," Logan says, changing the subject. "What do you think was chasing Cynthia? A wasp? Or maybe a drone?"

"It definitely had to be a drone." I try to imagine her swatting at the thing while running down the stairs and out of the hotel. Only – she would have to have gone past Logan's dad to get out the front door, or past everyone in the kitchen to get out that way. Unless she went down one flight of stairs and then jumped out of the big window at the end of the hall. Those windows do open, but it would take time to get the sash up, and then to get over the wrought iron balcony railing. So whatever had been chasing Cynthia would have had time to get a good

bead on her. And besides, if a drone had been set to attack
Cynthia, why not just kill her in her room, the same way Ted had
been killed? Why try and force her outside? I tell Logan, "I want
to check something out, up on the second floor."

We take the stairs, and I force myself to take my time. No
need to risk my breathing problems acting up from sprinting all
over the hotel. Still, I can't help jogging to the end of the open
hallway, with its balcony view to the floor below. It's possible that
if Cynthia ran this direction, someone might have seen her. But
not necessarily. It would have only been a couple dozen steps to
the corner, and by then she'd be out of sight to anyone below.
The window is still open, and when I lean through it, there's the
smashed remains of a drone, and the plastic rubble is dented in
roughly the shape of a shoe.

I ask, "If she destroyed the drone, why would Cynthia go
over the railing? She's coordinated, but she still risked injuring
herself when she jumped."

"Maybe she saw something below. Or maybe she was
afraid to go back into the hotel, and she figured if she was
already outside, she might as well escape before it was too late."

"Maybe," I agree. "I guess we will never know."

Logan says, "It's possible that that's not even what
happened. Hudson could be lying. That injury just now could be
to cover whatever Cynthia might have done to him earlier."

I can't believe Logan is saying that so calmly. I ask, "If you
think Hudson still might be the killer, then why did you let him go
off with your parents? Aren't you worried he might hurt them?"

Logan says, "Have you even met my parents? Together,
Hudson wouldn't have a chance against them, especially since
they're on high alert."

Well, if he's not worried, I'm going to try not to worry. I tell Logan, "While it's logistically possible for this to be staged, I don't think Hudson did it."

Logan says, "I don't either. Not really. My guess is Sebastian killed all three victims, together with his wife. Neither one alone seems to have the skills necessary to pull this off. But if you assume Ted put together the guest list himself, and we're just looking at the ability to actually commit the murders, the Wimbletons could have done it. They arrived early, and wandered the hotel. They probably got a look at the rooming list while we were finishing breakfast, and went up to the fourth floor while we were playing volleyball. Say he handles the drones, while she wrangles the ferrets and later Sasha stabs Cynthia while she's occupied with flying attacks. Either one of them could have poisoned Elena."

I ask, "If Ted planned all this, then why was Cynthia even on the guest list? We never uncovered a connection between her and anyone else here."

To prove my point, I start Googling Cynthia's name together with each of the other guests. I don't get any promising results. I try her name plus rare coins, plus ferrets, and plus true crime. Nothing comes up. I don't try Googling her plus drones – we already know she worked around a business that created and manufactured them.

"I get your point," Logan says. "She isn't in any criminal database, either. And I couldn't find anything she might be blackmailed over. She's the one piece in this puzzle that just doesn't fit."

"Unless Ted didn't plan his own murder. Or you know – the party that led to it. What if it was someone supremely organized, who also handles travel?" I try to put this in a way that's coherent. "My brain still says Irene had too many connections into all of this to be coincidence. But why? If she doesn't hold a grudge, and she assumed Ted had a will leaving his ill-gotten fortune to his dogs, then why would she have killed him – and two other people? If she'd just killed Elena, it would make sense, because she hated her. But even Elena admitted that Irene had a soft spot for Ted."

Logan says, "Did Arlo tell you that there was a will filed, but that the file disappeared off the computer at the law office that created it?"

Okay then. I say, "That puts Irene officially in the lead as chief suspect in my book."

"I can see why," Logan admits. "Though it could still be the Wimbletons."

"Or Hudson," I say reluctantly.

"Whatcha doing?" Chloe asks, coming up behind us. I cringe at how much of that she might have heard. I guess that's what we get for facing a window, trying to have a private conversation.

"We're admiring the view," Logan says, deadpan.

Chloe asks, "I was wondering if you've seen Hudson. I've been looking all over for him."

Logan and I exchange a glace. Neither of us had listed Chloe high on our suspect lists – but we can't eliminate her either. Especially not now that she's here, asking about the guy who believes he's marked for death because someone left a sword in his bed.

Logan asks Chloe, "You never met Cynthia before this weekend, did you?"

I suck in a breath. Is Logan seriously considering Chloe, in her pink sparkly tee and faded jeans, the puzzle piece that bridges it all together? It's a lot to say she's a killer, just because she's looking for Hudson.

Chloe says, "No. Why? Is it important?"

"Just curious," Logan says.

I ask her, "Why do you need to find Hudson?"

Chloe says, "I made him a compilation of some of my best videos. After this is all over, I'm hoping he'll want to do a collab. Could you imagine? Going to Japan to raise money to help cats?"

We chat for a while, and Chloe reminds us that Enrique says it's almost time for dinner. Then she walks off, still looking for Hudson. As she walks away, I notice a large adhesive bandage on the back of her bicep. Was it there this morning? I can't remember. But she's certainly changed clothes. I remember what Dawn said, about Cynthia possibly injuring Doc Frankenstein. Warm anxiety fills my chest. Surely it's just a coincidence, right? Chloe changes clothes a lot, which is hard to understand, since they're all pink.

Logan starts typing something on his phone. I look over his shoulder, and he's doing a Google search of his own. He's searching Cynthia Reed Cat Channel.

And there it is – on Instagram. No images of Cynthia at all, but weekly videos of an enormous long-haired cat playing with teaser toys, or drinking out of the water faucet, or trying to fit into a box half its size. She's only got around 2,000 followers – a fraction of what Mr. Tunaface has as a reformed jerk cat. But then again, Cynthia hadn't seemed capable of the level of marketing Chloe is able to master.

I ask Logan, "You don't think Cynthia was the girl Chloe had a fight with at the pet awards show two years ago, do you?"

"That's impossible," Logan says. "The other girl was also a minor."

Still, he Googles Cynthia Reed plus the name of the awards show, and she comes up as one of the volunteers at the show, helping to stage-handle the feline and canine stars, plus birds, at least one turtle and a stag beetle that holds a paintbrush. There's a whole gallery of photos. We start scrolling through them, and eventually we find one of Chloe – and there's Cynthia, in the background of the photo, holding a carrier as Chloe brings Mr. Tunaface on stage. Cynthia doesn't even seem to notice the camera.

Logan says, "It's possible that Chloe doesn't even remember that Cynthia was at that awards show. But I guarantee you Cynthia remembered Chloe. In their niche, Chloe's a rockstar. I can't imagine that Cynthia didn't say anything to her about it, maybe even asked how everything panned out after the fight."

"Why would Chloe lie about something like that?" I ask.

"Probably because she knows she's a suspect. And because Cynthia likely knew something damaging about Chloe's past. Maybe she even threatened to leak the information about the fight to the press."

I say, "That's just as thin of a motive for murder as Arlo's theory that Chloe killed Ted because of a skin care pyramid scheme."

Logan says, "But what if we've been listening to only Chloe's side of things, because we know her and we like her? What if she lied about what led up to the fight at the awards show, and she assaulted some poor girl because the girl dared to pet her cat? If she's that irrational, the same twisted logic could mean that people who wronged her in more significant ways deserved to die – even if a rational mind would consider what these people had done to her mere inconveniences."

"Then what about Elena?" I ask. "What possible inconvenience could a literature professor have caused a seventeen-year-old girl?"

Logan shrugs. "I don't know. But it's something to look into."

We look, but don't find a connection. Which doesn't prove there isn't one. After all, not everything is on the internet. And even if it is, you have to do the right search to find it.

I tell Logan, "I don't buy it. It all seems very circumstantial. I still think it's Irene." Although – I have to be honest with myself. I want it to be Irene, because I don't have a connection to her like I do to Chloe, or shared lived pain with her like I do with Sasha, or find her gentle and funny, like I do Hudson, or see her as ridiculously over the top, like Jordan. But just because she's the person my gut says has to be guilty, it doesn't mean my gut is right. It wasn't that long ago that my gut instinct was that she couldn't have killed Ted, because she still cared about him.

Logan says, "If that's your theory, how do you plan to prove it?"

I think about it for a moment, and then I say, "I'll try to sit next to her at dinner. Drop a few hints that the cops are scouring Ted's house for a print copy of his will."

"They're not doing that," Logan points out.

"But Irene doesn't know that. Maybe she'll give something away."

Logan looks skeptical.

I hear footsteps on the stairs, and realize Fisher is walking up with a sketch pad in his hand. Today's tee is obviously a souvenir, with two palm trees silhouetted against the sun above the words, *Galveston Island*. It could be cheesy, but it's actually well-designed, and he's layered it with a green hoodie.

He heads towards us, looking vaguely disappointed. "Oh. Are you using the balcony?"

"Not really," Logan says. "Are you?"

Fisher says, "I was out there this morning, sketching sunrise over the garden. I've felt so cooped up, and sad that I'm missing out on the beach, I've been trying to find places with good views of the outside. There's at least palm trees and tropical plants."

"I'm sorry," I tell him. "I don't think this is the weekend any of us wanted. And that it's ruined your first impression of Texas."

Fisher says, "I'm expecting you two to salvage it. Any chance you can catch this killer early enough we can still have the bonfire tonight?"

"We're trying," Logan says. He gestures at the window. "Did you close that, when you came back in?"

"Of course," Fisher says. "I don't like wasting air conditioning."

"And that smashed plastic wasn't there?"

He moves to look out the open window. "Wow. No. Do you think it's a clue?"

"Probably," I say. "You're sure this is the window you were sketching from? There's identical balconies at either end of the building, on this floor and up on the third floor."

"It was definitely here, but I don't want to disturb evidence. I can just go up a floor and finish the sketch."

I remind him, "It's almost time for dinner."

Fisher looks torn. "Well, I don't want to miss Enrique's cooking. Carmen told me there's paella. I had that once in Spain, on my senior trip for high school. It was amazing."

"You can finish your sketch tomorrow, when the light is better anyway," Logan suggests.

"Fair," Fisher says, following us as we head downstairs.

Chapter Twenty
Saturday

Logan holds my hand as we make our way to the dining room, and squeezes it when we get there, saying, "You got this. I'm right here if you need me." He lets my hand go and turns to talk to Sebastian, who is standing near the doorway nursing a margarita.

I spot Irene at a table near the kitchen. Like everyone else, she's sitting far away from the area still cordoned off by police tape.

Before I can go sit next to her, Aunt Naomi and Uncle Greg come up to me.

I tell Aunt Naomi, "You've just about been cleared as a suspect. And Uncle Greg has gone way down on Arlo's list of probable."

Greg says, "That's fantastic. I'm going to take some time off work, and I would hate to have to spend it in jail. I want to finish the garden, and reconnect with my lovely wife." He kisses Naomi's hand.

She blushes and giggles, like they are newlyweds. She says, "Do you know how long it's been since we had a real vacation together?"

"Building a garden isn't my idea of a vacation," I quip. "Especially since it's one you won't be able to enjoy, once the hotel is sold."

Greg says, "I guess it's what you call a staycation. I just want to take some time, dig in the dirt and create something alive and beautiful. And so what if somebody else is going to own it in six months or a year? I'll still be able to come visit it. Maybe pull a few weeds when no one is looking. I miss the land sometimes, when I'm on a platform surrounded by the Gulf."

I ask, "Are you thinking about giving up working offshore?"

"Probably not," Greg says. "It's rewarding work too, and we need the money. I just want to pay more attention to the rest of my life."

Fisher walks over to us. Jordan is now talking to Logan.

Fisher says, "I couldn't help but overhear. Have you thought about making part of it a scent garden? I don't know if Felicity told you I'm a landscape architect. I've actually been making some sketches of the grounds, from various windows, and I think you could turn this into something special. I have a magazine contact who would love to highlight this kind of project. It would really help you sell it."

He pulls up his website on his phone and flips over to a list of private photo galleries. He punches in a password, then shows my aunt and uncle some charcoal renderings of stone walls overhung with wisteria, of an herb garden and a scent garden, in addition to the in-progress kitchen garden, with a built-up area with an infinity pool overlooking the bay.

Greg frowns at the images, "That's a lot more work than I had in mind."

"But do you like it?" Fisher asks.

"Who wouldn't?" Greg asks. "But that might make the hotel an even harder sell, since all that would have to be maintained. It's already going to be hard to attract a buyer, once the news gets ahold of everything that's happened here this weekend. Who's going to buy the murder hotel?"

Fisher says, "It's a shame you aren't keeping the place. Let me give you the password for the sketch gallery, in case you change your mind."

I see Aunt Naomi pull the gallery up on her own phone, clearly intrigued. I think she would be just as excited as I would be if we could find a way to keep this place. I'm just not sure how to make it work.

I excuse myself and go take a seat next to Irene. Jordan has taken the seat on her other side. Which is going to make talking to her less than ideal. But she seems to be the one person he trusts, out of everyone here. He still isn't eating anything – but I keep seeing him eyeing the buffet. He has to be hungry, and there's not only the paella up there, but a rich beef stew and a lighter option of butter chickpeas with basmati rice. And a salad bar. Not to mention a selection of desserts, including Carmen's double-chocolate cake. And samples of one of Logan's other bars. This time the mystery flavor is blueberry pomegranate.

I ask Irene, "How are you holding up, with Ted gone?"

She says, "I'm trying to keep myself distracted with other things. I think I'm close to figuring out the game." She takes her Clue sheet out of the bag at the base of her chair. There are notes scribbled all over it. She pulls out her character sheet, which now has a diagram on the back. "It helped that I've been sharing information with Jordan."

Next to her, Jordan nods and offers a pleased smile. "Searching down clues has been helping me keep my mind off food."

"Tosh," Irene says. "I told you to eat something. There's been a different method for each of the real murders here. I seriously doubt there's going to be another poisoning."

The way she says it sounds so confident. Could she be the murderer, laughing in front of my face about her crimes? My gut tells me she is – but I still don't have any proof.

"Still," Jordan says. "Better safe than sorry." His stomach grumbles loudly. He says, "Ignore that." He gestures at the bulletproof vest slung loosely around my shoulders. "She gets it."

Irene tells me, "Those things only protect you if they're zipped, you know."

Jordan says, "I should have packed one of those."

Irene pats his hand consolingly, but in a distracted manner. She taps the character sheet. "Hudson gave me the clues he'd gathered too, which was actually too sweet of him." She looks around the room, as though surprised Hudson isn't on his way to her table. "Where is Hudson, anyway?"

"Don't worry," I say. "He's safe, somewhere in the hotel. But he took his dinner to go."

"Really?" Irene looks irritated. "I didn't realize that was an option." She stabs at her salad violently enough that an olive goes shooting off her plate and lands in front of Jordan.

She has to be the killer. Right? Who else would be that upset about the potential next victim disappearing. I say, "He was scared he might be next on Doc Frankenstein's list. He found a sword in his room."

Did Irene just flinch? Or did I imagine it. She asks in a flat voice, "Doc Frankenstein?"

I play it off casual, like I wasn't fishing for a reaction. Whoever the killer is, they want attention and pride themselves on being clever. If it's Irene, she may let something slip if I imply otherwise. "That's the nickname we've given the killer. It fits, since the whole plan is a mashup of a bunch of tired tropes. Our Doc couldn't even commit to one book, and the Frankenstein metaphors don't even seem to fit. It's sad, really."

"Oh?" Irene looks at me curiously. "You got two murder books this time?"

I hadn't even admitted to having one. But that proves nothing – it's a reasonable assumption that anyone would make after I'd brought up books. Anyone listening to Ash's podcast knows there tends to be a pattern.

I say, "No, just the copy of *Frankenstein*. But the tropes we keep coming up against in this case are so much more Agatha Christie than Mary Shelley. I get the idea that the killer thought Ted was a monster, or that he'd created a monster that turned around and killed him. But to have the second murder be a poisoning? That's exactly what happened in *A Murder is Announced*."

Irene looks at me, wide eyed. "Is it?" she asks. "I've never read it. I didn't even realize the name of this event was a pun until I got here. I should have realized *A Chocolate is Announced* didn't appear out of thin air."

I swear she sounds upset – but again, that isn't enough to prove anything. I need to keep her talking, but if I get any more blunt about her possible identity as Doc Frankenstein, she'll shut down. I gesture at the diagram. "So what do you have figured out?"

Irene points at a circle off to the side of the fireplace, which is conveniently labeled *fireplace*. She drops her voice, the better not to share clues with anyone at the other tables. "This is the palm tree in the lobby. The in-game killer had to have shot Chloe from behind it. Hudson's clue sheet even said that his character saw the fronds twitch just as the lights came back on. So the question is who was absent when the lights came back on. It couldn't have been Cynthia's character, or Logan's – they alibi each other. The same with Arlo's character and Elena's. I know I didn't do it, and – unless they lied to me – neither did Jordon or Hudson. Patsy told me her character saw Sebastian's and Colin's rush forward to help as soon as the lights came on. Which means I have it narrowed down to Sasha, Bea, or a member of Logan's family. I haven't found either of his parents to question."

Assuming I'm right, and Irene is the killer, the last thing I want is for her to be thinking about the whereabouts of Logan's family. I look up from the diagram and ask her, "Don't you care about the story? Not just who could have killed Clementine Vanderclump, but the why behind it? The foibles of human nature in an overprotective guardian, a flirtatious groundskeeper or a jilted boyfriend?"

Irene waves a dismissive hand. "I just care about results. Honestly, if you just told me the answer, so I could go tell Ash and claim the prize money, that would be ideal."

I shake my head and open my empty hands palm up on the table. "Sorry. I have no idea. I didn't even get a character sheet."

Irene sighs, then says, "That's unfortunate."

Jordan says, "I wish someone would claim the prize, so Ash would stop banging on about it. I get that he's trying to keep us occupied, but it gives me the creeps, talking about fake murder in the middle of a crime scene. Speaking of which-" Jordan nods towards the hallway, where Fisk is coming in, holding Satchmo's lead. "That guy creeps me out."

I say, "This time, I think he's just here to help out Bea."

Bea joins Fisk on the opposite side of the room, and he gives her a brief kiss. Then they say something to each other, and Bea laughs. Then they head over to our table.

Bea asks me, "Would you mind watching Satchmo for a minute? We're going to have a picnic out on the third floor balcony near my room. It's barely big enough for the two of us, so I don't think the beagle will fit."

"That's fine," I say.

I wrap the dog's lead around my wrist and sit back down. Satchmo moves under the table to lie on my feet, but his thumping tail knocks over Irene's bag.

Jordan hops up to pick up Irene's things. She leans over at the same time, and I swear she winces again, then straightens up, sucking in a breath. Could she be injured, somewhere on her torso? If so, I don't really have a way to check. It's not like I can just ask her to show me her belly button.

"What's this?" Jordan asks. He's waving a cruise ship ticket right in Irene's face.

She tries to laugh it off, saying, "It's just a business trip. And I was already going to be here. It's a repositioning cruise. Why waste a flight right to the cruise port city? I need to save on points."

She does seem all about being thrifty. But is a boat giving her a relatively quick way out of the country also a back-up plan in case she gets implicated in a murder?

Either way, she's lost Jordan's loyalty. He sucks at his lip as he shakes his head. "A one-way trip to Italy? You said we were going to deal with my problem together. That you wouldn't leave here until we found that envelope. Well fine, I better get back to looking by myself."

He throws her ticket onto the table and stalks across the dining room and down the hallway.

"Wow," I say. I'm thinking that whatever Jordan was being blackmailed over, it must be really bad.

Irene says, "You have no idea." She can't be talking about the blackmail – I hadn't said that aloud – but she seems okay with the rift between her and Jordan. She fake laughs. "Who knew he would be that upset about me not taking him on the cruise? What, with all those sea days, he'd be bored to tears."

Pretending I know nothing about the blackmail evidence, I ask, "What do you think Jordan is looking for? Ted's will? I'm sure the guy was worth a considerable amount."

The look on Irene's face is like she just bit a lemon. "I don't know what good that would do. Ted left all his money to his precious dogs."

I say, "Somebody told me Ted changed his will. Only now they can't find it."

I can feel Irene studying me, weighing how much I actually know. She fake laughs again. "That's preposterous. Ted would never change his will, unless he got married again. Don't tell me he eloped."

I shrug. "I have no idea why he would change it. But if it's missing – doesn't that mean you inherit? Maybe Jordan wants to make sure that doesn't happen."

I hope by pretending it's Jordan who wants the will, Irene might feed into the misdirect.

Instead, she says, "I'm not sure how it would be in Jordan's interest to do that."

The way she says it sounds like a threat. But to me or against Jordan? Clearly, she understands the implications of the missing will. Would that be enough for her to have killed Ted over – even if she still loved him? What about the first guy she'd married? Did she refuse the annulment to get money? Maybe I can get Logan to try to find the guy's info, and we can call him and ask.

Before I can even think about the logistics of doing that, my phone buzzes with a text. It's another message from the killer. Yet nobody else seems to be reaching for their phone. I read the text. *You take one of my players off the board, I take one of yours. Bring Hudson back in the next two hours or else.*

I look at Irene. Her phone's not even on the table, and her hands are visible, so she's not texting from her pocket or her lap. Was I wrong? Is Irene not the killer? Or could someone who's tech savvy enough to hijack the guest list for this weekend perfectly capable of typing out a text, to be sent later, at a specific time? Could Irene have seen us handing over Hudson to Logan's parents, despite Rosemary's attempt to disable the cameras?

"Are you okay?" Irene asks, trying to get a look at my phone screen.

"No," I say in a strangled voice. I stand up from the table and peer frantically around the room, trying to see who's missing. Aside from the obvious fact that both of Logan's parents and Hudson are hiding out somewhere – Hudson being the player I've taken off the killer's board – I realize Autumn's not here. My stomach sinks into a leaden knot. Autumn wasn't even supposed to have come this weekend. I'd assumed she was out of danger, not even on the board. I mean, what kind of cold, ruthless person picks on a pregnant lady, out of everyone here?

I look down at Irene who looks almost convincingly puzzled and concerned. Almost.

I let my look sharpen into a frown. Surely off the board doesn't mean dead. It can't, right? Otherwise why not just say eliminate, or whatever. And what's the point of giving a deadline?

I call Autumn, but her phone goes straight to voicemail. She usually never turns it off. I'm starting to panic.

I stride across the room to where Ash and Imogen are sitting and ask, desperately, "When was the last time you saw Autumn?"

At my feet, Satchmo whines, sensing my distress.

Imogen says, "I think she was in the business center, working on her book. We're supposed to meet up there later, to talk about my project."

"Okay. Thanks." I try to keep the panic out of my voice. Maybe I'm wrong. Maybe Autumn will be in there, writing, because I'm interpreting the message backwards.

I head for the door. Arlo gives me a questioning look. I zip up my vest, as a signal that I'm headed into possible danger.

By the time I've reached the hallway, Logan is walking by my side, not even asking what the crisis is. It doesn't take long for Arlo and Patsy to catch up to us, too.

I explain the threatening message, and my suspicions about Irene as we all cross through the lobby and move quickly towards the business center. Only, when we get there, the lights are out. And when I turn them on, the room is empty.

Autumn left her sweater on the chair where she'd been sitting earlier. I look down at Satchmo. He's trained to scent. If anyone can help us find Autumn, it will be him.

I lean down and let Satchmo get a big whiff of Autumn's sweater, lightly scented with her floral lotion. "Come on boy," I tell him. "I know you love Autumn. Tell us where she's gone."

Satchmo snuffles around on the floor, then heads out of the business center, towards the stairs. The four of us follow him up the steps and down the open hallway, and around the corner –

thankfully not even hesitating by the still open window. I think Aunt Naomi gave Autumn a room on this floor, since she has to stay over now unexpectedly. Could we be getting this upset over nothing?

Satchmo follows the scent trail over to one of the doors and sits down in front of it, looking pleased with himself. I move him over with my foot so I can get in front of the door to knock. There's no answer. Roiling with anxiety, I turn to Logan, who says, "Give me a second."

He picks the lock, which I am trembling far too much to do myself. The last few times we'd followed a clue, Logan's sister had been right on top of us. It almost feels weird that she isn't here now, offering to pick that lock herself.

When the door swings open, I hear a soft snore. And there's Autumn, fast asleep in her bed.

When I wake her up, she murmurs, "I finally typed the end. That means I get to celebrate with a little nap."

I grab her pillow and her blanket and say, "If you want to nap, you can do it downstairs. I'll have the guys pull in one of the sofas."

Autumn says, "I don't want to be that much trouble. It's just – I'm off caffeine. Except for the chocolate samples, of course. I wouldn't want to miss Logan's hard work. Do you know how long it's been since I've tried to make it through the day without two cups of coffee and a London Fog?"

I tell her, "I know exactly how you feel. On the caffeine withdrawal front at least. You remember when I was taking the treatments for my asthma and I had to severely limit my caffeine intake? I was a grump, especially for the first couple of weeks."

"It gets better, right? The headaches go away?"

"That they do," I assure her. "And the fact that you finished your manuscript deserves a celebratory piece of coconut cake. And some sparkling water."

Autumn heaves a satisfied sigh and says, "It does, doesn't it. It's nice to have a friend who gets what it's like to be a writer." She blinks as she realizes I'm not the only person in the room. She takes her pillow and asks, "What's going on?"

I start to explain about the threat, and how she didn't answer her phone, and that's when it hits me: someone else was missing from the dining room. Dawn.

But Dawn is too careful to have been captured by Doc Frankenstein. Captured – or worse.

I ask Logan, "When was the last time you saw your sister?"

Chapter Twenty-One
Saturday

He looks at Arlo, who says, "She was still looking around the garden, when I got called back to the station. We had an emergency meeting on what to do to get everybody out of here, without putting anyone else at risk."

Patsy blushes. "When he came back, we were discussing how he is personally planning to keep me safe if an evacuation happens. Sorry if that sounds selfish."

What it sounds like is that Patsy is the right person for Arlo to be with. I'm glad things between all of us turned out the way they did. I say, "Any guy who wouldn't want to protect his girlfriend wouldn't be normal."

Arlo grins at me. "Lis, I think that's the first time you've ever called me normal."

Logan's got his phone to his ear, obviously calling Dawn. "She's not answering her phone. And she hasn't checked in with Fisher. She usually does. He has her wrapped around his little finger, you know."

I gawk in surprise. If anything, that relationship had felt the other way around. Dawn seems like such a big personality.

"Well," Arlo says. "Before we panic, let's check her room too."

We do. She's not there. I go to the window in her room and check the parking lot. Her car is here. Which means she's really missing. I text Ash and ask him to check the sauna and the business center, while we get Satchmo scenting off items from Dawn's suitcase. The dog gets as far as the elevator, which means she could be anywhere.

I say, "Let's go downstairs and get him to scent from the door of her car."

Patsy says, "I'm still not sure if it's safe for anyone not on Doc's list to go outside."

Arlo agrees to wait with her in the lobby. But starting from Dawn's car, Satchmo just goes back into the half-built garden and does a loop right back to the hotel, where he scents through the lobby and back to the elevator. It's not his fault. But it is frustrating.

Logan says, "I have a bad feeling about this. I know I talk about my sister like she's an overbearing pest – and I'm not saying she isn't – but I would die if anything happened to her."

I tell Logan, "We'll find her, even if we have to go floor by floor."

The elevator dings, and the door opens, and there's Sasha, with Cheeseburger on his lead by her side. Satchmo and Cheeseburger come face to face, and Cheeseburger lets out a terrified screech that hurts my heart. Satchmo backs up, letting out a confused whine.

Cheeseburger sprints around him, pulling the lead out of Sasha's hand. The ferret rushes across the lobby and into the pot of the palm tree, disappearing from sight.

"What the heck?" Logan asks. "Where did he go?"

There's a thud behind me and I turn, realizing that Sasha has fainted. The elevator doors close on her, and someone else must be calling it, because it starts heading up towards three. Maybe Bea and Fisk are finished with their picnic.

I hold onto Satchmo's leash – though he shows no signs of trying to rush after the ferret – while Logan and Arlo examine the pot. Patsy's still standing by the door, her attention caught by something in the parking lot. Patsy opens the door, saying, "Ma'am, do you need help?"

I start to remind her she wasn't planning to leave the building, but she's already slipped outside. I keep Satchmo close, giving wide berth to the palm tree, as I head across the lobby to see where she's gone. She's helping someone who's walking with a limp to make it back to the front doors. That person turns her head, and I realize it's Irene. Patsy must not have been able to tell at first, or she never would have gone out there after I'd told her my suspicions.

What is Irene even doing out there? And how did she get hurt? She wasn't limping earlier.

I open the door to let her and Patsy back in, closing it quickly, since there's still a ferret on the loose. I look at Irene warily. I ask, "What happened?"

She says, "I think I saw the killer. He chased me outside and then he – he pushed me down. I thought I was going to die, but then Patsy startled him." She hugs Patsy so tight Patsy gasps. "You saved my life!"

"Patsy," Arlo says. "Come over here and look at this. Did you realize this is a fake palm tree?"

I know Arlo doesn't trust Irene. And it's obvious he's trying to get Patsy away from her. But when Patsy tries to move, Irene starts to fall over. Patsy catches her.

Logan reaches his hand into a gap in the dirt at the base of the palm tree, and then withdraws it again quickly, shaking his fingers like he's been nipped. But he's holding a yellow envelope. He says, "There's a bunch of stuff in here. I think the ferret is using it for a nest."

"What's in there?" I ask, even though I had promised Jordan that if we found a yellow envelope, we wouldn't open it. I'm guessing whatever's in there is absolutely scandalous.

Logan opens the envelope and pulls out a sheaf of folded papers. He says, "It's Ted's will." He skims quickly over the first page. "Apparently Hudson was telling the truth about Ted wanting to make amends for his biggest mistakes. There are four people who inherit the bulk of his estate, and two of them are Hudson and Sebastian. Ted sounds sincere in his apologies."

Irene gasps. "One of them must have killed him for his money. Whoever pushed me down was strong. It could have been either of them."

I'm not buying her act – but I still can't prove that she's lying. I start moving closer to her, keeping Satchmo close beside me. I need to get between her and Pasty. I feel the lump of the pepper spray in my pocket, next to my emergency inhaler.

Logan sees what I'm doing, and I can tell by the hardening of his jaw that he thinks it's dangerous. But he's trying to play the situation off as casual. He lifts up the ring of fake dirt and moss from the base of the fake palm tree, and not one but two ferrets shoot up into the fronds, both honking unhappily. At least it's not the terror scream again.

Logan catches Cheeseburger's leash, and Arlo manages to get ahold of the other ferret. Neither Arlo or the ferret seem too happy about it. Logan gives me a subtle signal that I should grab Patsy and duck. I shake my head, but really – this is reaching an impasse. Irene isn't going to confess, and she's not going to let us ruin her plan to inherit Ted's fortune by default.

Almost as if she's reading my mind, Irene says, "Do you think I could have a look at that will?"

"Why?" I ask. "So you can destroy it?"

"Of course not," Irene says. "Why would I do that?"

"Let's be honest," I say. "You challenged me to unmask Doc Frankenstein. I'm doing it. We have the will, so your plan's foiled anyway. This is the point where you give up and congratulate me for winning the wager you forced on me with the money you pasted into the book."

Irene says, "You're wrong. How could I even have done any of this? You saw me in the hall, right after Ted was killed. I was with Jordan. If I'd tried to do anything on our way up in the elevator, he would have noticed."

I say, "The key was the ferret. Everything else could be automated – including a face scan to make sure it really was Ted you were shooting. But you didn't count on this one escaping and gathering up more random objects."

Irene laughs uncomfortably. "What do I have to do with any ferret?"

And I realize how I can come close to proving her guilt. The only way it would be more sure is if ferrets could talk. I tell Arlo, "Put down the mystery ferret and see if he goes to his owner."

Irene scoffs. But when Arlo puts the ferret down, it starts to scamper towards her. She makes a *pffft* sound and stamps her foot, trying to scare it away, but the ferret climbs up her leg and then all the way up onto her shoulder – with easy motions that make it clear he's done it hundreds of times before.

Logan puts the envelope in his jacket pocket, and when he pulls his hand out, he's holding his gun. I grab Patsy's arm, and try to pull her down, but she squeaks, "No."

Oh, no! Irene has already grabbed the back of Patsy's shirt and pointed a gun of her own at Patsy's ribs. Irene looks at me sharply, so I take a couple of steps back.

Irene says, "Everyone, meet Side of Fries. I've spent the past two years training this little guy to do the tricks I needed to enact my plan."

I splutter. "You knew two years ago that Sasha would bring her ferret on a work trip? And since her ferret was named Cheeseburger, you couldn't help name it Side of Fries?"

Irene says, "I'm a patient person. And I thought the ferret double-bluff would be enough to throw you off. You would be convinced it had to be Sasha." She looks at me sadly. "I had hoped you wouldn't figure it out. That I would get to have my victory over the famous chocolate shop sleuth, and go down as the only one to challenge you and get away with it. And you wouldn't have to die to keep my secret."

She's addressing me, but the sweep of her gaze takes in all four of us.

I tell her, "Fine. But let Patsy go. She wasn't part of your original four players." I realize as I'm saying it that Dawn was. Which makes sense why she was the piece taken off the board – not Autumn.

"I'm afraid I can't do that," Irene says. "She's seen the will. What's going to happen now is that we're all going to walk down to that sauna room, nice and slow. And if you cooperate, I'll let Logan's sister out, before she runs out of air. She'll be grateful to me for saving her."

I ache at the thought of Dawn trapped somewhere. Despite myself, I have started to think of her as a sister. She's a big personality, and I already feel a sense of loyalty to her – even if we were fighting a few hours ago.

"If you hurt Dawn," Logan growls.

"Then what?" Irene scoffs. "Put your gun in the palm tree pot. You too, Arlo."

Grudgingly, both guys comply and we begin a careful march down the hallway, leaving Satchmo tied to a lobby chair – guarding my pepper spray. I half expect one of the guys to turn around and tackle Irene, but Arlo wouldn't dare, with Patsy at risk. And Logan won't jeopardize his sister. I know they're both thinking about angles and tactics, and how we can turn the tables on Irene. I am too – but our best chance at escaping her is fading as we leave the lobby and the hallway behind and enter the small room with the gym. My only faint hope is that Ash might still be in here. After all, this room was on his list of places to check for Dawn, and he never checked in after. I need to play for time.

I've done this before, half a dozen times. And somehow, Logan and I have figured a way out. It's still terrifying. Because this could be the time we don't.

"What about the $10,000 dollars?" I splutter. "You said I could keep it if I unmasked you. Now I have. And you're not keeping your end of the bargain."

Irene rolls her eyes. "I was going to let you keep it either way. Only now, it will probably go to finding someone to take care of your rabbit after I shoot you. You caused your own downfall by being too smart for your own good."

"So what was it?" I ask. "The Frankenstein thing. I still don't quite get the metaphor. You only kill the ones you love, or something like that?"

"Love is part of it," Irene admits. "But so is hate. I genuinely loved Ted – but I hated the monster Ted had turned me into while we were married. Any vestiges of hope and compassion I had – not that I was good at those much anyway – was crushed. And then I hated him for not chasing after me when I left. I wanted to show Elena – show all of you – just how many other people had a genuine grudge against Ted. How better the world will be with him gone."

The only part of what she just said that I hadn't expected was the part about Elena. Had I put this together all wrong – the right killer but the wrong reasoning? Had her real problem been with Elena – and Ted's murder was just for the money? That lines up so much better with what happens in *Frankenstein*.

"So what happens now?" I ask, trying to keep my voice steady, though my knees are shaking. We're all just standing in the middle of the room, and I see no sign of Ash in the shadows of the locker rooms. "Am I supposed to beg for my life? I won't do that, but I will beg for Patsy's. Like I said, she had no part in this challenge. Let me trade places with her."

Irene laughs. "I think we both know how this goes. I threaten to kill you. You get me monologuing, I explain myself, and then you try to take this gun from me. If this was a movie, that would work. I'll answer your questions, because I've been dying to explain all this to somebody. But after that, the five of you have to die. And then at noon tomorrow, I'll leave the hotel with everybody else, and no one will ever know it was me."

Logan looks at me, and I can tell he's planning a hero moment. His hand goes instinctively to his hip, but comes away empty. He balls his hand into a fist and tilts his head, looking at Irene's gun. I give a microshake of my head. Irene is still holding on far too close to Patsy.

"Five?" Patsy asks.

"The guy hiding in the sauna," Patsy says. "You might as well come on out,"

"No thanks," Ash says through the hole in the sauna door.

Logan clears his throat and asks, "If you've been training the ferret for years, what was the point? We planned this mystery weekend spur of the moment. How could you possibly have foreseen that – let alone hijacked the contest to get everyone here?"

"Right," I point out. "Greetings and Felicitations wasn't even open then."

Irene says, "At the beginning, I wasn't sure how I was going to get everyone who hated Ted together. I was beginning to think I may have to plan the party around the murder myself, and send everyone blind emails. But then I found out about your aunt and her history with Ted. She had this big hotel, you were an amateur sleuth. And your writer friend loved my suggestions about hosting a murder mystery weekend. It couldn't be more perfect."

I feel almost offended. I say, "So you didn't call me out to challenge me as a sleuth. What happened to you hoping to be the only one to best me? Was that a lie? I just happened to be a handy catalyst?"

"I didn't say that," Irene says. "I have been following your career, since your first case with that employee of yours who died. That's how I decided to look up your aunt in the first place. At first, I thought maybe you had murdered all of the victims in the murders you had quote unquote solved, and gotten away with it. I was impressed. But I eventually realized you weren't killing anyone. Somehow, you kept uncovering things the police couldn't. So my challenge was in earnest."

She leans forward and Patsy squeaks as the gun presses harder into her ribs. I cut a glance over at the sauna. I hope Ash got the cameras back up and running, because a recorded confession is worth gold right now. Maybe he even has the laptop still set up, that last bit of equipment that overloaded the circuit breaker when the sauna had been turned on. That way, if we don't make it, there's still a recording that Irene probably won't find.

Before Irene can get frustrated with Patsy, I ask, "Why a mystery weekend? How did you expect your plan to play into the game?"

Irene gestures with her chin towards the sauna door, and by extension Ash. "I took a look at the script for the game, after I had control of Chloe's computer." She tuts. "Do you know how easy it is to guess passwords off an influencer? Just about everything they might choose is going to be right there, in their feeds. Anyway, I just knew that when the lights went off during your silly game, someone was going to take advantage of the moment and kill Ted. I mean, I even brought the perfect, ironic murder weapon. The doc goes under the knife, dying the way he killed two others – it makes the perfect bit. I was sure either Sasha or Hudson was going to go for it."

Two others. Meaning that the Wimbleton's son wasn't the only one who had died as a result of Ted's carelessness. Which makes sense – after all, there were four beneficiaries.

"But they didn't," Ash points out, through the door, "Because they're not crazy killers wanting to re-enact literature."

Irene scoffs. "You re-enact stuff all the time."

"As actors," Ash points out. "Nobody ever gets hurt. Well, except for that one time Bob fell and broke his pinkie. But that was entirely an accident."

Irene looks angry. That's not good for Patsy – or any of us.

"We're getting off track here," I point out, taking a few steps closer to the sauna, like I'm casually talking to Ash. But there was a lot of pointy stuff in the hole where the hot tub used to be. Maybe there's something usable as a weapon. I turn back to Irene, trying to de-emphasize the distance I've covered – when there's so much left to go. "Nobody wanted to re-enact Clue for you and kill Ted, so you had to do it yourself. But you didn't want to. Because part of you still loves him. I saw your face when you saw his dead body. You were heartbroken."

"It had to be done," Irene says – and for the first time, she looks remorseful.

"But you didn't want to be there to see it. Which is why you used the drone. What was it? Motion sensored? Programmed to recognize Ted's face? Anything that let you be laughing with Jordan while your device killed a man. I think I get what you were trying to say by giving me the book. By killing Ted, you were trying to get back at Elena. She was the real monster, right? Just the way Frankenstein's monster in the book killed someone Doctor Frankenstein held dear, on purpose to punish him. You always intended on killing her – whether one of us left the hotel and disrupted your game or not."

Irene bares her teeth. "Of course I was going to kill her. She's the bully who tortured me as a kid and mocked me the whole time I was married. Elena may have acted like she hated Ted, but in truth, she was jealous over him. They were twins. He was supposed to be at her beck and call, all his life. And when he started acting independently – she punished him. She made him what he was, and in turn he made me what I am. An avenging monster."

I hold out a hand, trying to come across as understanding, though seriously – Irene had taken all the wrong lessons from the text of *Frankenstein*. My hand's trembling visibly, so I lower it back to my side before she sees how scared I am. "So you wanted to punish both of them. Especially since Ted was showing remorse over some of the bad things he'd done in life – but not over what he did to you. I get that. But what did poor Cynthia do?"

Irene gestures with her gun, and I hear both Logan and Arlo's sharp intake of breath as they try to gauge the distance to her. She quickly points the gun back at Patsy. "Cynthia was supposed to be a red herring. I stole her ID to access the prototype drones, so if you guys found one, it would point right back to her. Unfortunately, she saw me put the poison on Elena's water bottle filter." She blinks and looks off to the side. "At least, I'm pretty sure she did. She later claimed she hadn't, but people will say a lot of things when they're begging for their lives."

I say, "True. And I guess we'll never know if she was lying or not."

"It doesn't make a difference," Irene says. "After you've killed two people, what's a third? Or a fourth, or – a ninth? The four of you have such a complicated past, and it's oh so public. It won't be hard to make it look like you cheated on Logan with Arlo, and he decided to kill all of you. Ash, of course, was the innocent bystander, and Patsy the betrayed party getting in the way. We should just get on with it. I need you and Arlo in the sauna."

"We'll get to that," I say, trying not to tremble at how plausible she's making her scenario sound. People want to believe gossip, and it's probably obvious that I do still find Arlo attractive. It might convince a court. Of course, it doesn't explain away the other three deaths, but at this point, I think she's logiced herself past that. My chest feels cold at my powerlessness over the whole injustice of the situation and my thoughts keep trying to goo out like caramel. But I can't just collapse, like Sasha did. Worse than the thought of my own death is the possibility of some of my closest friends getting shot in front of me. I have to keep my voice steady, keep her talking, give one of these men of action time to come up with a different way to bring her down. "But you said I get to hear the whole explanation, and give commentary. You killed your ex and his controlling sister, who was your childhood bully. But all that was just a bonus, really. When it comes down to it, it was all about the money. You figured you could contest a will naming dogs as beneficiaries, or you could claim you still loved the dogs and take over the stewardship of them, so you hadn't really worried about being cut out of the will. But then you found out Ted had changed the document. Did he contact you to tell you?"

"No," Irene says. "If he'd at least been up front with me, I might have let him live."

"Really?" Patsy says skeptically.

Irene considers this, "Okay, honestly, that wouldn't have changed anything. It would just have made it harder to lure him to his death, if he knew I knew about the will."

I say, "That's assuming he was thinking about you at all. He probably assumed that by giving everything to the dogs, he'd already gotten rid of you."

Irene's nostrils flare and her hands flutter, like flustered butterflies. "Maybe so," she says, though clearly she hasn't actually thought about this before, and it shakes her more than anything about her current situation. "But either way, he didn't count on his lawyer being one of my travel clients. I gifted the guy a ton of travel miles as a thanks for having tipped me off. I waited until I had this plan in motion before I deleted the file from the computer at the law office, and stole their reference copy – but I couldn't find the one at his house. I just never expected he'd have the hard copy with him."

"I wonder why he did," Logan says. "It's not normally something you take on vacation."

Irene says, "The world may never know. Now about this sauna . . ."

I take a few steps in the direction she wants me to go, getting close enough to the hole to look into it. There's exposed piping and lots of sharp edges – but nothing that I could just pick up and wield. Now that we're all in motion, I'm a lot closer to Patsy and Irene, and they are approaching the hot tub hole. I'm wearing a bulletproof vest. Usually, this is the point where Logan is about to decide to do something stupid. This time, I think I'm going to have be the one. This might not work. Patsy might still get hurt. But I have to try to save us. I turn to face Irene. "One last question. About something I still don't get. Why have the ferret steal all those random objects? He obviously formed a habit for doing it."

"That was all Side of Fries's doing. You can't exactly explain to a ferret what kind of object you are looking for him to retrieve. He brought me that stupid shaving brush first." Irene nods to herself. "See? That's plenty of time for questions, and no one managed a last-minute save. You get to admire my brilliance, but now you have to die. Don't worry Felicity. I'll kill you first. Like with me and the drone, you won't have to see what happens to Logan."

I can't help picturing Logan lying crumpled with a gun in his hand, the light gone from his intense green eyes. My heart clenches, and my body feels like ice. But at the same time I'm on fire with the need to act. I think I might have rushed her, even if I didn't have a plan. But I do and Ash, bless him, is in just the right place to help me out. Just as I start to move, the sauna equipment comes on – and the lights go out. I trip Patsy, hoping that she'll fall forward, rather than backwards into the hole, and in the same motion I pull Irene's gun arm towards myself.

There's an explosion of sound that leaves my ears ringing, and fire in the center of my chest. I try to grab for the gun, but one of us drops it as Irene and I both go over the edge into the hot tub hole. I hear the ferret squeaking as it jumps clear. I'm in so much pain, I'm not sure if the vest even worked at such close range, and I'm having a hard time resisting as Irene pushes me off of her. I might be dying. I don't know. But if I am, it's almost worth it, because Logan will be safe.

The lights come back on and Logan is standing at the edge of the hole, holding Irene's gun. Irene sits up and holds up both her hands. There's a huge gash on the side of her face from something she hit on the way down, and the ferret is sitting in her lap. She says, "Fine. But I'm going to rule prison."

I look down at my chest. I'm not bleeding. But there are pockmarks in the vest.

Logan gives Arlo the gun, then he leans forward to help me out of the hole.

I tell him, "Careful. My everything hurts."

Logan grins at me. He says, "Vests stop the bullet – not the pain. You're going to be pretty bruised, and we'll have to get you checked out to make sure you didn't break anything. But now you're ahead on the who-saved-who meter." The grin falls from his face. "I'll have to thank you – as soon as we save my sister."

Irene laughs. "Good luck finding her."

Aunt Naomi knows this hotel better than anyone. I call her and ask, "On the property, what's airtight, but has enough air for a couple of hours?"

She says, "Out back of the kitchen door, there's some old equipment we pulled out, waiting for the recycle guys. Somebody tried to build a storm shelter into one of the ground floor rooms. That might be airtight."

"Storm shelter, out back of the kitchen," I tell Logan, and he's sprinting away, to save his sister.

Irene makes a face at me, sticking out her tongue like we're kids on the playground. And maybe that's it – she never developed into a fully functional adult. I can pity her for her trauma, and what it took from her life. But as a self-proclaimed monster, she took what could have been character-building triumph over adversity and instead let it warp her into someone who would contrive murder as a game.

Arlo asks, "You don't happen to have a towel, do you?"

I turn and realize that he's cradling Patsy, whose nose is bleeding, while still keeping the gun on Irene. I probably broke Patsy's nose when I pulled her over and she hit the floor. I feel bad about that – but honestly, it could have been much worse. "No towel," I say. Sorry."

"I have one," Ash says, finally coming out of the sauna. He has the same bag he'd had earlier when he'd been trying to fix the machinery in here. Possibly, he'd just left it here. He pulls out one of those round discs that expands into a towel. He says, "I also have zip ties, Tylenol and a bottle of rubbing alcohol, if it helps."

When we promoted this event, we promised a bonfire, and the remaining guests still want to have it. We already have the fire permits and the spot on the beach picked out on the other side of the island, so there's no reason to say no. Even with a permit, fires on the island can't be more than three feet wide, and have to be in an enclosed pit. So while we're calling it a bonfire, it's actually small enough that we can see each other across it while sitting comfortably in director-style chairs. It's almost dusk. Arlo found a frisbee somewhere and is throwing it for Satchmo. The beagle is loving the attention.

Fisher has been practicing his new sand sculpting skills, building an oversized sand castle decorated with sculpted sea turtles. By the time we get the fire going well, he's pretty much done.

There is an air of celebration, reasonable seeing that we have all been freed from incarceration and escaped death. Logan keeps telling me that I have never looked sexier than when I was leaping into the darkness. I'm not sure what I should make of that, but I decide to take it as a compliment.

Dawn, who is sitting on the other side of Logan, says, "Eeeeew. I don't want the memory of my brother calling people sexy."

"Get used to it, sis," Logan says, pointing with the stick he's using to roast a marshmallow. "I'm getting married."

"I know," Dawn says. She looks across Logan, at me. "And to be fair, I underestimated my future sister-in-law. Arlo gets credit for the arrest – but you get credit for saving my life."

I say, "I'm just glad you were safe."

Dawn says, "I had a lot of time to think in that shed. I need to be less of a perfectionist. And I need to let people choose what makes them happy – even if I don't agree with it."

Logan says, "My life makes me happy. This, right here – the beach with the waves crashing, friends and family close by, half-burned marshmallows going to make s'mores with chocolate I made myself – I never would have had any of it if I had stayed on the path I was on before."

He pulls the marshmallow back out of the fire and smashes it into a s'more, which he hands to his sister. "Cacao beans all the way from Tanzania."

Dawn takes it. "Obviously, you won the bet. But even if you hadn't – let's just say I'm less worried about you now. It felt like you were running away when you moved here."

"I was," Logan says. "But that's not why I stayed."

Ash stands up. "I'm happy to announce that Chloe's $10,000 prize has been claimed." He points over at Patsy. I still feel bad about the plaster on her nose, but it sounds like she's about to get something for all her trouble this weekend. "Drumroll please. Let's hear it for Patsy Nash, a wonderful CPA and amateur detective. She was the first one to correctly identify the game's culprit. Clementine was killed by Rosemary Hanlon's character, Ethel Waggsbottom."

Logan's mom stands up and takes a dramatic bow. She says, "While I'm standing, I have an announcement to make. Malcolm and I have decided to buy the hotel, and to leave the fourth floor for residences and rooms to share with friends and family visiting the island. Felicity, it's easy to see why you and Naomi both love this place. We've fallen in love with it too. And now that Logan's dad is retiring, there's not really anything preventing us from moving."

Logan whispers to me, "I guess we really can tear down that wall into the adjoining suite."

And I whisper back, "And we can get my dad in to help with the architecture."

Uncle Greg can have his garden to putter in when he's in town. Aunt Naomi and I can still sit downstairs sometimes on the lobby furniture and let Knightley play on the rug. Who knows? When Dawn comes to visit, maybe she'll sit down there too.

Logan tells his mom, "Tell them about the other thing."

She beams at him. "My son knows how fond I am of flying, but I gave it up because my back couldn't take all the long hours flying long distances. But since his business specializes in shorter flights, I'm going to be taking up some of his island tours. I know most of you want to get home right away, and I can't blame you after everything we've been through, but for anyone who wants to stay, my first tour flight will be at 9 in the morning, and the fee is on me."

She gets a round of applause and a loud wolf-whistle from Hudson. He says, "I'm game, if I can bring my camera."

Sebastian says, "I still want to visit the chocolate microfactory."

Epilogue

I get out of the catering van and close the door with a satisfied slam. It's hard to believe the hotel is already opening, under the name Hanlon House. But with many hands pitching in, and my friend Tiff stepping up to coordinate all the volunteers, our friends and family helped get it ready, fast. Plus, Chloe had put out a call for sponsorships, so several furniture companies donated more than enough pieces to finish furnishing the rooms – in exchange for small plaques with QR codes.

I go around to the back of the van and start taking out trays of s'mores truffles. I look up at the hotel, and I don't know. There's something different about it, now that I know it isn't being flipped. That my dad is working on plans for the renovated, enlarged suite that should be ready right around September, just in time for my wedding. Some stress inside that I didn't even know I had has relaxed.

I go in through the lobby door. Ash and Chloe are taking video of everyone coming in for the grand opening. They're doing a commercial that will have some of the clips, but also some more standard advertising elements. After I put the truffles down on one of the temporary tables set up near the fireplace, they show me the set they've put in the business center – where Knightly takes center stage. It was Chloe's idea to carry over the imagery from the chocolate shop to the hotel, so my lop is now going to be the logo of two businesses. Bunnies are shy. I'm going to have to take him back upstairs soon, before the event officially starts. But right now, he's happily munching the lavender flowers that are supposed to show how clean the hotel is.

I ask Chloe, "Are you sure you changed all your passwords to strong ones? Even accounts you don't still use?"

Chloe looks embarrassed. "I did. I'm sorry. I know I was the one who compromised the whole mystery weekend. It was a rookie mistake."

"You are still a teenager," I remind her. "As much as you act like you're seventeen going on thirty-five. You're going to make rookie mistakes because you don't have the life experience. So don't beat yourself up. It wasn't your fault."

I realize this sounds a lot like what Logan's mom told me, not that long ago. Well, it is good advice.

Aunt Naomi is at one of the tables, using her laptop to print out real estate listings, looking for her next flip property. The fact that she still has a suite here means she doesn't have to rush to find a new project, so she can be a bit pickier. I see the image of a brick warehouse emerge from the printer. It doesn't look like it has a lot of character. Which is disappointing. But that's just one possibility. Surely she'll find something better.

Imogen comes in and hands around three copies of a script that she says are, "To peruse and share and consider."

"What is it?" Aunt Naomi asks.

Imogen says, "It's a brand-new mystery weekend script for another event to be held at the hotel. You know Ash's podcast is bigger than ever, and given that this place was the sight of actual true crime, people are offering to pay for mystery events, rather than us having to give them away as prizes."

Aunt Naomi says, "Absolutely not."

Ash points out, "You don't have to worry about being in the middle of it anymore. It's Rosemary's problem now."

Naomi says, "Yeah, but I still live here."

Who knows, though? Maybe she will come around to the idea. After all, Ash doesn't give up anything easily.

There's a huge vase of flowers on the table next to Aunt Naomi, with at least two dozen peach roses, plus pale yellow and soft green filler flowers. I ask, "Are those a prop too?"

Naomi grins. "Greg sent them. He knows that this opening is only possible because of the sweat equity I put into this place, and that I'm proud of all the work I did. Even though he's back offshore, he wanted me to have some congratulations, too."

Chloe said, "They were delivered by a singing telegram guy."

A bit dark, considering the fact that woman who'd come to the mystery weekend as a singing telegram girl had turned out to be a ruthless murderer. But it matches my uncle's sense of humor. And the fact that Naomi giggles shows exactly why they are perfect for each other.

I put my bunny back up in my suite, and then come back down to wait with Logan's parents for party guests to show up. There have been a few bookings, but as the time for the party to start comes and goes, everything looks quiet, the food undisturbed.

Logan's dad is having one of his bad health days. He's waiting in the same chair he'd used to monitor the door that stressful day when we'd feared guests escaping the lobby. He looks more nervous today, waiting for guests to arrive.

He says, "Maybe no one will want to stay at a hotel with so much negative publicity."

"Oh, they'll come," I say. I've had experience with this kind of thing. As Carmen had predicted, sales at Greetings and Felicitations went through the roof when the news got out that I'd been involved with yet another case. And when we sent out the press release and media ads for this event, Chloe had added a line about the murder books being on display here today only.

The copy of *Frankenstein* looks right at home next to the other volumes – even though its connection to the case was far more convoluted.

Tracie and Miles come in, as guests. I don't think either of them have seen the hotel before, so it is great to get to show them around before things get busy. I hand them each a gift bag as a thank you for basically running the shop by themselves the other weekend. Carmen is manning the shop today – but I don't feel too bad for her, because her boyfriend is there to help her out.

The appetizers laid out on the temporary tables are clearly Enrique's work. Which means he's here somewhere. He comes into the lobby from the direction of the gym – which now has proper gym equipment and a functioning hot tub. He's cradling his phone like it's a butterfly that might fly away if he disturbs it.

"What has you so happy?" I ask.

He says, "Sasha came through, and I just got set up with an interview for the food competition show."

Enrique calls Sasha to thank her, and he puts her on speakerphone.

I say, "Hi Sasha! I'm here too! How's it going with Side of Fries?"

Sasha has adopted the male ferret, and is spending time socializing him. He's fixed now, which makes him a more suitable companion for Cheeseburger, since breeding ferrets is more of an undertaking than Sasha wants to deal with.

"He's still got a way to go to be a gentleman," she says. "But check your phone. I just sent you a picture."

I check my texts. And there's a picture of the two ferrets curled up in a heap. They're adorable together.

I tell Sasha, "I'm about to unveil my new limited edition chocolate bar, in honor of Cheeseburger and Side of Fries."

"Oh?" Sasha asks. "How do you have a ferret themed bar?"

I say, "This one took a lot of experimentation, because ferrets have such a meat heavy diet. And the protein they like shouldn't be bacon, and they can't do peanut butter. Not that they should be eating chocolate, but I wanted to stick with the spirit of the thing. So I decide to play with the whole cheeseburger and fries motif. I did a bar with inclusions of beef jerky bits and pieces of chocolate covered potato chips."

"That sounds interesting," Sasha says. "Be sure to send me one. Actually, make it a couple. I can pass them on to some friends who do reviews."

"That would be fantastic," I say.

Logan gets off the elevator and walks over to us. "Hi Sasha!" he tells the phone. Then he gives me a quick kiss on the forehead.

I guess it's a day for thank you gifts all around, because when Autumn and Drake walk in, Drake hands me a gift bag. He says, "I don't know how to thank you for taking care of my wife during the crisis." That's all he can bring himself to call what happened. I get that. Being vague can sometimes help blunt the emotion, and Drake had felt helpless because he couldn't go to

Autumn when she was in the hotel. We still haven't told him that for a minute, we had misplaced her. So I don't feel like I've really earned a thank-you gift. But I open the gift bag, and it's a beautiful purple necklace, with amethysts the size of my pinkie nail.

I really want it, so I just say thank you and get Logan to help me put it on.

Fisk walks in and waves. He says, "Perfect. You have something to wear to the show." He hands me and Autumn each an envelope, tickets for us all to go on a quadruple date to see *Kiss me Kate* – with Ash and Imogen, plus a single ticket for Arlo, since Patsy decided to actually go out for the part of Bianca. And nailed the audition. I knew she played an instrument – she'd stepped in last minute for another musician at Autumn's wedding – but who knew she could also sing?

I ask Autumn, "How are you feeling?"

She says, "Somewhat better, now that the worst of the caffeine withdrawal is over. But I'm trying not to stress the baby, now that I've already gotten an edit letter. The changes my editor wants are extensive."

Yikes! I say, "That sounds like a lot to deal with."

Drake says, "But at least we never get bored."

"Mrs. K!" somebody says, and I turn to see Hudson waving at me. He's standing next to a girl I recognize from the searches I had done on him. I didn't realize he was coming today – or that he is back with his girlfriend. The two walk over to us, and Hudson says, "I'd like you to meet Savannah."

I say, "It's great to see you together." I couldn't think of a more tactful way to say it. Anything involving exes is bound to be awkward.

"It's okay. You can ask what you're really thinking. After that weekend, I realized that time is short, and if the worst mistake I ever made was giving up on Savannah, I ought to rectify it, if I could."

Savannah says, "I'm a sucker for a sweet guy. I wasn't sure about the long-distance thing, but I found out the marketing company I work for can just transfer me to Tokyo."

"That sounds like quite an adventure," I say.

She says, "Yeah, I've been studying the language for a couple of years, but I'm not even conversational. So it's intimidating to be moving into a Japanese office culture."

Logan offers Savannah a s'mores truffle. "Try this. Hudson was one of the people who inspired this one, after a memorable fire on the beach."

Savanah breaks the truffle in half and pops part of it in her mouth. She pauses, evaluating. She must like what she tastes, because she says, "I actually wanted to talk to you about your chocolate. Hudson told me how much you helped him get his priorities in order – not to mention stopping him from getting killed. I want to help your business any way I can. One project I'm working on once I get to Japan is a big chocolate expo in Tokyo. If I can get you in, are you interested in flying to Japan?

Logan and I look at each other and make *huh, what do you think* faces at each other. Then we both turn to Savannah, and I say, "Absolutely," at the same time as he says, "Please."

Hudson pokes Savanah's arm and she laughs. Savannah says, "You're right. They are perfect for each other."

Hudson spots the glass case, off to the side. "Dude! Are those the murder books?"

"Yes," I say. "You finally get to see them."

I watch them walk over to the case. They both get very excited about the copy of *Frankenstein*.

Savannah turns back to me and says, "Mary Shelley is my favorite author. Imagine, writing something like *Frankenstein* when she was even younger than I am now. Basically launching an entire genre. Science fiction as we know it wouldn't exist without her."

"I know," Autumn says, and the two start discussing books. Something tells me they're going to become friends.

Hudson steps closer to Logan and asks him, "Do I look nervous? Because I'm really nervous. Savannah's not just moving to Japan. When we land, we're eloping and spending a week at an onsen."

Logan tells Hudson, "Just breathe. You've obviously put thought into this decision. It will be fine."

Chloe comes up to Hudson and says, "Hi!" in an ingratiating tone.

"Hi," he says hesitantly.

She says, "I couldn't help overhear your beautiful bride inviting Felicity to an event in Japan."

"Right," Hudson says, equally hesitantly.

"Well, here's the thing. I've actually got my dream collab with the cat toy company in Tokyo, working with a number of Living-in-Japan Youtubers. Now, I just have to talk my mom into letting me spend a couple of weeks in Japan. But if she knew you were participating in the videos, and everything could be scheduled to line up with the chocolate expo, then Felicity can chaperone."

"Wait a second," I say. "I did not agree to that. Logan and I need to discuss it before you start making plans."

"Absolutely," Chloe says. "I understand. You discuss it."

I should have said no. Because she's not going to listen to a word I just said. But I almost feel like I owe it to her to be nice, since I did suspect her of being capable of committing multiple murders.

Hudson asks, "Did anybody ever hear from Jordan? I didn't obviously, but I wonder what happened to him."

We all shake our heads.

I say, "Nobody ever figured out what he was being blackmailed for, but after his ordeal, and feeling used by Irene, he wrote a play about it. And now he's about to become a director."

Logan says, "You know who's doing surprisingly well? Colin, the former bank robber. He's back in prison, but he wrote me asking me to be a character witness for his parole. I think he may get it, due to the extenuating circumstances."

"That's great," I say. "Look, we're starting to get a crowd. I want to grab some of Enrique's appetizers before they're all gone."

I make my way over to the table and pick up a plate. I'm putting a shrimp puff on my plate when I hear my name, not spoken to me, but in conversation. I half-turn to listen. Logan's dad is talking about me to someone I don't recognize. I try not to look like I'm eavesdropping. I put another shrimp puff on my plate and add a tiny cup of ceviche.

Logan's dad says, "I don't think my son could have chosen anyone more level-headed in a crisis. And she's organized, too."

Wait. Did Logan's dad just compliment me? Like sincerely, without a hint of backhandishness? I move down the appetizers line, feeling like I'm floating. I get to the end of the line and circle back around into the room, and Logan's dad stops me. He says, "Felicity, I want you to meet my old partner. We were together as rookies, and look at us now, both retired. Russ flew in from Florida just to support us."

I spend a few moments chatting with them, trying not to feel like they're scrutinizing every word.

It's a relief when Fisher and Uncle Greg come in and invite everyone to see an herb planting presentation in the in-progress gardens.

As I'm heading for the door Dawn spots me and heads my way. There's a shirt-size box in her hand with a big green bow on it. She thrusts it at me. "Here."

"What's this?" I say taking it. I open the lid. Inside, there's a bulletproof vest, with the words *Chocolate Maker* stitched on the back. I grin. "You shouldn't have."

Dawn says, "We both know you're going to get into trouble. So how could I not worry about my little sis?"

I give her a hug. "Thank you. It's perfect."

Once we're outside, Logan's mom gestures me over and says, "We're taking a family photo."

"You want me to take it?" I ask.

"No, silly, you're supposed to be in it." She hands her phone to Russ. "Can you take it for us?"

Logan slips his arm around my shoulders and leans his head towards mine.

I ask Russ, "Can you take one on my phone too?"

Logan's parents wind up in the middle of the photo, with me and Logan on one side and Dawn and Fisher on the other. It's my first real photo with Logan's family, and it has a beautiful swathe of the hotel garden behind us. Out of all the photos of today's event, this is the one going on my Instagram.

ACKNOWLEDGEMENTS

Special thanks to Jael Rattigan of French Broad Chocolates in South Carolina, who has consulted extensively on this series. And to Sander Wolf of DallasChocolate.org, who put me in touch with so many experts in the chocolate field.

I'd like to thank the readers over at Meg's Cozy Mystery Corner for suggesting a ferret as a possible animal for Felicity to interact with. It was such a great idea, and I learned a lot about these cute, friendly animals while researching Cheeseburger the ferret.

I'd also like to thank TexaKona Coffee for taking us behind the scenes on how coffee is roasted and espresso shots are pulled, and Maasa at Makua Meadows (Dotour's coffee farm on Big Island Hawaii) for the extensive behind the scenes tour, and answering all my coffee questions.

I have to thank Jake, as usual, for reading the manuscript umpteen times, being my biggest fan and cheerleader, and doing all the formatting things to make this thing happen. He always keeps me going, even when things are stressful. This time, I was writing the book in the middle of a move (we bought a house!) and he took on a lot of extra tasks so that I could keep working.

And thanks to my agent, Jennie, for her input on this series, and her encouragement to keep moving forward.

And for this series especially, I'd like to thank my family for giving me a love of the ocean and a curiosity about history. The Cajun side of both mine and Jake's families comes through in Felicity's family in the books. This has given me an excuse to reach out to family members for recipes and inspiration, many of which you can find on the Bean to Bar Bonuses section of my website. Thanks y'all!

Thanks to James and Rachel Knowles for continuing to sharing their knowledge of bunny behavior, despite the loss of the ever-adorable Yuki.

I'd also like to thank Cassie, Monica and Tessa, who are my support network in general. I don't know how I would have gotten through these years of social isolation without you three.

And Thanks to Stacie Jefferson for being a huge cheerleader for my work from early on and an excellent friend!

Thank you all, dear readers, for spending time in Felicity's world. I hope you enjoyed getting to know her. Her eighth adventure will be available for you soon.

Did Felicity's story make you hungry?

Visit the Bean to Bar Mysteries Bonus Recipes page on Amber's website to find out how to make some of the food mentioned in the book.

AMBER ROYER writes the CHOCOVERSE comic telenovela-style foodie-inspired space opera series (available from Angry Robot Books and Golden Tip Press). She is also co-author of the cookbook There are Herbs in My Chocolate, which combines culinary herbs and chocolate in over 60 sweet and savory recipes, and had a long-running column for Dave's Garden, where she covered gardening and crafting. She blogs about creative writing technique and all things chocolate related over at www.amberroyer.com. She also teaches creative writing in person in North Texas for both UT Arlington Continuing Education and Writing Workshops Dallas. If you are very nice to her, she might make you cupcakes.

www.amberroyer.com Instagram: amberroyerauthor

9 781952 854200